THE QUEST BETWEEN WORLDS . . .

"You find yourselves on a hilltop, overlooking a vast walled city," the professor began. "Beside your party is a collection of large wooden boxes. You have no recollection of how you got to this hillside, and the only possibility that suggests itself is too incredible to be taken seriously . . ."

"What are we going to do about these boxes?" Andrea asked.

"Open them, of course," Doria answered.

"Okay, fine, I'll open them."

"No, don't—"

"As the first box is opened, you are overwhelmed by a rush of . . ."

James Michael couldn't hear the rest; a rush of sound like the roar of an impossibly loud, impossibly near jet buffeted his ears; acrid smoke invaded his nostrils until he found himself on his knees in a coughing spasm, his tearing eyes jammed shut.

When he opened his eyes again, James Michael was standing on the side of a grassy hill, a dwarf with an axe in his hands . . .

BOOK ONE OF GUARDIANS OF THE FLAME

THE SLEEPING DRAGON

A FANTASY NOVEL BY

JOEL ROSENBERG

A SIGNET BOOK

NEW AMERICAN LIBRARY

SIGNET TRADEMARK REG. U.S. PAT. OFF. AND FOREIGN COUNTRIES
REGISTERED TRADEMARK—MARCA REGISTRADA
HECHO EN CHICAGO, U.S.A.

SIGNET, SIGNET CLASSIC, MENTOR, PLUME, MERIDIAN AND NAL BOOKS
are published by New American Library,
1633 Broadway, New York, New York 10019

First Printing, November, 1983

4   5   6   7   8   9   10   11   12

PRINTED IN THE UNITED STATES OF AMERICA

for Felicia

. . .

Acknowledgments

I want to thank the people who helped me through this: Allan Schmidt, who gave me the crazy idea in the first place and helped to make the gaming aspects work; Cara Herman, who gave much needed encouragement as I struggled through the first draft; Harry F. Leonard, who annoyed the hell out of me by quibbling endlessly over minor flaws until I saw the light and corrected them, much to the betterment of the story, if not my disposition; Robert Lee Thurston and Judith Heald, who gave me good criticism and better friendship; Doug Kaufman, who put his money where his mouth was; Barry B. Longyear, whose advice always helps when I'm wise enough to take it; Kim Tchang, who told me to relax and write the damn thing; my agent, Cherry Weiner, whose help and support went beyond the call of duty; my editor, Sheila Gilbert, who not only knew a good thing when she saw it, but knew how to make it better; and the members of Haven: Deborah Atherton Davis, Mary Kittredge, Mark J. McGarry, and Kevin O'Donnell, Jr., who gave this book the line-by-line, word-by-word examination and dissection that a first novelist so desperately needs.

And, most particularly, I'd like to thank Robert Anson Heinlein, whose work has been both example and inspiration, for Thorby, Colonel Baslim, Oscar Gordon, and so much more.

The great problems of life . . . are always related to the primordial images of the collective unconscious. . . .

The unconscious is not just evil by nature, it is also the source of the highest good: not only dark but also light, not only bestial, semihuman, and demonic, but superhuman, spiritual, and, in the classical sense of the word, "divine."

—Carl Gustave Jung

. . . for every human being there is a diversity of existences . . . the single existence is itself an illusion. . . .

—Saul Bellow

It seems to me that there might well be the equivalent, with regard to the collective unconscious, of the concept in physics of "critical mass." Are we approaching it? Quite possibly— consider the resurgence of spiritualism, in all its guises, and don't neglect the function of the fantasy role-playing games. The characters, the situations . . . all seem to touch something that is basic and fundamental.

But where would the locus of crisis be? And how can it be exploited? *The Elder Edda, The Song of the Harper, The Book of the Dead,* even *The Great Hymn to the Aten* offer only hints, suggestions, intimations.

Perhaps the best approach would be neither induction nor deduction, but, rather, empirical experimentation. Perhaps . . .

—Arthur Simpson Deighton

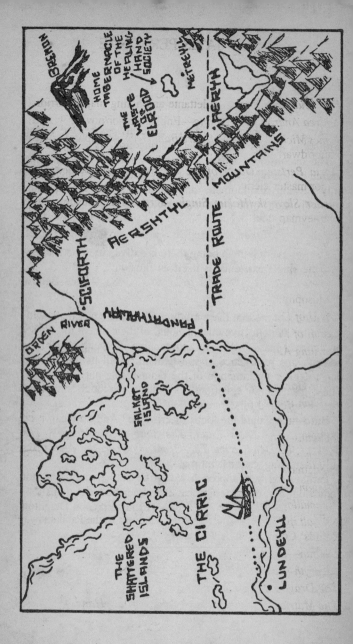

DRAMATIS PERSONAE

Karl Cullinane/Barak—dilettante and acting major/warrior

Andrea Andropolous/Lotana—English major/novice wizard

James Michael Finnegan/Ahira Bandylegs—computer sciences major/dwarf warrior

Doria Perlstein/Doria of the Healing Hand—domestic arts major/master cleric

Walter Slovotsky/Hakim Singh—agricultural sciences major/journeyman thief

Jason Parker/Einar Lightfingers—history major/master thief

Louis Riccetti/Aristobulus—civil engineering major/master wizard

Arthur Simpson Deighton, Ph.D.—Associate Professor of Philosophy, gamemaster

Wen'l of Lundescarne—peasant and freefarmer

Frann of Pandathaway—innkeeper

Lordling Alahn Lund—heir to the throne of Lundeyll

Marik, Arno—men-at-arms

Avair Ganness—captain and owner of the *Ganness' Pride*

Airvhan ip Melhrood—customs official

Challa—man-at-arms

Callutius—Junior Librarian of the Great Library of Pandathaway

Oreen—Specializing Librarian of the Great Library of Pandathaway

Ellegon—a young dragon

Tommallo—owner of the Inn of Quiet Repose

Khoralt ip Therranj—Wineseller's Delegate to the Pandathaway Guilds' Council, Games official

Ohlmin—master slaver

Blenryth—master wizard

The Dragon at the Gate

The Matriarch of the Society of the Healing Hand

PART ONE:

The Student Union

CHAPTER ONE: *The Players*

Karl Cullinane reached out his fork and speared the last stick of asparagus from the stainless-steel serving plate in the middle of the table, not bothering to set the asparagus on his own plate before taking a bite. It was cold and mushy, almost tasteless; he swallowed quickly.

"Karl, you're a pig. A skinny one, granted, but a pig." Andrea Andropolous' smile took most of the sting out of her words, pitched low enough so that nobody else in the crowded cafeteria would have been able to hear her over the clatter of dishes and the chatter of a hundred or so students.

Karl put it down to a natural gentleness. Hell, she'd been able to make him like it—almost—when she'd turned him down. Usually, the let's-just-be-friends routine drove him into a silent, stomach-churning rage.

"I gotta rush, Andy-Andy. There's a game tonight." He took another bit, added a mouthful of lukewarm black coffee, and swallowed quickly. "If I'm late, sure as hell they'll start without me, put Barak out to pasture for the night."

"You mean that they'll put him out to *stud*." She chuckled, revealing a mouthful of even, white teeth.

Karl liked her laugh, her smile. He had always thought that the notion of somebody brightening a room with a smile was just a fantasy. Until he had met Andy-Andy, that is. Not that he had anything against fantasy, quite the—

"It's bullshit, Karl," she said, smiling sweetly. "Just an absurd male power fantasy." She reached out and stroked his

15

skinny forearm with a long, dark finger. Was it tanned, or not? Andy-Andy always seemed to find something better to do during afternoon tanning hours than loll in the sun like some well-oiled, roasting slug. Probably the olive tone of her skin was natural coloration. Maybe not. Of course, there was a way to tell. Trouble was, Karl had never had the chance to check her for bikini marks.

Damn. "No, it's just a game. A way to spend a little time, have a little fun."

"A little fun?" She arched an eyebrow. "You call pretending to chop up a pixie, rape a virgin or three, slice an ogre—you call that fun?" Quirking a smile, she sat back in her chair, crossing her arms almost defensively over her blue velour pullover. Which was amply filled out, but not tight. Karl liked that; Andy-Andy was more than a little pretty, but not an exhibitionist.

"First of all"—he tapped his index finger on the table, forcing himself to pay attention to the conversation—"you're missing the point. Pretending isn't the same thing as really doing it. I mean—take last week's session, for instance. Barak strangled an elf, chopped a half-orc in two—hey, now the critter's really two halves of an orc. Or should that be 'quarter-orces'? Never mind, the point is that he took three points of damage. One's a light wound, two's more serious, going up to five, which is certainly lethal. Three's the equivalent of getting sliced up pretty bad." He reached for his shirt's top button. "Care to check for scars?"

"Some other time." She tossed her head, sending shoulder-length black hair whipping around her face. "Maybe." A strand came to rest on her slightly too long, slightly bent nose. She blew it off. "Then again, maybe not."

"Teaser."

"That's only half the word, Karl. You don't have to use that bullshit with me."

"In my neighborhood, *mother* was only half a word." That might sound good, but it wasn't true: Karl was a product of middle-class suburbia. "And besides, I was . . . kind of pointedly told to watch my language around—women." If you consider having your mouth liberally washed out with Lifebuoy to be a pointed telling. Which it was, after a fashion. "But to get back to the point, it's all just a fantasy, a game. No harm; no damage. Anyway, Barak isn't that sort of character—he'll violate a *law*, but he's no rapist." That was true, but omitted a new character Doc Deighton had helped him roll up, one Lucius of Pandathaway. Lucius was not a nice person. Not at all. "The trouble with you is that you feel perfectly free to judge something you haven't tried. How many times since the start of the semester have I invited you—ten? Twenty?"

She shook her head. "I don't have to jump out a window to decide that I'm not going to like it."

"Irrelevant. If you try role-playing and you don't like it, you quit. Period. No scars—not even on your psyche. Which is part of the fun." He shrugged. "Besides, it's probably beneficial. You get to work out some aggressions without hurting anybody. Not yourself, not anybody else."

"Stop trying to sound like a psych major. You're supposed to be studying to be an actor, these days."

"I used to be a psych major—"

"—and a poli sci major. Plus American lit, engineering, philosophy, sociology—am I missing something?"

"Prelaw. And two weeks of premed, back when I was a freshman. What's your point?"

"You're a dilettante, Karl. This role-playing stuff is just another one of your temporary obsessions. Remember last year, when it was bridge? You spent a whole semester nattering about Stayman conventions and South American Texas transfers, whatever the hell they are—"

"South African Texas, not South American." He dipped two fingers into his shirt pocket and pulled out a cigarette, then lit it with his shiny new Zippo. Karl let the flame flare for a moment before snapping the cover shut. He figured that he might as well enjoy it while he could; he'd lose it soon. Karl could never seem to keep track of *things;* the Zippo was the third lighter he'd bought that semester. "I still play bridge," he said, exhaling a cloud of smoke. "It's just that this is more fun—particularly with this group. Sometimes . . ." He let his voice trail off.

"Yes?"

"Sometimes, when you get the mechanics of the game out of the way—rolling the dice, keeping track of what you're carrying—it's almost like you're there." He lifted his head and smiled. "And that's *something*. How often do you think I'm going to get the chance to, say, rescue a princess or slay a dragon?" He glanced down at his wrist. 6:48. Karl pushed himself to his feet.

"Well, I've got to run, if I'm not going to be late. See you later?"

Andy-Andy's brow furrowed. "How late are you going to be? Getting back, I mean."

"Mmmm, probably be back before midnight. If you want to meet me in the lounge, I'll help you go over *Deerslayer*, if that's what you mean. It's a rotten book, though—I've got a Twain piece on it that pretty much—"

"No." She shook her head. "I'm caught up with that, but I do have a quiz in astronomy tomorrow. If you're sure we can be back by twelve, I'll come along, give it a try. If the invitation's still open." She stood, taking her bulky yellow ski jacket from the back of her chair and slipping it on.

"You know it is."

She sighed. "Yes, I do." Andy-Andy shook her head slowly. "Which is part of the problem. Never mind; let's get going, shall we?"

James Michael Finnegan was the first player to get to Room 109 in the Student Union. It was a matter partly of habit, but mainly of pride. The others, well, they'd wait for him, sure. *Only* for him, dammit.

They wouldn't wait for him because he was now the most accomplished player in the group. Davy Davidson had been the best in the group until he'd dropped out last year, and nobody would wait for Davy and his character, Erik of the Three Bezants, on the not too infrequent occasions that he'd arrive late.

James Michael shifted uncomfortably in his chair, his hands limp in his lap.

No, they wouldn't wait for him because he was a nice person to be around, with a dry sense of humor and an always friendly smile. That monomaniac flake Karl Cullinane cracked better jokes; that hick jock Walter Slovotsky always seemed to have a grin pasted on his face—and everybody *always* liked being around Doria. But if one of *them* showed up late, it was well-too-bad-it-seems-your-character-is-down-with-a-cold-tonight. Just last week, Doria had fluttered in breathless, just five minutes after they'd started, and even Riccetti had ignored her implied promises and threats; Doc Deighton had just turned a very cold eye her way and suggested that lateness was an implicitly hostile act.

He spun his chair in a tight circle and swore softly under his breath.

It wasn't all that bad, not always. The one time he'd had to wait for the Special Student Services truck (all the way muttering a spell to change the driver into a toad, a particularly small, unusually ugly toad—with one eye) and had been wheeled into the elevator late, coming out on the first floor *late*, his car-battery-powered chair zipping down the tiled hall and into Room 109 LATE—

—nobody had said anything. Except, "Hi, James," and "Nice to see you, James," and "Let's play, James."

The tolerance, the implied pity, was bad. Not playing would have been worse. Much worse.

All cripples fantasize, you see. They have to, just like normal people, although not always about the things normal people do.

And when you've spent your whole life with muscular dystrophy, you're really lucky, in a way. There's *lots* more things to dream about. Like being able to punch a computer keyboard at better than a scorching ten words per minute. Like sleeping in a top bunk. Like feeding yourself quickly, wolfing down food so you could run off somewhere. Like using a goddam bathroom without having someone else wipe you off.

Like not having to be so goddam cheerful all the time since because you're a feeb in a chair, people will let you get away with anything as long as you don't touch them.

But the game . . . ah, there it was. All at once. "I'll walk across the room, heft my axe, and chop at the ogre," you'd say, and everybody would react to it, *just as though you'd really done it*.

A miracle? Well, not quite. An addiction, *yes*.

James Michael lifted his right hand to the steering knob and wheeled himself over to the long table in the middle of the bright room, getting himself so close that his chin was directly over the edge of the battered mahogany surface. He reached into the denim bag on his lap, secured there by a long cloth loop around his neck, and pulled out a large plastic bag, bringing it up to the tabletop.

And the whole . . . wonder of it depended on this little bag, and the dice inside it. Standard six-sided dice for the attack tables. A twenty-sided die, generating a random number to compare to Ahira's intelligence, or endurance, or strength. And

Ahira was *strong*, although not terribly wise, perhaps, and certainly not handy with anything except an axe or hammer.

And then there were the pyramidal four-sided dice, and the eight-sided ones to—but why bother thinking about the mechanics of it? They didn't matter; the rules were soon learned and subsumed, the way a normal person would learn to ride a bicycle by technique, and then forget the technique, to ride. . . .

James Michael closed his eyes and dreamed of riding a bicycle, seeing the ground slip by smoothly beneath him. Sort of like riding in a car, but being there, and—

"*James!*"

His eyes snapped open like twin shutters. Doria Perlstein stood over him, concern creasing her too round, too smooth face, her short blond hair only making her seem chubbier.

"James, are you okay?"

"I'm fine." He smiled up at her, making a special effort to keep the traitor muscles of the right side of his face under control. Doria . . . *tried*, that was it. The little dwarf in the chair revolted her and scared her, as though his disability could rub off. But she tried to hide it.

He brought his hands down into his lap, out of sight. No shame, just a reflexive kindness, although he really wanted to reach out and shake her. *I'm not contagious.* "I'm just fine. It's been a busy week; I guess I was just dozing off."

She dropped into a chair, visibly considered the possibility that it would seem to him to be too far away, took a half second to fight with her own fear of James Michael Finnegan, and compromised by wiggling herself a scant inch closer.

Someday, he thought, *I'm going to tell her that she doesn't have to sit next to me, if she's so uptight. Then again, maybe this is better for her than sitting across the table from me; it's natural for her to avoid my eyes, this way.*

She forced a smile, drumming crimson fingernails against the tabletop. "I see I'm early this time."

"I'm glad you're here. We ran into a fairly heavy-duty goblin last time; could have used a cleric."

"How bad?"

"Both Barak and Ahira took quite a bit of damage. He got three points; I got away with just two."

"Wait a minute—where was Sandy?"

"Dropped out. Which leaves you as the only cleric around. The team's topheavy with warriors."

"Ooo." She grimaced. "Sorry I was late last time." She tossed her head, brightening. "But don't worry. Soon as Doc works me back into the campaign, I'll heal both of you up."

James Michael smiled. "Make that 'heal Barak up.' Ahira's just fine."

She wrinkled her forehead. "How? I know Barak had some healing draughts in his bag—but Ahira—"

"—persuaded him to fork them over."

She toyed with the ruffles of her blouse. "What did you offer him? As though I didn't know." She raised a finger in mock accusation.

"Not bashing him with my axe."

"Sounds fair." She reached up and scratched the tip of her stubby nose. Slovotsky claimed it was artificial; James Michael had a standing bet that it was natural. Unfortunately, there was no way to find out; Doria ignored all questions on the subject. "But one of these times he's not going to stand for it, if you keep it up. Bully. He might—" She caught herself. "Never mind."

James Michael sighed. It was obvious why Cullinane didn't want to fight him, despite the way he'd been provoking the confrontation. If Ahira killed Barak, Cullinane would lose—and if Barak managed to win, James Michael would be, at least temporarily, out of the game. Cullinane wouldn't want to kick a cripple out of the game, would he? "I guess he recognized that it was more useful to the whole team to have Ahira up and healthy, what with us being underground, and all." A dwarf's natural habitat was in underground warrens, where his ability to see in the infrared gave him a clear advantage.

"That sounds like a bit too . . . sound reasoning for Barak. His IQ's not that high, is it?"

"Wisdom, Doria, wisdom. Barak is the wisest fighter around. Not a berserker, like Ahira." He formed his hands into clumsy fists, and pounded himself lightly on the chest. "Arg."

A new voice bellowed from the doorway. "You going berserk, *again?*" Walter Slovotsky swaggered into the room, smelling vaguely of Ivory, his hair damp. "Doria, James." He nodded, dropped his books to the floor, kicked his shoes off and in the general direction of a far corner, and perched himself tailor-fashion on the table. "How goes it?"

Of all the people on campus that he knew—hell, of *all* the people he knew, specifically including his parents—James Michael was most comfortable around Walter Slovotsky. Jealous, sure—but not unusually so; James didn't particularly want to Be a Football Hero. The thing was that the big man was so sure of himself, without being offensive about it. Whether he was stomping quarterbacks out on the field or spending extra time in the Ag Library, cramming for a final in Meat Science (a course that Slovotsky couldn't mention without chuckling), Slovotsky seemed certain that the universe centered on him, and that all was well with the universe.

A massive hand reached out and chucked Doria under the chin. "And where the hell were you last Friday, m'love?"

"Thursday." She shoved his hand away. "And you know damn well where I *wasn't;* you were the one yelling 'Come on time if you want to play,' weren't you?"

"No, I meant Friday. I thought you were going to come over, spend the night."

"*Shh.*" She started to jerk a thumb toward James Michael, stopped herself. "I don't think—"

"Pre*cise*ly. You don't think." He turned to James, running blunt fingers through his damp black hair. "Jimmy me boy, would it be any surprise to you to learn that Doria and I sleep together, every now and then?"

"*Wal*ter!"

"No, not really," James Michael said. Doria's pale skin went from light pink through various shades of red before settling on a nice, hot crimson. He looked her in the eye, suppressing an urge to reach out and pat her arm. "Not that he ever said anything about it. I'm pretty good at reading people for a . . ."—an impish impulse made him pause—"computer sciences major."

Walter's broad face went somber. "Exactly. Beautiful, I don't tell on ladies. Wouldn't mention it in front of Cullinane, say—he's an explosion, looking for a place to happen. Trouble with you Jewish girls is that your desire to *do* it is in inverse proportion to your willingness to *talk* about it."

Doria's skin had gone back to its normal shade, which made her glare at Slovotsky a trifle less comical. "Another one of Slovotsky's Laws?"

"Actually"—he cocked his head to one side—"I think that I got that from one of my many roommates—Bernstein-the-rabbi, I think."

Many roommates was a fair statement of fact, James Michael thought. Not a whole lot of people liked spending their nights mainly on the couch in the lounge.

Slovotsky brightened. "But I don't mind stealing it. Make it Slovotsky's Law Number Twenty-three, right after 'Never date a woman with a brother named Nunzio.' " He bounced to his feet. "I'm going for coffee. Either of you need anything from the snack bar?"

"Shoes," James Michael supplied.

"Sorry, they don't serve them there. A burger close enough?" He patted the hip pocket of his jeans. "On me. Had a nice bet we wouldn't beat the spread against Yale."

"No, you've got to *wear* shoes."

Slovotsky looked down at his blue-sock-clad feet, then blanked his face. "James, when you're six-foot-one-and-a-fraction, weighing in at two-twenty-three, *nobody* tells you you've got to wear shoes." His eyes glazed over. "Walter not un-der-stand. Per-son half his size telling him he not come in? Walter must have mis-un-der-stood." He shrugged, a bit sadly. "You wouldn't *believe* how easily people believe that if you're big, you've gotta be dumb. And violent. Now, do you want anything?"

Doria shrugged. "Coffee sounds fine."

"James?"

"Herb tea. Red Zinger, if they've got it. With plenty of sugar." He mimicked Slovotsky's big-and-dumb voice. "Ahira need to keep strength up."

"That's the ticket." Walter paused in the doorway. "But if it takes me more than a couple of minutes, don't let them start without me. Assuming that the rest get here on time."

"I wouldn't dream of it." Doria's voice held a definite chill.

"Hey, Dr. Deighton, wait up." Jason Parker broke into a lope, letting Riccetti fall behind.

The thin, stoop-shouldered man stopped under a streetlight and turned, the harsh green casting his face into shadow. He wore a tan wool suit, amply decorated with burn marks from his ever-present bulldog briar pipe; the suit, like the pipe, the battered briefcase, and the man, had come a long way since new, the wrinkles having developed a life of their own, as though they would be resistant to even the stubbornest, most persistent dry cleaning.

"Good evening, Mr. Parker." The voice was out of place; it was a strong young tenor, the voice of a prepubescent boy, not a sixtyish philosophy professor. "And good evening to you, Mr. Riccetti," he added, as Lou Riccetti panted up to join them under the streetlight. "I trust you're ready for the test tomorrow?"

Lou Riccetti shrugged, his round face covered with a light sheen of sweat. "I hope so, Doc. I've got the *Apologia* practically memorized, and this is my second go-round with the *Republic*."

Jason chuckled. It was a good bet that Lou would flunk again; he never seemed to be able to understand anything that didn't have a number attached. Engineering students—"Hey, no teaching tonight, Doc. You're gamemastering tonight, not using your conclusions to prove your postulates." He took an impatient step toward the Student Union building.

Deighton took a few puffs on his pipe, then followed. "You have that reversed, Mr. Parker." He blew a smoke ring; it shattered and drifted away in the light, cool breeze. "One uses one's postulates to prove one's conclusions, not the other way around."

Jason shrugged his bony shoulders and tucked his hands into the pockets of his fraying army jacket. "That's what you say. Seems to me you philosophers do both. Sort of bootstrap levitation."

"A nice phrase, that. Not true, mind you, but a nice phrase." Deighton sighed deeply. "But your major premise was correct: We are gaming tonight. Mr. Riccetti, I apologize if I seemed to be pressuring you about the test tomorrow."

"No problem, Doc." Riccetti cocked his head to one side. "Any clues about what we're going to run into after we get through the treasure room?"

"Ricky, *don't* ask." Jason tried to keep irritation out of his voice; he failed. "Either he won't tell us, in which case you're just wasting your breath, or he will—and that'd ruin the game. Let it flow, don't—"

"—force it. Okay, okay. I was just asking."

"Actually, I can tell you something without spoiling anything."

Deighton smiled crookedly around his pipestem. "But if you'd prefer to wait . . ."

"Go ahead." Jason was curious. Doc never gave anything away, except at the start of a campaign, of course, where the gamemaster would have to set the scene, give out a clue or two.

"We are beginning a new campaign tonight. From scratch."

"Wait one minute." Riccetti slapped his bookbag. "I've spent one hell of a lot of time turning Aristobulus into a K-Class wizard—I don't want to have to start again back in A-Class, with just one spell. Sleep, probably."

At least Ricky was keeping his wits. Of all the spells available to an A-Class wizard, the Sleep spell—technically, Herstell's Spell of Induced Somnolence—was the most useful. Once you had an enemy sleeping, he, she, it, or they were as good as dead if you wanted them to be.

"That was not what I meant, Mr. Riccetti. We will be starting a new campaign, yes, but not with A-Class characters. They wouldn't be likely to survive. You can run Aristobulus, if you like. The balance should be about right that way, as a matter of fact."

Jason ticked players and characters off on his fingers. "Let's see . . . Cullinane and James are going to run their warriors—I'm sure about that: I talked to Karl about it earlier. And James always runs Ahira, of course."

"Jase, I don't think he always does. Didn't he—"

"Nope. You should pay attention." It was obvious why the poor little guy always wanted to be a warrior; the game was the closest he was ever going to get to being like Slovotsky. It was kind of pitiful, the way James Michael tried to pretend he wasn't jealous of Walter—or, possibly more accurately, Walter and Doria. "Let's see . . . Doria's the only one who likes being a cleric—God knows why—cleaning up after everybody else's fights. Slovotsky could play either as a wizard or a thief."

"Or a monk. I like Master Kwan."

"Too limited. Depending on the situation, we might need a thief, but a monk is a waste. He can't advance fast enough, can't carry enough—most of the time, everybody else has to carry him."

Deighton's slate-gray eyes went vague. "Actually, I think you might well need a thief. Or two. For this campaign, a balanced team would be best. I think you'll find all of the archetypical situations in this one. '

'Fine,'' Jason said, we'll have him run Hakim. That gives us two warriors, one cleric, one wizard—take a bow. Ricky; looks like Aristobulus is going to be on his own—and one thief.''

"Plus you, Jase."

"Right. Any suggestions. Doc? I really don't care what sort of character I get. Long as I get to *do* something."

"Hmmm . . . quite possibly a thief would be best."

"Or a thief/assassin? I've got Lendwyl ready to run."

"No, I doubt that you'll need to have anyone poisoned. You might want to choose someone more dexterous than Lendwyl."

"Jase, how about running Einar Lightfingers? You haven't run him for a while."

"He is kind of fun."

They walked up the stone steps of the Student Union, Riccetti bustling ahead to hold the door. "Give it a try, Jase. Not that I'd turn my back on him, but Lightfingers is awful good at what he does, all things considered."

"You first, Doc—age before beauty. On the other hand, if he hurts his other arm, he'd be pretty much out of the picture." Jason shrugged. "But what the hell; I'll run him." As they crossed the yellowed marble floor to the stairwell, Jason stopped. "But I don't like having just one wizard. What if Ari gets killed?"

Deighton shrugged. "You could find an R-Class cleric, and have him resurrected. Or, conceivably, help Doria of the Healing Hand rise to that height."

"Fat chance—I don't think I've ever run into a cleric past N-Class. And what is she now, J?"

"K, Ricky. As a cleric, she's one step farther along than Aristobulus is as a magic usurer."

"That's magic *user*."

Jason returned Riccetti's glare. "I meant exactly what I said. I didn't like the way you charged everybody a thousand gold—*each*—to charm the Eater."

Riccetti shrugged. "Wizard's got to make a living, just like anybody else. You'd rather I let him eat Doria?" He took the lead in the hall, their footsteps echoing hollowly on the tiles.

"No, but—"

"But nothing. Value is relative; first law of economics. At that point, Aristobulus' value was pretty huge. I think you should have been happy to pay."

Deighton stroked his chin. "I think you are asking a bit too much of Mr. Parker. Perhaps the . . . fee for your services was proper; certainly, adding gratitude to it does seem excessive."

"That the gamemaster talking, or you?"

"Just me. Just me—and here we are. If you would get the door, please?"

Riccetti swung the door open; Jason ushered him and Deighton in before following.

"Seven-thirty on the nose. Nice timing, Doc, Ricky, Jason," Walter Slovotsky said, from his usual spot on the table, where he sat like an improbably massive sprite.

"Hi, Hakim." Jason dropped his jacket in a corner, setting his books on top. He took a moment to check out the other players as he took his own seat across the table from Deighton, next to Doria. As usual, to Doria's left was James Michael, huddling in his wheelchair like a vulture waiting to pounce.

Next was Karl Cullinane. Jason shook his head; Karl was *still* trying to persuade his sparse growth of facial hair to become a beard. Actually, he might have been able to make it, if he wouldn't give up and shave after a few weeks—but that was the trouble with Karl: He never followed through with anything.

On the other hand, he thought, *that might be a bit of a hasty judgment*. From the way Karl was perched protectively close to the woman sitting next to him, it seemed that perhaps here was something he'd follow through with. She was a bit too, well, Mediterranean for Jason's taste, but Karl seemed to go for that type.

And another mystery solved. Now we know why Karl's been ignoring Doria's come-on. His mind, such as it is, is elsewhere.

"Hakim?" Slovotsky interrupted his thoughts with a friendly bellow. "Something going on that I don't know about?" There was just a hint of threat in the question.

"Ask Doc. Ricky, toss me a cigarette."

Riccetti obediently pulled a box of Marlboros out of his faded blue workshirt and rolled one across the table.

"And a match?"

Without pausing in his hushed conversation with the woman

next to him, Karl Cullinane pulled out a shiny new Zippo and slid it across the table to him.

"Thanks, Karl. You going to introduce us all to your friend, or do we have to wait until Doc issues us psi ratings?"

"Cute." Karl's face made the word a lie. "Andrea Andropolous, Jason Parker."

Jason nodded, As Andrea smiled in response, he decided to reconsider his original appraisal. Nice.

"The one with the maps, charts, and calculator"—Karl jerked a thumb toward Riccetti—"is Luigi Riccetti."

"*Lou.*" Riccetti didn't bother to look up.

"Doesn't matter; call him Ricky, just like everybody else. You've met the rest, except for Dr. Deighton, and—"

"By the process of elimination, she should be able to infer that I'm he, no?" Deighton set his briefcase on the table and opened it, careful as always to keep the open back toward the table, the contents hidden from view. "And, as everyone is here, shall we begin?"

"Hold it, Doc," Karl objected. "We haven't rolled up a character for Andy yet."

Deighton smiled indulgently. "That was what I meant by beginning, at least in part. Do you think you can help her with that—honestly, mind you—while paying attention to my briefing?"

"What briefing? We're still stuck in the treasure room, a whole bunch of dead critters and jewels lying around, Barak cut up pretty bad, and—"

"Actually, I am terminating this campaign. We start a new one tonight. From scratch." Deighton raised a palm. "All I ask is that you give it a try. If, say, after half the evening—even just an hour, perhaps?—the consensus is that the old one is more entertaining, we will resume where we left off." He tapped his briefcase with a gnarled forefinger. "But I've spent quite a bit of time on this new campaign. I expect—I am certain that it will appeal to you." Deighton smiled, momentarily appearing much younger than his sixty-odd years. "Quite certain."

Slovotsky shrugged. "Let's give it a try, then. James, that okay with you?"

"Fine."

The big man gave Jason a meaningful glance. "And now I understand what you were up to before. I'm supposed to run a thief this time. Hakim Singh, just as a guess?"

"It would help balance the team." Jason puffed on his cigarette. "But it's up to you."

"What do you know that I don't know?"

"Quite a—"

"Gentlemen." Deighton rapped the stem of his pipe on the table. "In answer to your question, Mr. Slovotsky, Mr. Parker knows nothing that a few minutes of listening to me won't teach you." He raised a bushy eyebrow. "If that's acceptable. Mr. Riccetti, if you will be kind enough to close the door and spin the dimmer switch down to low, we will begin." Deighton took a deep breath.

"Now."

CHAPTER TWO: *The Game*

> *The chess board is the world, the pieces are the phenomena of the universe, the rules of the game are what we call the laws of Nature. The player on the other side is hidden from us. We know that his play is always fair, just and patient. But we also know, to our cost, that he never overlooks a mistake, or makes the smallest allowance for ignorance.*

> —Thomas Henry Huxley

While Deighton began to speak in low, mysterious tones, Karl Cullinane borrowed five four-sided dice from James Michael, then slid a well-chewed pencil and a sheet of paper in front of Andy-Andy.

She picked up one of the dice. "Funny-looking little pyramid. But how do you get the numbers to come up on top?"

"You don't. Look at it a bit closer." Instead of being stamped in the center of the faces, the numbers, zero through three, were along the edges; when the die was thrown, the player would read the upright number, the one closest to the table. "But I want to keep half an ear on what Doc's saying, so we'll make this mechanical—I'll fill you in on the background later. Okay?"

"Fine. But bear with me if I'm slow."

He couldn't let that pass without turning to look her straight in the eye, letting a tight grin creep across his face. She didn't have the grace to blush.

"This campaign," Deighton intoned, his face lit demonically by the light of the flashlight in his opened briefcase, "is the Quest for the Gate Between Worlds. . . ."

"Now write this down on the paper: ST, S, I, W, MD, WP, E, and C."

". . . find yourselves on a hilltop, overlooking a vast walled city, and—"

"Doc?" Karl half-raised a hand, then brought it down.

"*Yes?*" Deighton snapped.

"Sorry for interrupting, but I've got to know: How do you want me to generate her character? And what level? This sounds like a pretty heavy-duty campaign; you're not sending in an A-Class character, are you?"

"Good point." Deighton nodded a quick apology. "Try . . . three rolls for each characteristic, and set Miss Andropolous up as a C-Class whatever. If her Intelligence is high enough, try for a wizard; the company is a trifle light in that department—"

"Wait a minute!" Riccetti's head snapped up. "I—"

"—*despite* the great skills and talents of Aristobulus. Now, if I may proceed . . ."

Andy-Andy tilted her head close to his. "Intelligence? If he's suggesting—"

"No, he was talking about your *character's* intelligence. But let's roll Strength, first." He gestured at the five dice. "Go ahead."

Andy-Andy shrugged, took the dice, and rolled them gently. "Three, three, one, and two zeros—how's that?"

"Not too good; strictly average, in fact. The top possible score's fifteen. Try again; twice more, in fact. I think we can better a seven."

The next roll brought a total of five, the one after, a nine. "That's not too bad, but it's not too good; your character's barely above average Strength. Speed next. It's related to Strength; we throw out all rolls that aren't within two points of your Strength score of nine."

Her first roll was five zeros. "Doesn't count," Karl said. "Three more tries."

In the three tries, she couldn't do better than eight. "So you've got average Speed. Roll for Intelligence, now."

Her best score out of three rolls was *the* best score. "A full fifteen, and that's good. Means you can be a wizard—like being a magician, except for real."

"Almost."

"Right."

Deighton droned on, ". . . to the north, you see a great body of water stretching out to the horizon. It could be an inland sea, but the wind blowing across it brings no smell of salt; you suspect that it is a lake, instead . . ."

"Roll for Wisdom."

"Wisdom? What's the difference between that and Intelligence?"

"Edith Bunker."

"*What?*" She flinched as the others glared as though in chorus. "What?" she whispered.

"I said, 'Edith Bunker'—from *All in the Family?* Not too bright, but wise as all hell. Or to take a counterexample, Richard Nixon. Get it?"

"Fine."

Three rolls gave her a ten. "That's not too bad," he said. "Manual Dexterity is next."

"As opposed to electric dexterity?" She arched an eyebrow.

"As opposed to Weapon Proficiency—wizards can be dexterous as hell, but not with weapons. It comes with the territory. Roll."

". . . beside your party is a collection of large wooden boxes. Except for weapons and personal effects, they are the only equipment you have with you . . ."

The best she could do was five. "Too bad. Guess I'm clumsy, eh?"

"And cold." He smiled. "Now, Weapon Proficiency."

Her first roll was a total of twelve. "Which is a waste of some good numbers," Karl said. "The best WP a wizard can have is five, which is what we'll give you. Now try Endurance."

". . . you have no sure recollection of how you got to this hillside, and the only possibility that suggests itself is too incredible to be taken seriously . . ."

"Hmm, a thirteen." She lifted her head. "Which means I'm hardy as hell, right?"

"Close. One more to go."

"What's the C stand for?"

"Charisma. Roll."

Her first roll was a perfect five threes. "Which figures," he mumbled.

Andy-Andy just smiled back.

". . . and now," Deighton straightened himself, "all that remains is for you to decide who you are, and what to do next."

"Not quite, Doc." Karl tapped Andy-Andy's sheet. "Still got to work out her spells, decide on a character."

"Quite right. Miss Andropolous, if you'll step over here, you and I can work that out. Mr. Cullinane tends to be a bit too . . . generous with spells, as I recall."

"*Not* fair." James Michael's voice held a decided edge. "I was there the time Karl rolled up Martin the Illusionist. Righteous rolls, all of them."

"As it may be." Deighton motioned Andy-Andy over to his side of the table. "And now, it is time for you to decide on your characters, weapons, and effects."

James Michael Finnegan held himself back from the arguments over who was going to do what. There was no question that he was going to be Ahira Bandylegs, a dwarf warrior of great Strength and Weapon Proficiency, average Intelligence, Wisdom, and Charisma, low Speed—because of the three-point penalty for his short dwarf's legs—but with an Endurance level that was just this side of magical. That was settled, for certain. On the other hand—

"Dammit, I *don't* want to be the cleric this time." Doria thumped her hand on the table. "Let me run a warrior, a thief, a wizard—and get to *do* something. One of you be the cleric."

Cullinane shook his head. "Who? The only one of us with a reasonably high-level cleric is Walter. And as I recall, his cleric's only about a D-Class—we'll be better off with Walter as a thief." Cullinane shrugged. "It makes sense to do it that way."

Slovotsky shifted position uncomfortably. "I do have a cleric character." He licked his thumb and riffled through the character sheets in front of him. "Gin. But it's Rudolph—"

"—the Incompetent," Jason Parker finished, his voice taking on a whining tone that made James Michael itch. "Forget it. A

D-Class cleric in a killer campaign? C'mon, Dore—stick with what you're best at.''

Riccetti sucked air in through his teeth. "Why don't we let her decide for herself? If she's tired of being a cleric, if she wants to do something else, let her.''

"Thanks, Ricky." Doria smiled a promise at him.

Now *that* was strange. Riccetti always followed Parker's lead, but . . .

Of course. James Michael nodded. The only character of a higher class than Riccetti's Aristobulus was Doria's cleric, and Riccetti wanted to be the most advanced character in the game.

Cullinane spun around. "You want to be the cleric?"

Riccetti sneered. "And have our only wizard be a C-Class novice? Don't be silly.''

James Michael sighed. If this haggling went on much longer, it would threaten to cut heavily into playing time. And that would be intolerable. "Excuse me." Five pairs of eyes fastened on him. "Ricky, it seems to me that you're being kind of . . . generous. Usually, you're the one pushing for a balanced team. At least you were, until Doria went up to K-Class.''

"Yes, but . . ." Riccetti obviously couldn't think of a but.

"But nothing. The fact is that Doria of the Healing Hand is K-Class. Aristobulus is J-Class, one level lower. I'm sure, Ricky, that you'll put aside your jealousy. For the good of the group.'' He turned to Doria. "If you're willing to be the cleric, that is.''

Suddenly, he was ashamed of himself. Not that he'd meant it that way, but Doria was taking it as a request from a cripple. And she wouldn't turn down a little feeb, would she? *Please, Doria, say no. You wouldn't give in to anyone else on this. Treat me like everyone else, for once. Please?*

She nodded. "I'll be the cleric—but I want to have a say in your characters. You choose mine, I get to veto yours if I don't like it. Agreed?''

"Agreed," James Michael sighed.

"Fine," Parker said. "Ricky and I were talking to Doc on the way in; he kind of agreed that it would be a good idea for Walter to run Hakim, if that's—''

"Yippee!" Walter leered at Doria. "This thief's going to steal your heart, he is." He riffled through his character sheets and selected one. "I like that greasy bastard. Please don't veto him, Doria-beautiful, please?" He clasped his hands below his chin and ducked his head.

"Okay, okay." Doria turned to Parker. "And I suppose you've decided on a character already?"

Parker shrugged. "Einar Lightfingers, I guess—Doc suggested that we might want to have a couple of thieves along. Particularly if we're going to have to steal this Gate thing."

Cullinane's head snapped back from his almost constant staring at the new girl, who was still talking with Doc in the corner of the room. "Steal it? Do we know that it's portable? I was helping Andy roll up her character; must've missed something."

"No." James Michael made it final. "We don't know what it is, where it is, or how it does what it does—although I'm willing to bet I know *what* it does."

"Big fat hairy deal." Walter waved it away. "Getting to it, and then doing whatever the hell we're supposed to do after we get to it—"

"—is the problem." Parker tapped a pencil against the table. "But we're getting a bit ahead of ourselves. Doria hasn't okayed me as Lightfingers, James as Ahira, or Ricky as Aristobulus— you want to veto them, Dore?"

James Michael suppressed a scowl. Cute—by lumping his and Riccetti's characters in with James Michael's Ahira, Parker was making it more than a little awkward for Doria to exercise a veto.

Doria opened her mouth, closed it again. A quick glance at James Michael, then, "No. No veto."

"Fine." Parker slid a sheet of paper in front of him and picked up his pencil. "Now, on to weapons. . . . I don't see any problem for Lightfingers: shortsword, dagger, and a few throwing darts should do it." He looked over at Riccetti. "Unless you think I can get away with armor."

"Out of character. But how about tools?"

Parker lifted his head. "Doc? Do thief's tools come under the heading of personal effects?"

"Don't worry about it. I suspect rather strongly that you'll find all that you need in the wooden boxes next to your party, on the hillside." Deighton turned back to Andrea.

"Fine." Parker glared at his back. "Just fine."

James Michael tapped Slovotsky's leg. "Do you think I could arrange to borrow Hakim's plus-three battleaxe?"

"Nope." Walter didn't bother to take the sting out of the refusal. "Hakim doesn't *lend* anybody anything. You want to talk buying?"

"With Hakim? What would the price be? Two or three times whatever I could come up with?"

Doria laughed. "He's got you. Probably four. James, you'd better stick with your usual stuff; the battleaxe, crossbow, and . . ." she wrinkled her forehead.

"Flail. I like to go well armed."

"Flail," she agreed. "If you think you can carry all . . ."

Everyone was silent for a moment. *Damm it, why can't you forget about it for one bloody second?*

Walter raised himself and stretched. "Hakim, m'friends, will be carrying a scimitar, and two braces of throwing knives."

"Be more specific, please. How many knives in a brace?" James Michael kept his words as acid as possible, but couldn't help smiling his thanks.

"Two. Always two in a brace." Walter quirked a smile at Karl. "And if you're running Barak, I assume he still turns up his nose at anything except his two-handed broadsword?"

"Yup." Cullinane sat back. "Established character trait."

"Wait a minute." Doria sounded more calculating than peeved. "I'm thinking about changing my mind and vetoing Barak."

Karl snatched his lighter from the table, stuck a cigarette in his mouth, and lit it. "Make up your mind." He *snapped* the lighter closed. "I've been running Barak all semester, but if you've got an objection, let me know. You think I've got another character that'll be better for the team?"

"No, but . . ."

"Doria's within her rights, Karl," James Michael said. *You stupid bastard. You treat her like a piece of furniture, then get offended when she insists on a bit of attention.*

"Thank you, James. But go ahead, Karl, run Barak." She smiled ingratiatingly.

James Michael tried to keep his face straight, but brought his hands up to rub at his eyes in case he failed. *All the dynamics of a kindergarten. Doria's still chasing after Cullinane. He's hooked on Andrea—badly, unless I miss my guess. And to make it worse, Parker has been shooting meaningful glances Andrea's*

*way, and Cullinane's looking as though he wishes he had a real
sword to run through Parker's guts.*

*So Doria tries a quick I-don't-have-to-let-you-but-I-will to get
some attention. All of which means—*

Walter Slovotsky leaned over. "Looks to be an interesting
evening, all things considered." He tapped his temple with a
stubby finger that was almost the size of a hotdog. "Wal-ter may
look dumb. Doesn't mean he is."

"Just what I was thinking. On both counts." James Michael
raised his voice. "And since neither Aristobulus nor Doria carry
weapons, I think we're all set. Except for picking a team leader,
of course."

Parker sat smugly in his chair. Which wasn't totally unreasonable; he'd been doing an adequate job as team leader in the Draa
Dungeon campaign, the adventure that Deighton had just
terminated. But that was as a warrior, not a thief.

Walter reached out and laid a massive hand on James Michael's
shoulder. "You think you're up to it, Jimmy me boy?"

"*What?*" Parker was stunned; Cullinane, Doria, and Riccetti
smiled their approval in unison, as though they had rehearsed it.
Even Riccetti? Hell, Ricky followed Parker around like an obedient spaniel.

"Makes sense," Riccetti said, drumming his impatience on
the table with nail-bitten fingers. "Can't have a thief as team
leader; nobody'll trust him farther than I could throw Walter."
For Ricky, the game came first.

"Yes, but—"

"But nothing, Jase." Cullinane was enjoying this, perhaps a
little too much. "James has been gaming longest here; he hasn't
been team leader in quite a while. Give him a chance." His
glance over toward Andrea took most of the pleasure out of
hearing that. James Michael wished there hadn't been . . . superfluous reasons.

"Doria-beautiful, speak up." Walter slipped down from the
table, stretching broadly. "If you're in agreement, then let's
have Doc finish getting Andrea's character ready, and play." He
rubbed his hands together in mock impatience.

"It's okay with me. Besides, there'll be plenty of time to
argue—and fight—once we start playing." She turned to James
Michael, and actually smiled as if she meant it. "You're on,
Ahira."

"Fine." James Michael folded his hands in his lap. "Okay, everybody—character sheets to Doc. Start an encumbrance list."

"With what?" Parker was still chafing.

"With just your weapons and armor, so far. Once we open the boxes, you'll add to that. Doria of the Healing Hand?"

"Yes, Ahira?"

"I'll need to know your spells—that goes for you, too, Aristobulus."

Riccetti—*no, Aristobulus; get into the spirit of it*—nodded. "You want me to write them down for you?"

"Ahira doesn't carry sheets of paper. Orally, of course. You first."

"Okay." Riccetti closed his eyes. If James Michael could remember his spells, so could he.

Good.

"I'm carrying . . . Herstell's Spell of—"

"Just the short names."

"Make that Sleep, Lightning, Fire, Glow Temporarily, the two-way version of Charm, Injure, Preserve, Shatter Metal, and Dispel Magic. That's nine, isn't it?"

"Yes. And that's fine. Don't waste them, now." One of the rules of the game was that a wizard's spells were immediately forgotten when used. It was sort of like firing a gun; the gun could be reloaded, but a spent cartridge was gone. And it would take valuable time out of a campaign for a wizard to relearn his spells from his spell books. Often that time couldn't be spared. "Doria?"

She had to consult her notes. "I'll memorize them, Ahira. . . . Here they are: Heal Minor Wounds—I've got that one three times—Make Edible—"

"Handy. Good choice." Situations could come up where there wouldn't be food at hand. But with that spell, the company could survive for a long time on *anything;* she could even make cafeteria food edible.

"Thanks, Ja—Ahira. . . . Ah, and Warm, Glow, Heal Disease, the Gift of Tongues, Heal Serious Wounds, and—ta-da!—Locate. That last could be handy, no?"

"Very. But be careful. You'll have to know what the Gate is, roughly where it is . . . and we'll have to be reasonably close before you use it." He turned to Cullinane, smiling. "I know what your special skills are."

Karl Cullinane cracked a smile and stroked at the stubble that he no doubt thought of as a beard. "*Arrgh.*"

"Arg, indeed. Hakim."

Walter Slovotsky bounced to attention and bowed from the waist, clasping his hands in front of him. "Thy servant, O short sahib."

"Don't waste the oil on *me*. You might need it later. —We're going to need a thief on this quest, probably."

"Yes, O Source of All Wisdom, but what is thy point?" His look of total innocence was perhaps a bit overdone.

"It would be a shame to have to execute you for stealing from members of the party." James Michael mimed hefting an axe. "A great loss."

"As it would be to thy servant." Walter felt at his neck. "So this unworthy one shall keep thy counsels in mind."

"See that you do." This was getting better all the time. "And Lightfingers."

Visibly, Parker considered giving him a hard time, not playing along. James Michael was counting on Parker's basic desire to play to overcome his irritation at not getting to be team leader for once. For a moment, opposed desires balanced. Finally, Parker shrugged and answered in a harsh whisper. "And what do *you* want?"

Good. "I want you to listen very closely to me, *thief.*"

"I always listen closely. To humans, at least. Not to a filthy little dwarf."

"Barak? Do you think I should have to take this?"

"No. You want me to persuade him, Ahira?"

James Michael glanced over at Deighton, who was again standing in front of his open briefcase, his hands hidden inside. One of the things James Michael liked—a lot—about Doc Deighton's gamemastering was that Doc almost always chose to do the dice-rolling himself, freeing the players from as much of the mechanics of the game as was possible. It helped to maintain the illusion, the atmosphere. "Will that be necessary, Einar Lightfingers? Barak would lop off your remaining hand if I asked him to." And Karl Cullinane would probably enjoy kicking Jason Parker out of the game by killing off Parker's character.

Lightfingers/Parker sighed. "What do you want me to do?"

"Good. And it's not what I want you to do, it's what I want

you *not* to do. Understood?" He rapped on the table. "I know your habits; we won't have any of that nonsense in this company."

Pause. "Understood."

And we're off. He gave a slight nod at Deighton.

"You have just awoken on a hillside," Deighton intoned, "a company of . . . six adventurers, seeking treasure and fame."

"Wait a minute," Aristobulus grated. "How did we get here? And I thought that there was—"

"Patience, please. Last night, you all slept in an inn, which was located in a village just south of the great walled city, D'tareth. You don't know how you got here." He stopped.

Doria picked up the hint. "Where the hell are we?"

"Yeah."

"What're we doing on this hilltop?"

"Last thing I knew, I was kicking the serving girl out of bed so I could get some sleep." That was from Slovotsky/Hakim; Ahira leaned back, closed his eyes, and smiled.

"From the top of this hill, you can see the dawn sun, rising over another walled city. It is not D'tareth; the walls of this city are of some wet-looking gray stone."

"Forget the distance—what's close up?" Ahira understood Parker's impatience, but wished that he'd contain himself. They would learn, soon enough.

"Beside you on the hillside are half a dozen large wooden boxes. They are plain, almost cubical, each side roughly the height of a dwarf."

Eyes still closed, Ahira spoke up. "Nobody touch the boxes. We don't know what's in them."

"I'll dispel any spells."

"You're not thinking, Aristobulus," Ahira shot back. "First, if it's harmless, you're wasting a spell. Second, there could be, say, a magic carpet inside. You want to turn it into a throw rug?"

"But what can we *do?*"

"Hakim." He voiced it as a command.

"Here, sahib."

"You want to give the boxes a try? Careful, now."

A deep chuckle. "So you want me to be the sacrificial meat? Very well. I walk over to the nearest of the boxes and run my fingertips lightly over its top surface."

Deighton: "You feel nothing unusual, although your . . . ." As he paused, dice clattered. "Your suspicion is that there is a hidden catch."

"For some reason or other, I suspect that there is a hidden catch, Ahira. You want me to find it?"

Deighton: "From behind you, you hear a voice."

"Quick!" Ahira said. "Everybody, turn around. Barak, loose your sword—but don't draw it. Aristobulus, get ready to throw a spell—if anything funny happens, throw it."

"Which one?"

"Lightning." James Michael knew that the new voice would be Andrea's character, joining the group, but Ahira was a suspicious sort, who wouldn't know that, anyway. Best to be prepared.

"As you turn around, you see a young human woman, dressed in the gray robes of a user of magicks. Go ahead."

"I . . . I'm supposed to say . . ." Andrea was uncomfortable; James Michael resigned himself to having a hard time getting her into the spirit of things.

Hakim/Slovotsky's basso boomed, "Speak for yourself—are you possessed by a demon, wench?"

"Wench? Oh. No, I'm not possessed by a demon. I'm, uh, Lotana," she said, the accent firmly on the second syllable, "and," she added in a low monotone, "I'm going to get even with you for this, Karl Cullinane."

Never mind; get back into it.

"Greetings, little girl, would you like a piece of candy?"

"Barak," Ahira snapped out, "if Einar Lightfingers opens his mouth again, stick a sword through his lips."

*"De*lighted."

Bringing a new player—a new *person* into the company was always a touchy situation. Ahira didn't need Lightfingers complicating matters, not with a nov—a not terribly experienced magic user. "Lotana, we are a band of adventurers, seeking . . . something, although we don't quite know what, *yet*."

Deighton: "You have a vague, unexplainable feeling that what you are looking for is something called the Gate Between Worlds."

"Although we all share a vague suspicion that we're looking for the Gate Between Worlds, whatever that is. Would you like to join us?"

"Sure. Uh, what were you going to do about those boxes on the hillside?"

Doria's voice was almost a whine. "Open them, silly."

"Okay, fine, I'll open them."

"No, don't—"

"As the first box was opened, you are overwhelmed by a rush of . . ."

James Michael couldn't hear the rest; a rush of sound like the roar of an impossibly loud, impossibly near jet buffeted his ears, acrid smoke invading his nostrils until he found himself on his knees in a coughing spasm, his tearing eyes jammed shut.

He bounced to his feet on the damp grass, reflexively reaching for the axe strapped to his chest, loosening the straps with two quick jerks and taking the axe in his gnarled, well-muscled hands.

Well-muscled hands?

He opened his eyes.

He was standing on the side of a grassy hill, a dwarf with an axe in his hands.

"Ohmygod."

PART TWO:

Lundeyll

CHAPTER THREE: *"It Isn't a Game Anymore"*

> *I do not know whether I was then a man dreaming I was a butterfly, or whether I am now a butterfly dreaming I am a man.*
>
> —Chang-tzu

"Jason, *wake up*," James Michael's voice rasped.

Jason Parker shrugged the hand from his shoulders, reaching for the covers, to pull them over his head. But the covers weren't there.

"Want me to try?" The voice was Karl Cullinane's, but changed: a deep, rich baritone.

"No, we'll do it. You go back to your little friend," Doria said. "Maybe she's over her crying jag by now."

Jason pried an eye open, squinting painfully in the bright sunlight. Doria knelt on the grass next to him. But it wasn't Doria, not exactly. She was older, gaunt, the rounded features of her face having changed into the well-defined ones of a thirtyish woman. And her eyes were strange; *nobody* had yellow irises.

But Doria did. And that seemed . . . right, familiar.

"What the hell?" Jason jerked upright, now totally awake. Maybe.

He was sitting on damp morning grass, wearing a musky-smelling leather jerkin and dew-damp gray woolen leggings, an ivory-hilted shortsword in its scabbard at the right side of

47

his waist, a sheathed dagger strapped to his chest beneath his jerkin.

He reached his right hand up to his face, to slap himself awake. This had all the makings of a *bad* bad dream.

He missed; air brushed his cheek. *Missed?* He looked down at his arm. Instead of a hand on the end of his withered, age-spotted right arm, there was nothing but a naked stump, covered with brown keloid scars.

My hand . . . The world went gray.

James Michael's voice came from behind. "Take it easy, Jason. Deep breaths. But you've got to get yourself together. You're next to the last—we still can't get Arist—Ricky to wake up."

He kept his eyes closed. A massive hand gripped the back of his neck, pulling him forward. Reflexively, he retrieved his dagger with his left hand, thrust it over his shoulder—

And found his wrist caught in a bone-crushing grip. The dagger was wrenched out of his fingers, thudding on the ground beside him.

"*Don't* try that again."

"You just go easy on him, Ahira." There was a strength, a confidence in Doria's voice that Jason had never heard before. "It's going to be harder on him than it was on you." Gentle fingers stroked his face. "We'll just have to take this one step at a time."

"Maybe you're right, but I don't like it. Aristobulus is still—"

"Shh. One step at a time."

Jason opened his eyes. Somehow it was fitting that James Michael was a dwarf, a broad-shouldered creature with a huge, broken nose and a jutting jaw. But it was still James Michael's eyes that peered at him from beneath heavy brows.

"You're Ahira."

"That's right." The dwarf smiled, running a hand down the front of his gapped chainmail vest. "We're here, on the other side."

"Other side?"

Ahira shrugged. "Somehow or other . . . never mind, for now. But if I'm Ahira, who are you?"

Doria glared at the dwarf, then clasped Jason's good hand in her two. She was wearing a long, high-necked robe, belted tightly around her waist. "Easy, now. Don't let him rush you."

Jason snatched his hand away and slapped at Doria's sleeve. It didn't even dent; it was like slapping a brick wall. "It works." In the game, Doria of the Healing Hand had a robe like that, a magical one.

She smiled reassuringly and waved her arm, the tightly woven cloth flapping. "It's just like in the game. Feels like a cotton robe from the inside, but from the outside it's like armor. Just like in the game." Her face sobered. "And all of us, we're our characters. Sort of."

"Which means that I'm Lightfingers." A small leather pouch dangled by a thong from her sash. He let his head loll forward as though he were fainting again, slipped his hand across her body while his head movement distracted her, and fingered open the pouch without disturbing the strap that attached it to her belt. He dipped two gnarled fingers in, lifted and palmed a coin, closed the pouch with a gentle tug, and tucked the coin into a pocket inside his sleeve with a practiced flip.

Elapsed time less than three seconds. It felt natural, as though he'd done it thousands of times before. *But I've never stolen anything. It's—*

"A nice try, Jason." Ahira shook his head. "But I was watching for it. Give it back."

"Watching for *what*?" Doria's brow furrowed in exasperation. Now *that* was strange; she always deferred to the little cripple.

Oh. He isn't little anymore. Or crippled. Just short. The snotty bastard must be having the time of his life.

"He just picked your purse." The dwarf chuckled. "Give it back. Now."

"I don't know what you're talking about—and who are you to be giving orders, anyway?" He braced himself on his stump and slid his feet under him. It was the practiced routine of a thief when caught: First deny, then challenge, then *run*.

Ahira grabbed his sleeve and shook the coin out. Picking it up, he handed it to Doria. "Don't worry; I'm not going to give him a hard time. This once." He turned back to Jason. "But we're in enough trouble as it is; I don't want you adding to it. Understood, Lightfingers?"

"My name is Jason." But the name felt strange in his mouth. "And I want to go home."

The dwarf helped him to his feet. Standing, Ahira's head barely came up to his chest. Ahira picked up his battleaxe from

49

the damp grass and tapped a well-chewed thumbnail against the blade. "Two things. In answer to your question, *this* says that I'm in charge here. Back home, the group chose me as team leader. That's the way it is; that's the way it's going to be.

"And second, we are going home." Ahira opened his mouth; shut it. He shook his head. "Just take it easy for a while, get your bearings. Doria, let's go see to the wizard."

Karl Cullinane had often thought of holding Andy-Andy in his arms, but nowhere in his imaginings had she been crying. "Everything will be fine." He patted her clumsily on the back.

But these weren't his arms, this wasn't his body. Not quite. Karl was of average height, and skinny. *Was.* Now, he towered over her as he held her, careful not to squeeze her tightly; somehow, he knew that his grip could break a strong man's back.

After a while, her weeping died down. He let her go, then took a loose sleeve of her gray robe and wiped at her eyes. "Feeling better?"

"N-no. I'm *scared.* What happened?" She rubbed at her temples. "I . . . feel so strange—how do I know that I could turn invisible, or make you fall asleep, or charm—it's like there's something in my head, trying to get *out.*"

Her mouth started to move; he clapped a hand over it. "Don't. Just listen to me, but don't say anything." Her eyes grew wide; she brought up her hands, vaguely pulling at his arm. "*No.* Nod if you understand me, and I'll take my hand away."

Her head moved; he let his hand drop. "Don't do that again," she said, planting a palm against his chest, shoving.

He could have laughed, almost. But he took a step back. "Okay, but be careful what you say. You've got three spells in your head, and they're trying to get out."

"How do you know?"

He shrugged. *I don't know. But I do.* "It's . . . like I've got two minds. One is Barak; the other is me." That a wizard had to constantly rein in spells was something Barak would know. It had to be: Karl hadn't known it; it wasn't part of the game. He stooped slowly, and lifted his scabbarded sword from the grass. "Barak knows how to use this, not me." The sword was long, almost three-fifths his height. Without drawing it from its scabbard, he knew that it was single-edged like a Japanese katana, but straight, not curved; primarily a slashing weapon, it still could be used to thrust. "And why not to strap it to anything; it'd take too long to draw it." He gripped the cord-wound handle with his left hand almost at the pommel. To draw the sword, he would slip the scabbard away, add his right hand in its place on the grip, and strike. That was one of the rules: Get your sword into play, and worry about picking up the scabbard later.

It was important to keep the blade clean and dry; an image of his hands—*his* hands—cleaning the blade with a dead enemy's hair welled up, unbidden.

"But what *happened?*" She gestured at her robes, at him, at the boxes on the hillside. "We're in the place that Dr. Deighton described. Look."

He looked to the east. The early-morning sun sat over the far walls of the city below. Karl raised his hand to his forehead to shield his eyes. The walls were solid and wide; a few bowmen stood on the pathways girdling them. People, and horses drawing two-wheeled carts, swarmed in and out of the gate.

To the north, a vast expanse of dark water spread across the horizon, waves rippling in toward a rocky shore. Off in the distance a broad-beamed schooner glided slowly in toward the docks.

But there was more than Deighton had described; he hadn't mentioned the fishing village to the north, and Karl hadn't visualized it.

How did he know that it was a fishing village?

It was too complicated, too strange. He shook his head. "You're right. I don't know how, but somehow we're *here.*" He stretched his arms, letting his shoulders strain against the seams of his leather jerkin, and drew in a deep breath. It was clean air, fresh and sweet with a tang of ozone; this world had never known the stink of the internal combustion engine. "But doesn't it feel fine?"

"For you." She was nearing tears again. "But how do I get home?"

"I don't know. And I didn't mean it that way—not that I wanted to stay here forever." It was one thing to play at being a warrior, but a fuzzy memory of his sword opening someone's belly like an overripe fruit . . . that didn't feel right, not to Karl Cullinane. *But I'm not just Karl, not anymore. There's a lot of Barak in me, now. Then again, maybe that's not all bad.* He and

Andy-Andy used to be close to the same height, although when she wore heels she'd look down at him. Now he towered over her by a foot, or more. When he stood close to her, she had to crane her neck to look up at him. She wasn't changed, though, at least on the outside, except for the loose robes that had replaced her jeans and shirt.

And the fear in her eyes. That was new. "Karl, how are we going to—"

"I don't know." He shook his head. "But someh—"

"This a private conversation, or can anyone join?" Walter Slovotsky's voice boomed from behind him.

Karl spun around. He hadn't heard the big man—*no, not big anymore; I'm half a head taller than he is.* "Don't do that."

"Don't do what?" Slovotsky smiled innocently. Except for Andy-Andy, he was the least changed of the group, at least physically. His skin had darkened a shade or two, his black hair was slightly straighter and a bit longer, and there were hints of epicanthic folds around his eyes, but that was all. Even his all-is-right-with-the-world smile was intact.

"Don't sneak up on me. I don't like it."

Slovotsky shrugged, muscles playing under the bare skin of his chest. He was dressed as Hakim would be: shirtless, a blousy pair of pants belted tightly to his waist, the cuffs tucked into the lacing of his sandals. From the left side of his waist, a wickedly curved scimitar hung in a leather scabbard; from the right, a tangle of knives and straps. Slovotsky rubbed at his temples. "I guess I should apologize, or something. It's just that moving silently seems to come naturally to me. It's sort of like a new toy, Karl. Or should I call you Barak?"

"Karl." He forced a smile. "Barak would give you a clout on the head as a reminder."

"Good point. You had better call me Walter. Hakim would slip a knife between your ribs, for—" He stopped, puzzled, raising a palm. "Sorry. That wasn't me."

"I understand." Karl unclenched his hand from the hilt of his sword. "But the question is—"

"What the *hell* are we going to do?" There was a new strength in Andy-Andy's voice. Just a little.

Karl gave her a smile. "Right." She was adjusting. A few minutes before, she would have put the emphasis on *do* instead of *hell*.

"In theory, it's simple," Slovotsky said.

"Nonsense." She waved a hand at their surroundings. "Simple?"

"Everything's simple, actually." He held up a well-manicured finger. "First, you figure out what you want."

Karl didn't like the way Slovotsky's eyes roamed up and down her as he said that, but he let it pass.

"Second, you figure out what you have to do to get it." Another finger. "And three"—he added a third, tapping all three fingers against his other hand—"you do it. That's the way life works." He jerked a thumb toward the city below. "Somehow or other, we're in the world that Doc described, no?"

"Yes, but—"

"But nothing, Karl. That has to be our operating assumption, until and unless we find out differently. Which is unlikely. I mean, I've got skills I never had, Doria's got cleric spells trying to bust their way out of her head, you're a full foot taller than you should be, James is—"

"I get the point. But what does that do for us?"

"Simple, again. The name of the campaign Doc designed is, if you'll remember, the Quest for the Gate Between Worlds. How we got here, I don't know. But if we want to get back, then obviously we've got to find this Gate thing." He pointed at the six wooden boxes, just over fifty yards away. One of the boxes stood open and empty; the other five, smooth, dark, and seamless, closed. "I'm willing to bet that there's something inside that'll give us a clue. Or more than a clue."

Hushed voices whispered behind the cluster of boxes.

"They haven't woken Riccetti yet?"

"They're trying. Jimmy—make that Ahira; he likes it better— Ahira thinks that we should have a fully conscious wizard on hand before we try to open any of the rest. And no offense, Lotana—"

"Andrea."

"Andrea, then—no offense, but the way you fell apart, I wouldn't want to count on you to sniff out any spells on them. You think you could spot a Glyph of Shrouding?"

"*I don't know what you're talking about*—wait." Her hands flew to her temples, her fingers digging into her scalp. "It's strange. I know things that I don't know, if you understand what I mean."

53

Karl laid a gentle hand on her arm. "We all do."

She grabbed his hand, squeezing it with white-knuckled fingers. "A glyph is like a magical charm, usually placed on a doorway or entrance. It can hurt anybody trying to get past it, unless it's tuned to leave them alone, or unless they break its spell," she said, her voice calm and businesslike. "Like the ones on the city." She jerked her hand toward the walled city, below. "Right?"

"*What* ones?" Karl and Walter said in unison.

She chuckled. "C'mon, don't play games with me—I don't need that."

Karl sighed and looked back toward the city. Just a walled city, no writing on it. "You see anything, Walter?"

"No." Slovotsky raised an eyebrow. "And that was a part of the game I always had trouble swallowing."

Karl nodded. "Me, too." He shrugged. "Well, another—"

"If you don't mind, I'd like to know what you're talking about. Please?"

"We can't see magical writing," he said. "To Walter and me, that's just a wall."

"Don't be silly, it's plain as . . ." She turned back. "Really?"

"Really. As Deighton said, unless you've got the genes for wizardry, all magical writing is totally transparent to you. What does it say?"

"I can *see* it, not read it. Besides, it isn't something that can be pronounced, but it would fry Aristobulus or me to a crisp if we got inside the city." She wrinkled her forehead. "Wait a minute. How did I—"

"Comes with the territory," Slovotsky said. "Looks like wizards aren't too popular there; probably cost the locals quite a bit to hire one to do the work." He smiled. "But it looks like there's a pony in the bottom of this shitbucket; want to check out the boxes for Glyphs?"

Karl frowned. "I thought you said Ahira wanted to wait."

"I'll check it out with him, first. But"—he clapped a hand to Andy-Andy's shoulder—"it looks like you've got what it takes."

Karl suppressed an urge to knock Slovotsky's hand away from her. "Why don't you go clear it with him, then?"

"Which was something else I wanted to talk to you about. You got any objection to him being in charge? Somebody's got to do it." Slovotsky's face was studiously blank.

Karl thought about it for a moment. In the game, he'd always enjoyed his occasional chances to be the team leader. *But this is for real. I may be good at the game, but this is for real.* "No. No objection As long as there're no PMDs. or anything like that."

"PMD?" Andrea asked. "What's that?"

Slovotsky grinned broadly. "Stands for Polish Mine Detector." He covered his ears with both hands and mimed stomping fearfully on the ground. "*Boom.* Seriously, it's a technique for checking for traps. You send the lowest-class character on ahead. If there's no trap, there's no harm. And if there is, then you bring the player back into the game with a new character. It's kind of hard on the old character, but—"

She looked up at him. "You mean that it kills him. Or her."

"Right, but—"

"But we won't have any of that," Karl said. "Not as long as I'm around."

"I can speak for myself, Karl." She scowled at both of them. "And I'm not going to let myself be a guinea pig."

"Understood, Andrea." Slovotsky nodded and walked away.

"Karl, he seems so . . . sure of himself."

"That's Walter. Possibly Hakim, too." Which was one of the things he'd always envied about Slovotsky. Always so sure of himself, no matter what. And so comfortable around women.

Karl shook his head. Even around Andy-Andy he felt awkward, gawky. And she was a *friend.*

"What are you thinking?"

He returned her smile with interest. "Nothing much." This was ridiculous. Here he was, God knew where, more scared than he cared to admit, even to himself. And thinking about how good it had felt to hold her. "And you wouldn't believe it, anyway."

"Bets?"

"Well, what's the diagnosis?" Ahira asked.

"I think he's in shock." Kneeling over the limp form of Aristobulus, Doria looked up at him. "Shallow breathing, thready pulse." Her fingers dipped into the wizard's short gray hair. "And I think he might have hit his head on one of the boxes; there's a bit of a lump here." She bent over, examining his head more closely. "Although the skin isn't broken. Do you think there might be a blanket or two in one of these boxes? We should keep him warm."

"No."

"What do you mean, no? He could *die.*"

Ahira repressed a smile; she wouldn't have understood. But that felt good; Doria would never have contradicted James Michael Finnegan, would never, ever have argued with a little cripple.

But I'm not a cripple anymore. He bounced on the balls of his feet, reveling in how good, how natural it felt. *I'm Ahira Bandylegs, and I'm strong.* Better *than normal.* "No, he won't die. Try your Healing spell, the one for minor wounds. I think this should count as a minor wound."

"But, James—"

"But nothing. You're a cleric, a healer. You've been complaining about spells buzzing around your head. Here's your chance to get rid of one. You'll have to pray for it, to get it back—but we'll have plenty of time for that later."

Her face paled. "I—I don't know if—"

"I trust you, Doria of the Healing Hand. And so would Aristobulus. Do it. Now."

She nodded a reluctant agreement, and planted spread-fingered hands on the old man's chest. The polish was gone from her nails, just as the fear of him was gone from her manner. Perhaps, somewhere inside, Doria Perlstein was confused, frightened. But not the cleric.

"Easy," he whispered. "It's going to be easy. You've done this a thousand times."

Slowly, her eyes sagged shut, as her weight bore down on her arms, on Aristobulus' chest. The old man looked to be in bad shape; his skin was ashen, his breathing barely perceptible.

Strange, liquid syllables issued from her barely parted lips, starting slowly, then becoming a torrent. Ahira could hear the words distinctly, tried to memorize them.

But he couldn't. Not a phrase, not a word, not a syllable. They vanished from his mind like a snowflake melting on a palm.

The volley of sound flowed into Aristobulus, his breathing becoming deeper, a tinge of pink replacing the fishbelly pallor of his face. The fingers of an outflung arm twitched, then curled, as his eyes snapped open.

Aristobulus sucked in air with a desperate gasp, and a stream of sound issued from his mouth, obscenely guttural and harsh.

And like a striking snake, a bolt of lightning crackled from the tips of his fingers, shattering the nearest of the boxes into a thousand charred, smoking pieces.

"You idiot!" Ahira reached out, grabbed the wizard's throat, setting broad thumbs against his windpipe.

"Stop it! *Stop it!*" Doria's fists beat a rapid tattoo on his back.

Reluctantly, Ahira released Aristobulus, bouncing the old man's head against the grass.

The wizard's eyes were wide. "You told me, have the spell ready—you told me, Ahira." He rubbed at his head. "Ahira? Or are you James . . . ?" He bit his lip.

Ahira spat in disgust and stood. "Take care of him, Doria. Just get him out of my sight." He raised his voice. "Barak, Hakim, Lightfingers, Lotana—get over here. Let's see if there's anything we can salvage out of this . . . mess."

"I . . . don't understand," the wizard whined. He began to cry, to weep like a frightened child.

After more than half an hour on their hands and knees, sorting through charred pieces of bone and horn, smashed vessels of glass and clay, Ahira called a halt.

"Anybody find anything salvageable?"

Barak shook his head, rubbing a sooty finger against a smudge on his nose, which only made it worse. "No, whatever was in here is gone." He lifted a jagged scrap of horn and scraped a clean spot with a thumbnail. "What do you think this was?"

Hakim shrugged. "A Joshua's Horn?"

Lightfingers swore softly under his breath. "And unless I miss my guess, these scraps of leather and parchment were spell books. *Were.* Unless there are duplicates in one of the others, we can kiss Lot—Andrea's and Ari's relearning their spells goodbye." He pitched a shard at the wizard. "You stupid little *shit.*"

This couldn't go on. Ahira agreed with Lightfingers—emphatically—but what was done was done. The problem was what to do now. He wasn't sure that he knew.

Never mind. The leader has to seem to know what he's doing. At least. "Shut up, Lightfingers. We go on from here. Lotana?"

"Andrea," she said, with a friendly nod. Good—at least somebody was on his side. "Yes, Ahira?"

"Do you think that you can check out the rest of the boxes for magic? Without touching them, I mean."

Hakim held up a hand. "I'd better check for mechanical traps."

"Fine. You two do that. And if it seems safe, have Barak open them."

Barak nodded slowly. "You don't think there's any trap."

No, I don't. But if there is, you're probably the most expendable Without the spell books, we can't afford to risk either of the wizards. And we've only got one cleric, and one two-handed thief. "I'm certain of it. I think that what's in the boxes is our supplies, or what's left of them. But be careful, anyway." He beckoned to Lightfingers. "Come here for a moment."

"What do you want?" the thief asked, walking over, stopping a few feet away.

Just about half a foot farther away than I could swing my axe. Which was good; at least it showed caution, if not respect. "We're going to need somebody to scout around, check out the city down there. The wizards are out, what with the glyphs Andrea sees on the walls. And I don't think Barak or I tend to be subtle enough. You think you're up to it? *Jason*," he added, deliberately. Not a whole lot was clear to Ahira, not yet. But one thing he was certain of was that he wanted to encourage the other's Jason-part, not the Lightfingers persona.

Lightfingers stood silently for a moment, rubbing his stump against the point of his jaw. "Yes." He stopped himself in mid-nod. "You do want me to pick up more than information, of course."

"No. Just find out whatever you can. We're going to have to find this Gate thing. Whatever and wherever it is. Which means, among other things, that we'll have to find out where *we* are. And, Jason, you're too valuable to lose. Don't pick any pockets; don't try any swindles. We've got quite a few coins in our pouches; we need information a lot more than money."

"Yes?" Lightfingers tilted his head to one side. "And how much is one gold piece worth, here? It could buy half a town, if gold is scarce. But if not . . ."

"Then maybe we couldn't buy half a sandwich. If they have sandwiches here. Good point."

"It is, isn't it?" Lightfingers' hand came to rest on the hilt of his shortsword, perhaps accidentally.

But perhaps not. Ahira pretended not to notice. "You know, maybe I made a mistake. Declaring myself in charge, that is. You've always been a bit sharper than me. Maybe—"

"Don't be silly. You think Slovotsky or Cullinane and his little friend would follow me? A one-armed thief?"

The dwarf took a slow step forward and laid a hand on Lightfingers' arm. "Perhaps no. But if I am going to be in charge, I'll need your full support. Or I won't be able to do it. If you want—"

Lightfingers cut him off with a full-throated laugh. "James Michael, you little *bastard*. You're damn good at manipulating people, aren't you?" His smile was almost friendly.

Ahira shrugged. "You have to learn a lot of things when you spend your whole life in a wheelchair. Lots of things you can't do for yourself; you have to get other people to do them for you. In your case," he said, smiling, "all the technique in the world isn't going to do any good, is it?"

"Maybe, maybe not. For the time being, I'll follow your lead." He jerked a thumb at the city below. "You want me to leave now?"

Ahira hadn't thought about it. In the game, daytime was safer than night. But a thief was at his best in the dark. "Hmmm. How far away would you say that the city is?"

"Five miles, or close to it. You want another opinion?"

"No, I'm sure you're right." That sounded phony, even in his own ears. But the point, that he was going to trust Lightfingers, had gotten across; Lightfingers was smiling. "What do you think the chances are that they lock up the city at sundown?"

"If they don't, I'd be surprised. Why build a wall around a city if you don't lock up?"

"Right. So, time it so you get there just about an hour before sundown. Plan to spend the night inside. Find out whatever you can, then get back up here, first thing in the morning. Understood?"

"Fine." The thief nodded. "Which means—figure it'll take two hours to get down there—that I ought to leave, say, about three hours after noon. Sounds good?"

Noon was still a while off; the sun was at about a forty-five-degree angle. "Right. So get Hakim. We'll see if there're any

59

blankets in those boxes. You two duck into the woods and get some sleep.'' It would be best for them to stay awake all night. In preindustrial cities, the night was a time of danger, when the only safe place to sleep would be behind locked, barred doors.

"*Hakim?*" Lightfingers glared down at him. "What do you mean?"

"He's going along." *I may have to trust you a bit, Jason, but I'm not going to go overboard about it.* "Two is better than one. Besides, I want you to keep an eye on him."

A snicker. "Don't play games with me. It's me that—"

"*Ahira, Lightfingers—we found something.*" Andrea jumped up from in front of a now-open box, waving a sheaf of paper. "It's a letter. From Dr. Deighton."

CHAPTER FOUR: *"It Should be Relatively Easy"*

There is no one who can return from there
To describe their nature, to describe their dissolution,
That he may still our desires,
Until we reach the place where they have gone.

—*The Song of the Harper*, Stanza Five

Jason threw his arms up in disgust. "I can't read that. What the hell language is it in?" It was frustrating. The letters on the page looked familiar, but strange. Clearly, they formed words. But not for him.

Andrea's brow wrinkled. "It's easy. Listen: 'Tikrach amalo, ift recet quirto blosriet az . . .'"

Dear friends, please accept my sincere apologies . . .

She raised her head. "Can't any of you *read?*"

Barak tugged at his beard. "No." He shook his head sadly. "I can understand it, but I'm not literate. Not in Erendra."

Erendra. Eren meant man, or human; *dra* was a shortened form of *dravhen*, mouth. Man-mouth: a language for humans. But how did he know that? No, Jason didn't know that—Lightfingers did. *And that's who I am.*

Ahira shrugged. "That makes sense, actually. Aristobulus, Doria—take a look. Bet you can read it."

They could. "It's easy," Doria said. "But you can't . . . ?"

No, Hakim, Barak, Ahira, and Lightfingers couldn't.

61

"Damn." Lightfingers rubbed his fingertips against his stump. It did make sense, of a sort. They all had the abilities of their characters, plus their memories of the other side. But no more than that. Barak, Lightfingers, Hakim, and Ahira weren't literate in the game; warriors and thieves didn't need to be. On the other hand, clerics and wizards had to be able to read.

He licked the tip of his index finger and wrote his other name in the dust on top of an unopened box. *JASON.* He could read *that,* at least. Thank God.

"Right." Ahira looked down at the letters, just a few inches below his eyes. "We haven't lost anything, but"—he smiled—"alu n'atega nit damn ekta, pi agli." *We haven't gained too damn much, either.*

Interesting. Damn was the same word in both languages. And that suggested a possibility. . . .

He looked at the others. Barak was the most bothered by it; the big man sat on the ground, his face buried in his hands. Or was it Barak that was bothered? Quite probably, illiteracy was more distressing to Karl.

Hakim stood easily, confidently. "Well, which of you magical folks is going to give me reading lessons? Damned if I'm not going to be able to *read.*"

"That's the spirit." Ahira clapped him on the back. "But maybe we're not going to have to hang around here long enough for that to be a problem. Andrea, how about reading the letter? Out loud, for the sake of us"—he smiled—"disabled types."

Barak shook his head. "Why the hell didn't he just write it in English?"

Andrea, sitting with the letter on her lap, smiled reassuringly at him. "He did, I think. But the letter translated across, just as our bodies did. Either that, or he was trying to show off. Ari?"

The old man twined his fingers in his gray beard. "I don't know; it could work either way." He closed his eyes. "Which . . . depends on the complexity of the spell he used. And that depends on how magic works there." He opened his eyes and shrugged. "Which is something I can only guess at. Let me see the letter." He held out a hand. "I—"

"*No.*" It was bad enough that he'd been robbed of his literacy, at least for all practical purposes. But Jason didn't want to become some sort of second-class citizen. "No, you read it. Out loud. Give all of us a chance to understand it at the same time."

Ahira nodded. "Go ahead."

She began, reading in Erendra, pausing only occasionaly for breath.

Dear Friends,

Please accept my sincere apologies for not warning you about what was to happen. I am sorry for any distress you suffered, but I really had no choice: Had I warned you, you never would have believed me.

As I am sure you have gathered by now, you are in the world on which I modeled the little games we played together. Except they weren't just games.

I am not going to bore you with a long rendition of the difficulties this caused me as a child, but I have always had an ability to see into another world—this world that you are now in, since you are reading this. Quite clearly, I am not the only one who has ever had these visions, although I flatter myself by feeling that no one has ever had them so clearly. Not that it is ever terribly clear; the different time rates of our two worlds have always made events on the other side—your side— seem to happen so quickly that they are difficult to follow, even when my fleeting visions are so powerful that they overwhelm my senses.

My friends, I hunger for this world; given the chance, here, I know that I would be the most powerful wizard that this world has ever known. Were I able to transfer myself, as I did you, I would have.

But I can't. Magic works differently in the two worlds; in ours, it is an erratic force. As I write this, I have been trying to transfer material objects for twenty years, succeeding only slightly better than one percent of the time. And always, the objects change; only recently have I been able to control that change.

People, or any sentient creatures, are a different matter. There is a force in our world, called the collective unconscious, which inhibits the transfer of such. To put it simply, all of you belonged in our world, and there was nothing that I could do to transfer you as long as that obtained.

But there is ample evidence of individuals who have been liberated from the collective unconscious, and, given the proper set of conditions, have popped from one world to the other. Benjamin Bathurst and Ambrose Bierce are the two best known examples; no doubt there have been others.

As I write this, I don't know if I will be able to duplicate those conditions with any success; I do know that I can't do it for myself. A corollary of self-referential theory may, indeed, make that an impossibility for one confined to our world.

But, as you read this, you know that I have been able to duplicate those conditions for you, with the aid of much preparation and your participation in our game. I don't know who you are—as I write this, I have been trying different combinations of enchantments and individuals for a number of years, setting up caches of supplies at many different sites. The sites have been, as I'm sure you have gathered by now, always the places where our campaigns have started.

I would be very surprised if you all are not angry with me right now. But please try to understand: With what I know from my sight, I could be the greatest wizard, the most powerful user of magic that this world has ever known; instead, I find myself in the grips of academia, this world hovering in front of me like a ripe fruit.

But there is a way across. In this universe, there is a device called a Gate, a Gate Between Worlds, that can open up a pathway between our universes. I ask that you go to the Gate, and bring me through.

And in return, I promise to gratify your every wish.

To make this possible, along with the various supplies you will find in the other boxes, there is one box which I am certain you will regard as a treasure chest. Its contents are the result of years and years of research and experimentation. You will find a Horn, a lengthy book of spells, ten Cloaks of Transposition—but I don't need to go on; the contents are self-explanatory. Use and enjoy them.

These devices, together with the map of this world, will enable you to get from where you are to where the

Gate is, and help you subdue the Gate's guardian so that you can bring me through with ease.

As for the rest of the supplies, they should prevent your having to buy anything locally. Please distribute the brandy among yourselves as a treat from me, and in partial apology for the discomfort I have caused you.

When you bring me through, you will receive the rest of my apology. Those among you foolish enough to wish to return to our dull, drab world will be given a ton of gold. And for those of you who wish to remain with me, I promise to gratify your every wish. And I mean that literally.

Andrea lifted her head, and looked directly at Barak. "And it ends, 'with most sincere best wishes.' "

Barak rose to his full height, slipping his scabbard from his sword, and dropped the scabbard to the grass. "Can you hear me, you bastard? *This* is what you get, when I get my hands on you." He spun on Aristobulus. "Get a sword."

"What?" The old man cowered.

"Get a sword, so I can kill you fairly. That box!" He waved his sword at the shards littering the hillside. "The one with the treasures. You broke it, you—"

"Enough, Barak." Ahira moved in front of him, his battleaxe held easily in his massive hands. "We're in enough trouble as it is. I'm not going to have you—or anyone else—killed. Is that understood?"

Barak snickered. The dwarf was threatening him? Ahira might be a lot stronger, but his sword had the reach. "Me killed? Don't be more stupid than—"

"Karl!" Andy-Andy moved between the two. "Stop it."

Karl? Who is— "Oh." He took a deep breath. He was Karl Cullinane, and Karl Cullinane did not carve up a helpless old man like a side of beef.

He stooped slowly and picked up his discarded scabbard, slipping the sword easily home.

Aristobulus got to his feet. "I understand your anger. I was most . . . disoriented upon awakening." He turned to the others. "And I do apologize, to the entire company." He sucked in air through his teeth. "But it is worst for Andrea and myself. The box I inadvertently destroyed contained the spell book. Unless we can find duplicates, I am limited to the spells in my head. Just those, and when they are gone, no more." The wizard took a step back and raised his hands. "It would be a shame to waste one—Fire, say—in defending myself."

Barak smiled and took a step forward. "Try it. I bet I get my hands around your throat bef—" The prick of a knifeblade at the back of his neck stopped him.

"Easy, Karl." Walter was calm as always. "No fights. You heard Ahira."

If he moved forward quickly enough, while kicking back hard enough, he could—*no*, Barak thought, *not a good risk*. "Then how about—"

Ahira held up a palm. "I'll deal with Aristobulus." He turned to the wizard. "Put your arms down."

"I—"

"Put them *down!*" The dwarf planted himself in front of the old man, dropped his axe to the ground, and folded his arms over his massive chest. "We had better settle this now. Are you willing to take orders like everyone else, or do you want to strike out on your own?"

Aristobulus sneered. "That's an empty threat. You don't dare abandon me." He waved a hand at Andy-Andy. "And leave her as your only wizard?"

Ahira turned his back on him. "Then get going. Hakim, put the knife away. Barak, you agree that I'm in charge?"

He rubbed at the spot where the knifepoint had been, surprised to find no blood on his finger. "For now." Was the dwarf really going to get rid of Aristobulus? With the loss of the treasure box, that would make things more than difficult. But he was right. They were in enough trouble; there just wasn't room for internal dissension. "As long as you think you can get us home, Ahira."

The dwarf nodded. "I don't just think it, I swear it." He turned back to the wizard and did a double take, as though he were surprised to see Aristobulus still there. "I thought I told you to get going."

"Now wait a minute. You—"

"No. You're either one of us, or you're not. You decided not. So leave."

"But . . . how can I—how do you expect me to—"

"Frankly, I expect you to die. A wizard, without spell books, alone? You don't have a chance. You needed us more than we needed you.'' Ahira planted a hand against Aristobulus' chest and pushed him sprawling. He turned to Karl. ''If he's not gone in two minutes, you get a chance to see whether you can work that sword faster than he can work his mouth.'' The dwarf closed one eye in a broad wink.

Good for you. I just hope that this works. ''Understood.'' He took a step toward the fallen wizard.

''Wait!'' The fear in Aristobulus' voice matched the ashen pallor of his face. ''I agree. You're in charge.''

Karl didn't look at Ahira as he advanced on the wizard. ''You want to give him another chance?''

''Yes.'' The dwarf walked away. ''Help him up.''

Karl smiled at Ahira's back. *I'm not sure I like you. But I'm sure as hell not going to cross you.* He looked from Doria to Lightfingers to Walter, then let his eyes rest on Andy-Andy's. They had all gotten the point, too.

But you'd better make it work. You'd damn well better.

Ahira had been off by himself for a while, sitting on a fallen tree and staring at an anthill, when Doria walked over.

''James? Mind if I join you?''

''Sit.'' He kicked a heel against the rough bark, feeling it crunch satisfactorily. He quelled a muted resentment at her presence; it had been good to be by himself, not have to juggle six, twelve personalities. No, *fourteen*—including both of his own.

She smoothed her robes around her legs and seated herself gracefully on the grass in front of him, peering at him out of unblinking, yellow-irised eyes.

He looked away. A strange reversal this was. Usually, she was the one who avoided his eyes. ''What is it?''

''We have a problem.''

''*Really?*'' He arched a brow. ''Just one? That would be nice. Very nice. Which one are you referring to? Right now, I'm busy chewing my nails over Hakim and Lightfingers. I can think of half a score of things that could go wrong down there, and not much we could do about any of them. How long have they been gone, anyway?''

''A couple of hours. But I meant that we have a new problem.'' She rubbed at her eyes. ''I can't get my spell back.''

''What?'' A cleric wasn't like a wizard, dependent on

rememorizing spells from books. For a cleric, getting a used spell back was just a matter of praying for it. At least, it was supposed to be.

"I tried. Honest, I tried. But it just didn't work."

He didn't bother to keep the anger, the frustration out of his voice. "You tried what?"

"Praying. To the Healing Hand. But nothing *happened.*" She scratched at the back of her hand, leaving long red weals. "I can feel the other spells in my head. All of them—but I can't get the one I used back." A stray blond strand came to rest over one eye; she pushed it away. "Maybe . . ."

"Maybe *what?*" This was frightening; the one thing he had been able to count on was their magic working.

"Maybe if I believed . . ."

He grabbed her shoulders and shook her. "You mean to tell me that with all that's happened to us, *you don't believe in magic?*"

"Stop it. *Stop it.*" He let her shrug his hands away. "It's not that. It's just that the notion of a god of the Healing Hand, a . . ."

"Benign deity?"

". . . doing good, healing people—it just seems so absurd." She fastened slim fingers in her hair. "After all that's happened to us—after all that's happened to *me*—I just can't accept that. Not really."

"You're not just talking about here." This was a side of Doria he had never really seen. But beyond the friendly facade, the polished nails and slightly awkward manner, he had, sometimes, sensed a deep sadness.

"No, not just here." She worked her mouth, but no words came. Doria buried her face in her hands.

"You don't have to talk about it if you don't want to," he said, then cursed himself for putting it that way. Confession was a powerful cleanser of the psyche; he should have asked her to talk about it, made her talk about it. "But tell me, anyway." That sounded lame. Damn.

"I can't."

He reached out, gently pulling her hands from her face. "Don't worry about it." Ahira forced a smile. "I'm sure that everything will work out. And if you want to talk about it later,

I'll be here. Wherever here is." He stood and helped her to her feet. "I saw some cans in one of the boxes. How about you read them for me? If one of them's salmon, we'll split it."

Her smile was almost natural. "But did you see a can opener?"

He hefted his axe. "Yup."

CHAPTER FIVE: *Lundeyll*

The day is for honest men, the night for thieves.

—Euripides

Lightfingers sidestepped a rut on the dusty road. "How do you want to play it?"

Hakim smiled. "The first thing we do," he said, "is find ourselves a tavern, and get ourselves a drink." He cocked his head to one side. "Unless, of course, we can find ourselves a willing tavern girl."

They were half a mile from the city, the walls looming dark and massive ahead of them. Lightfingers found it strange, actually, that there was still spring in Hakim's walk; the hike down the hill and along the road hadn't made an impact on the younger man.

Lightfingers raised his hand. "Hold it a moment; got to catch my breath." He forced a chuckle. "Besides, since when have you been willing to share? 'We'?" Not that anything interested him after that walk, except a place to sit down, and something to drink. Preferably something cool.

Hakim clapped him on the back. "That's the spirit. Jason, m'friend, we may be down here on business, but I didn't hear the dwarf say we couldn't have fun, too. How much do you have on you?"

He shrugged. "I don't know exactly. One platinum piece, five gold, eight silver, six copper—something like that."

"Pretty good for not knowing exactly, Jason."

"Call me Lightfingers." He rubbed at his stump. Jason Parker was a young man with a full complement of limbs. *Was* . . .

"Lightfingers, then. Look, Doc apparently went to one hell of a lot of trouble to get us here and get us supplied. I doubt that he would've outfitted us with money that wasn't good—at least at bullion rates."

"Whatever they are."

"Right."

A creaking from ahead sped them around the bend. A stocky peasant, dragging a creaking handcart, smiled a greeting through gapped teeth. He stopped to run the blunt fingers of one hand through his greasy blond hair while he balanced the cart with his other.

"Greetings, friends," he said in Erendra, his vowels overlong to Lightfingers' ears. "Bound for Lundeyll?"

Lightfinger walked over and brushed an imaginary speck of dirt from the peasant's shoulder. His jerkin was similar to Lightfingers', but cut more broadly. "Yes, we are. —There. That looks better, friend. And how is the trading today?"

The peasant patted his pouch, then waved a hand at the muslin sacks on his cart. "Good." He lowered the cart, letting it balance on the two struts that depended from the handles. "In fact"—he rummaged around in the cart, producing a bulging winesack—"good enough that Wen'l of Lundescarne would share a drink with two strangers. For luck." He uncorked the bag and drank deeply, two trickles of purple running from the corners of his mouth and into his beard. "If you would honor me?"

"Delighted." Hakim elbowed Lightfingers aside, accepted the winesack, and tilted it back. "Good. Very good." He wiped his mouth on the back of an arm, handing the sack to Lightfingers.

Lightfingers drank. Hakim was right; the wine was good. The dark, lukewarm liquid washed the dust from his mouth, replacing it with a tingling, a rippling effervescence that burbled down his throat, setting up warm vibrations in his middle. Lightfingers propped the bottom of the winesack on his stump and considered taking another swallow. No, it wouldn't do to seem too greedy. Better to *be* greedy.

He handed the wine back to Wen'l. "I thank you."

The peasant frowned; an unsummoned memory welled up: A

72

drink for luck was a ritual that had to be accompanied by an introduction.

"Einar . . . One-handed thanks you."

Wen'l smiled, his forehead wrinkling as he turned to Hakim.

"And Hakim Singh thanks you, as well."

Wen'l's puzzled smile didn't change. "I can see that friend Einar is of Osgrad, but you are from . . . ?"

"Secaucus."

Wen'l nodded knowledgeably. "Ahh. And that land is to the . . ." He snapped his fingers, as though the direction were on the tip of his tongue.

"West," Hakim supplied. "Far to the west."

The peasant's eyes widened. "Beyond the Bitter Sea?"

"Far beyond."

"Beyond fabled D'tareth, even?"

Hakim shot Lightfingers a quick glance. D'tareth had been the jumping-off point of the last game. The last one before this one—no, this wasn't a game. "Yes, beyond even D'tareth."

Wen'l nodded wisely. "Oh, yes, I have heard of Seecacuse—it just escaped me for a moment." He shrugged, dismissing the subject. "Do you need a place to stay in Lundeyll?" At Lightfingers' nod, the peasant brightened. "Good. If I may, let me suggest the tavern of Frann of Pandathaway, on the Street of Two Dogs. It is just beyond the public well. Tell Frann that you are friends of Wen'l, and I am sure he will give you a special rate, a good one." Wen'l turned to put the winesack back in his cart.

"Permit me." Lightfingers stepped up and stumbled slightly to distract the peasant while he opened and emptied Wen'l's pouch, then flicked his haul into his sleeve before taking the sack. He tucked the winesack under a blanket in the cart. "To keep it out of the sun, and cool." Lightfingers raised his good hand to his forehead. "And a good day to you, friend Wen'l."

The peasant nodded, picked up the handles of his cart, and started down the road. "And a good evening to you, friends— you should hurry, if you wish to reach Lundeyll before sundown."

"We will." Lightfingers tugged at Hakim's arm. "Let's *hurry*, friend Hakim." In a few moments, Wen'l and his cart were out of sight. Lightfingers emptied his sleeve pocket into his hand. "Look at these."

"Where did you—you stupid son of a—"

"*Look at them.*"

Hakim held the scattering of coins in cupped hands. They were just like the ones they had in their own pouches: roughly circular, covered with a rippling pattern on one side like a stylized representation of waves; the other side decorated with a poorly stamped bust of a bearded man. He couldn't read the writing—*damn, I should have had Doria read it to me before we left.*

"See?" Lightfingers said. "That solves the money problem—this is local coin. But look at the amount. Wen'l said he did well, but there's a full dozen coppers to one silver coin. Which means that we're rich."

Hakim's face darkened. "No, that means that you're disobeying orders. Ahira said no stealing."

He shrugged. "Put them in your pouch." Hakim hesitated. "Unless you want to run after the peasant and tell him you're sorry we robbed him. Look, didn't the dwarf say that we were supposed to gather information?"

"Well, yes."

"And isn't the fact that we have legitimate money important information? Well, isn't it?"

"Yes, but—"

Lightfingers spat on the ground. "Don't be more of a fool than you have to be. He tried to steal from us—'stay at Frann's Inn'—he's probably getting a kickback from the innkeeper, who'd know to charge us extra."

As Hakim tucked the coins in his pouch, Lightfingers kept a smile from his face. The bigger thief—hah!—wasn't thinking. Why would Lightfingers have him hold his haul? No reason—unless Lightfingers intended to add to his take, add enough to it that would make a paltry dozen coppers and one silver coin seem too small to bother with.

If only I'd known how well off we were, I wouldn't have bothered to come along. Just lift all the money in their pouches, and run. Which is what I'll do when we get back—won't let that opportunity escape me again.

"Ja—Einar?" Concern creased the big man's face. "Are you all right?"

"Never mind. Just thinking about something." He waved a hand at the guard squatting at the latticework gate ahead of them. "Let's get him on his feet, and get some directions."

He raised his voice and switched to Erendra. "You—how do we get to the Street of Two Dogs?" Lightfingers smiled at Hakim. "After all, we don't *have* to tell him that Wen'l sent us, eh?"

Frann of Pandathaway mopped at his gleaming pate and seated himself across the table from them. "I thank you," he said, tossing back a quart-sized mug of the sour beer that already had Lightfingers' head buzzing. "And would you care to ply me with more beer before you start to extract information from me? Not that it will do any good." He gestured at the scraggly occupants of the low-ceilinged room. "There's little enough wealth here. Not enough to interest a pair of thieves." Frann raised a bushy eyebrow. That appeared to be the only hair on the beefy man's body; his mottled forearms and huge hands were as naked and hairless as his head.

The tavern was dark and dank, the gloom hardly alleviated by a dozen oil lamps sputtering out clouds of smoke where they hung from the overhead beams. The low, roughhewn tables were littered with pools of spilled beer and gobbets of meat.

Lightfingers sipped his beer. Hardly a well-kept place, this was. But even at this early hour, Frann's tavern was crowded, several scores of men gathered around the tables, shouting at the three harried barmaids to bring them more beer.

Hakim smiled broadly. "And what makes you accuse us of being thieves? As we told you, we are men-at-arms." He dropped a hand to the hilt of his scimitar. "If you have any doubts, I'd be happy to demonstrate. Quite happy."

As Lightfingers set his mug down and reached his hand into his jerkin to loosen his dagger in its sheath, Frann chuckled deeply, raising both palms in mock surrender. "As you say." Shaking his head, he pinched a passing barmaid, the bedraggled girl rewarding him with a squeal and a scowl. "More beer, or I'll feed you to the hogs." He turned back to Lightfingers and Hakim. "As long as you don't annoy my customers, it's of no interest to me whether you're soldiers, or thieves . . . or whores in disguise, for that matter."

Hakim returned his smile. "A rather good disguise."

"Indeed." Frann accepted the fresh tankard and took a healthy swig before setting it down and folding his hands on the table in front of him. "And now, my two well-disguised trollops, what is it that you want to know?"

Lightfingers considered it for a moment. This interrogation of the innkeeper was a waste of time, but it couldn't be helped. He had to stay in Hakim's good graces until they got back to the hill. And, for now, that meant getting information out of Frann.

If the innkeeper knew anything. "Let us suppose something," Lightfingers said, idly running a fingertip through a puddle of beer on the tabletop. "Let us suppose that my friend and I were thieves?" He stared sternly at Frann. "Untrue as that is, of course."

Frann pursed his mouth. "Why not? And?"

"And let us suppose that we two thieves were newly arrived from the west—from the far west—looking for something worth stealing, say."

"Then you would probably pay well for information, I suppose."

Lightfingers produced a silver coin, spun it on the table in front of him. "Possibly so." As Frann reached for it, he slapped his hand over the coin. "Possibly we would pay for such information, *after* we had received it." Lightfingers left the coin on the table as he sipped his beer. "Remember, we are supposing that my friend and I are thieves, not fools."

"Well put." The innkeeper rested his many chins on his fists. "Then I would say this: Take passage from Lundeyll. We are poor here." Frann shook his head sadly. "It's all I can do to make ends meet, keep the lord's men from booting me out into the street. Now, if I were a younger man, I'd go back to Pandathaway." He scowled, then sighed. "There is much worth having, there. I remember once, back home, a dwarf paid for a night's lodging with a diamond. It was the size of my thumbnail." He stared at his dirty, split thumbnail. "I swear, it was."

Lightfingers didn't ask why Frann had left Pandathaway. In the second place, the innkeeper probably wouldn't tell him. Possibly he had been chased out, exiled, or left just a few moments ahead of the authorities.

But in the first place, Lightfingers really didn't care. "And how would you suggest we get to Pandathaway?"

Frann shrugged. "The usual way. Book passage at Lundeport." He smiled. "I know a captain who might give you a good rate for deck passage."

"Like you gave us here? I don't see the need."

Hakim elbowed him in the side. All this talk of stealing was not what the big man was interested in. "Perhaps there would be something else, some other—"

"Quiet." Lightfingers shook his head. "I find what our host is saying to be most interesting."

Frann smiled knowledgeably. "What are you really looking for?"

"Actually," Hakim said, quashing Lightfingers' objection with a glare, "we've heard of something called the Gate Between Worlds."

"Then you're not thieves. You *are* fools." Frann spared his hands. "Even if it exists, then it would seem a waste of—" He interrupted himself with a shrug. "But it's none of my concern." He turned to Lightfingers, palm up. "But I would be happy to tell you . . ." He accepted the coin, beckoned to a barmaid, and tucked it into her cleavage. ". . . what everybody else knows, that it's said to be east of Pandathaway, somewhere past Aeryk." The innkeeper set his palms on the table and levered himself to his feet. "And I will add this for free: If you have any talent, you would be wise to stay in Pandathaway. Steal from the dwarves, from the elven. The risk is great, but so are the rewards—if you're good enough." He turned away, muttering, "The size of my thumbnail, it was. . . ."

Lightfingers drained his tankard and shook his head. "A genius, that's what you are. A genius."

"What did I do?"

"You told him the truth, stupid. Look, as long as we didn't seem too eager, I could have kept him talking, probably all night. A silverpiece is worth a lot here—haven't you been listening? Hell, we could buy this place, serving girls and all, for what we've got in our pouches."

Hakim shrugged his bare shoulders. The big man was completely unaffected. By Lightfingers' scorn, by the hike down, by the chill drafts blowing through the tavern, by the quarts of beer he had consumed. "As you pointed out, money isn't a problem for us." His expression grew grave. "And no more stealing, by the way. Understood? There's nothing worth taking here, and we don't need any trouble with the locals. How'd you like to try climbing those walls?"

Lightfingers rubbed his stump against the edge of the table.

"Wouldn't be hard; they've got a walkway around the top, and staircases leading up to it—the walls are intended to keep people *out*, not in. It would be tough to get over them from the outside. And I could have done that barehanded, before I lost my—"

"*Jason.*" Hakim's face creased with concern. "What the hell are you thinking of? You sound as if you think . . ."

"That I'm Einar Lightfingers?" He sneered. "Who do I look like? And who do I have one hand like?" He slammed his stump down on the table. "For all I know, this *Jason Parker* was only a dream. Here is real." He waved his stump under Hakim's nose. "*This* is real."

He pushed himself to his feet, wobbling. The beer, that was the trouble. He'd had enough to get angry on, but not enough to relax on. Yes, that was it—time for some more, to smooth things out.

The room canted off to the left; he snatched his tankard from the table and veered right, toward a stoppered keg in the corner.

He was halfway there when the huge oak door swung open and three men stepped into the tavern. Two were soldiers, tall and muscular in chain armor, swords belted to their waists, each leaning a short stabbing spear against the wall.

The third man, though, made Lightfingers' palm itch. Man? Maybe boy was more accurate: he looked to be about sixteen, blond, with sunken dark eyes in a narrow face. His soft purple cape, the many-jeweled ring on the thumb of his ungloved right hand, the bulging pouch at his waist—all of it screamed *Wealth*.

Frann bustled over as the background chatter died, the new stillness almost painful. "Lord Lund! I am honored!"

With a crooked smile, the boy removed his other glove and slapped it lightly across the innkeeper's face, his men-at-arms smiling at his side. "*Not* Lord. Not yet. Just Lordling, until my blessed father dies. . . ." He cocked his head to one side and laid a hand on the larger soldier's arm. "Marik, I believe that this fat beerseller has just insulted my father."

"M-my apologies, Lordling," Frann sputtered, his fingers knotting at his waist. "I meant no insult to your noble father, may he live forever."

"Oh? Then you think me incompetent to rule Lundeyll?"

"No, not at all . . . I . . . I mean, what may I bring you?" The innkeeper clumsily dodged the paradox. Clearly, the lordling would choose to take offense at whatever Frann said. He

78

gestured four men away from a nearby table, and wiped at its top, then his own face. "Beer? Wine?" He held a chair for the boy.

Lund stood silent for a moment, then shrugged. "Let's let it pass, for once." He sat. "And you, innkeeper, will bring us nothing." He jerked a finger at the least bedraggled of the serving girls. "Wine. Your best. Which, I suspect, is none too good. Oh—and clean glasses, if you please?"

The barmaid scurried off toward the back.

Lightfingers kept his face blank as he filled his tankard, then returned to his table. He sipped his beer slowly as the level of noise in the room began to pick up, returning to only a fraction of its previous level. Everybody in the room was patently terrified of the slumming lordling. Which was an advantage, of sorts. It might make it—

"Don't even think about it!" Hakim hissed.

Lightfingers smiled, taking a deep draught of the sour beer. The taste actually got better after a while. "Easy, my friend. I wouldn't." *Unless the opportunity presents itself. Then I wouldn't bother going back to the hill with you. I'd just book myself a passage to Pandathaway, and spend my time picking up diamonds the size of an innkeeper's thumbnail.* "Wouldn't think of it."

"Good." Hakim sat back. "I think it would be a good idea if we get out of here quietly, make our way back to our room. It's a bit stuffy there, but I don't like—"

"*You.*" The smaller of the two soldiers stood in front of them, glaring down at Lightfingers. "Didn't you see me beckon to you?"

"No, I—"

"Very well." The soldier tugged at his forelock in a sarcastic genuflection. "Lordling Lund requests the great honor of your company at his table. He likes to drink with the common people. If you will come this way?"

Lightfingers called up an expression of terror. *Speaking of opportunity . . .* "M-my pleasure, s-sir." He stood slowly, and walked shakily over to where the boy sat, a cruel smile flickering across his thin lips.

"Be seated." He nodded at a chair. "And you are . . . ?"

"Einar. Einar One-Hand, Lordling." Lightfingers was too obviously the name of a thief.

A clay winebottle and four glasses arrived, the barmaid setting them in front of the boy, then scurrying away, her smile unchanging, as though it had been painted on.

"Allow me," the boy said, pulling the cork, then pouring wine in two of the mottled glasses. "My . . . friends don't like to drink while they are working." He raised a glass to his lips and took a sip. Lund frowned. "Too tannic." He lowered his glass and smiled. "I hope you won't be offended by their abstinence?"

"Oh no, Lordling. I follow the same custom."

Lund picked up his glass again and drank deeply, the overflow of the purple liquid running down his chin and onto his tunic. That was good; either the boy was normally a slob, or he was more than a little drunk. "Please drink, Einar One-Hand. After all, you are paying for the wine, are you not?" The two soldiers looked at each other, smiling knowingly. Obviously, this was not Lund's first stop on a night of slumming, drinking with the common folk, forcing them to pay for his wine.

"Of course. I am honored." Lightfingers drained his own glass, then let his hand fall into his lap. It should be easy, actually. The purse dangled from the near side of Lund's belt, hanging next to Lightfingers as though it were a ripe fruit, begging to be picked. He reached out his hand—

"Would you be kind enough to pour me another glass?" Lund rapped his wineglass against the table. "It shee—seems that I am a bit uncoordinated this evening."

Lightfingers kept his scowl off his face. "Delighted, Lordling." He poured, then set the bottle down. A bit of distraction seemed called for; he brought his stump up to the table as he let his hand drop to his side.

The boy recoiled. "I . . . I understand your name now. How did you lose it?"

Easy, now . . . Lightfingers dipped two fingers into the mouth of the boy's pouch and pried them apart gently, slowly. *Easy* . . . "An accident. It was crushed in a mill." Inside the pouch was a jumble of coins; he grasped one between his fingers and eased it out.

It was platinum, thick and heavy.

Lightfingers fingerflipped it into his sleeve pouch, then took another, careful to be slow enough, smooth enough to prevent it from clinking against the others.

"Long ago?"

"Many years, Lordling. Many years." He took another, then another, slipping them carefully into his sleeve pocket. *That's enough for now. No sense in being too greedy, Jason.*

Jason? I'm Jason? Then what—

His hand slipped.

Its full weight came to rest on the pouch.

And tugged firmly on the boy's belt.

Lund's eyes shot downward. "My pouch!" He snatched at Lightfingers' wrist, his glass clattering on the table.

Rough hands grasped Lightfingers' shoulders; a sharp blow to the back of his neck sent the world spinning.

"Marik—grab his friend, too," Lund rasped.

He opened his eyes. Hakim was in the doorway, his scimitar in his hand, off-balance as though he had decided to run, then changed his mind. He snatched a knife from his belt, sent it spinning toward the soldier holding Lightfingers

The knife clanked against chainmail, then clattered harmlessly, uselessly to the floor.

"Don't be a fool, *run*." He put all his strength into a scream. "*Now!*"

The big man hesitated. The smaller soldier picked up the knife and flung it at him.

With a meaty *thunk*, it sank into Hakim's shoulder. Dripping blood, he staggered through the doorway and into the night.

"Get him, Marik." The soldier, sword in hand, ran after him.

The other wrestled Lightfingers to his feet.

Lordling Lund stood easily in front of him, hefting a spear. "We will deal with your friend. I promise." He twirled it, the foot-long steel head catching and shattering the light of an overhead lamp. "But you won't see that, will you?" He touched the spearpoint to Lightfingers' tunic.

His arms were held behind him; no way to reach his dagger. Not that that would do a lot of good. "Lordling, let me *explain*. Please." *What can I say? But I've got to say something, talk my way out. It can't end like this.*

The boy hesitated, then nodded, "Of course."

"You misunderstood me. I—" An explosion of pain burned through his belly.

He screamed.

Bloody vomit choked his throat, spewed out of his mouth and down the front of his tunic.

He looked down. Half of the spearhead was sunk into his midsection.

Lund pulled the spear out and considered its bloody head. "A gut wound. I always liked gut wounds."

He was a long time dying. He only stopped screaming toward the end.

CHAPTER SIX: *Second Blood*

> *. . . a soldier,*
> *Full of strange oaths, and bearded like the pard,*
> *Jealous in honor, sudden and quick in quarrel,*
> *Seeking the bubble reputation,*
> *Even in the cannon's mouth.*

> —William Shakespeare

Barak came awake at a touch, flinging away the blankets, reaching for his sword—

"Easy." Ahira's voice was a harsh whisper. "It's only me."

He set the sword back on the grass and tightened his cotton loincloth around his hips. That had been enough to sleep in, on a warm night.

He looked around. Within the circle of wooden boxes, everyone else was asleep, sprawled out under their blankets like a collection of corpses—except for Andy-Andy, who was huddled under hers in a fetal position, shivering in her sleep. Barak shrugged. It was her own fault: Not only had she turned down his suggestion that they share each other's warmth, but she had stubbornly ignored his reminder to make certain she kept at least two-thirds of her covering underneath her. The ground stole a body's warmth more readily than even the chilliest air.

Rubbing his eyes, he glared up at the dwarf, not able to make out his expression in the dim starlight. "My turn to go on watch? Already?"

"No." Ahira beckoned him to his feet. "Look down the hill, down toward the city."

Barak drew air into his lungs and stared off into the distance. Nothing. A few lights twinkling in the city, stars shimmering over the sea, but that was all.

Wonderful. Our leader is jumping at shadows. "So?"

"You don't see anything on the road?"

Below them, the road was a black ribbon on a black background. "Don't be silly. You do?"

"I . . . I thought I saw a shape, like somebody fallen—there it is. Can't you see it? It's glowing like a—"

"Glowing?" He stared. Nothing. *Oh.* "I don't see in the infrared, remember?"

"Sorry—*wait*." The dwarf pointed. "But you can see that, can't you?"

Barak followed the other's gesture. Farther down the road, lanterns twinkled like fireflies. Three—no, four of them. They were too far off, too dim for Barak to make out the shapes holding them, but . . . "I do see the lanterns. But why are they out—"

"Ohmygod. The shape on the road—it's *Hakim*." The dwarf spun around. "Everybody, up. *Now*."

Barak stooped to pick up his scabbarded sword. Best to keep it in its dark sheath, lest the bright steel reflect light, announcing his presence. He cast a longing look at his leather armor, heaped next to his blankets on the grass. "I'd better take it."

"Like hell you will. No time."

"No, I didn't mean the armor. I meant I'll get him, bring him back. Your legs are too short to run fast." Four of them, eh? He would have to take out two quickly, before they became aware of his presence. And even two-on-one would be a chancy shot. "Get your crossbow, follow me."

Ahira's face was still unreadable. He hesitated. Then: "Go."

Barak sprinted away. Behind him, Ahira called to the others. "Get up, damn you all."

Barak reached Hakim when the soldiers were still a few hundred yards away, the flicker of their lanterns announcing their coming. "Walter!" He reached out a hand and felt at the thief's neck. Good; there was a pulse. He slipped his hand down, his fingers coming away sticky. There was a knife in the thief's shoulder, dripping blood.

He rubbed his hand on his thigh. Where the hell was Lightfingers? No time to worry about that now. He could try to move Hakim off the road, but that might be too dangerous. There could be other wounds; moving him might kill him.

He smiled. Besides, there was some business to take care of first.

Slipping silently into the bushes beside the road, he loosened his sword in its sheath. *Well, Karl, now we find out if you have it.*

Karl? No—*Barak*. Karl Cullinane hadn't raised a hand in anger since the third grade. Karl wouldn't squash a spider; he'd lift it on a piece of paper and fling it out of a window instead.

Karl was a peasant, Barak a warrior. So it had to be Barak, not Karl.

And to a warrior, everything is a challenge, or a reward. But he had to decide what the challenge was. Merely chasing them away wouldn't do; perhaps they could dig up reinforcements. He had to take out four soldiers—*no euphemisms, kill them*—and he had to do it without getting hurt himself. Doria had none too many healing spells left; Walter might need all of them.

"Arno, I think I see him," the closest of the soldiers said in curiously accented Erendra, then broke into a trot. Chainmail and a shortsword, plus his lantern—Barak could save him for later. But the lantern, dangling from a pole—that had to go quickly, before anyone spotted him crouching in the bushes.

Barak felt around the ground. His fingers located a jagged rock, half the size of his fist. He hefted it experimentally, and threw.

The lantern shattered, drenching the soldier in flames. He dropped his sword and screamed, his skin *crackling*.

The screams were like a signal to the other three; they dropped their lantern poles, the nearest two drawing their swords, the other, probably the leader, bringing up his crossbow. Its tip weaved, uncertainly.

The wind brought a stench of burning flesh to Barak's nostrils. He slipped his sword from its scabbard, keeping the blade low, next to the ground.

"*Where?*"

"I don't see—"

"It's the thief—he's shamming." The leader's crossbow leveled itself at Hakim's crumpled form.

Barak gripped his sword and charged out of the bushes, directly at the leader, a growl forcing itself from his throat.

The crossbow wavered as Barak closed, breaking stride to kick one of the swordsmen sprawling, ducking under the other's wild swing. *Too bad. You want to live too much.* The leader's drill was obvious: Kill one enemy, ignore the other one charging you.

He smacked the flat of his sword against the side of the crossbow, sending it spinning away in the dark, the bolt discharging harmlessly to his left.

The leader's eyes grew wide; he reached for his sword as Barak's backswing caught him at the base of the neck, the swordtip cleaving his throat effortlessly, dark blood fountaining.

The heavyset man clapped both hands to his throat, trying to hold the wound closed, his cry of pain only a gurgle as a dark torrent poured out through his fingers.

Barak spun around, leaving him at his back. No time to finish him off, not yet. When it's one-on-many, you can't worry about killing a disabled enemy when there are still unhurt ones around.

The one he had kicked away was gone, vanished in the dark, his sword lying still on the ground. *Where is he? Never mind—worry about him when you've killed the other.*

The small dark man in front of him smiled, crouching, his sword in his right hand, a long, curved dagger in his left. "Many thanks for the promotion, friend," he said in Erendra, stepping lightly forward, his sword weaving like an eager cobra. "I never liked Arno anyway."

No time for chatter; there was still one man unaccounted for. Barak slashed, the blade of his sword parallel to the ground.

The soldier slid to one side, easily deflecting Barak's sword with the flat of his dagger. Before Barak could bring his sword back into line to parry, the slim rapier had nicked at his biceps. It stung, terribly.

"Not used to two-swords, eh?" He lunged, in full extension.

And gasped down at his right wrist, almost severed by Barak's blade. The sword dropped to the dirt.

Barak smiled down at the crumpling figure. "Then again, maybe I a—"

An arm closed on his throat, dragging him back, off-balance. At the edge of his vision, a gleaming dagger rose, and started to fall.

Time seemed to slow. *You stupid idiot. You know better than to chat while a fight's going on.* He released his grip on the sword, bringing his hands up to block the downward thrust, knowing that he'd never make it in time.

It just wasn't possible; the knife only had to travel a few inches to reach his throat, but his hands would have to seize the wrist, stop the downward movement—

Both hands met at the soldier's flaccid arm, as the other arm loosened at his throat. He grabbed, twisted, brought an elbow back into his enemy's midsection, and spun around.

"No need," Ahira's voice rasped from behind.

Barak looked at the soldier. A crossbow bolt transfixed the man's head from temple to temple, its dark iron head bent, crumpled.

The dead soldier stared up at him, eyes wide in reproach.

Twang! Barak turned to see Ahira standing over Walter, drawing the string of his crossbow back, slipping in another bolt and sending it whistling into the leader. "Never worry about conserving bolts. Better to make sure that they stay dead." The dwarf sent another bolt into the smoldering body of the first soldier, the one whose lamp Barak had shattered, then looked up, a crooked grin on his broad face. "Not bad, Barak. Not too bad at all." He frowned. "Except for that *stupid* bit of bravado. But never mind; just do it better next time. Right now, we've got to get these bodies hidden, have Doria heal Hakim—and you, come to think of it; don't want your arm getting infected—then get ourselves packed up and out of here. There's probably going to be hell to pay—hey, what's wrong?"

Karl Cullinane was on his hands and knees in the dusty road, the stench of burning flesh in his nostrils, vomiting like a fiend.

Squinting in the dawn light, Ahira tugged at the cords lashing his two rucksacks together, then shook his head. It would tend to keep him off balance, having two packs on his back, but that couldn't be helped. Somebody had to carry the extra—either that, or leave behind supplies that might be needed.

"Hakim?"

The thief stopped fiddling with his pack and lifted his head. "What is it?"

Ahira held out a hand. "Toss me one of your knives. If I have to, I want to be able to cut these loose."

"Fine." Hakim flipped a knife point-first into the ground at Ahira's feet, then turned back to his work.

Ahira opened his mouth, then closed it. Ever since Doria had healed Hakim, he had been distant, quiet, not himself. Not at all. Best to leave him alone, at least for a while. What had happened in Lundeyll must have been bad—climbing down a sheer wall with a knife in his shoulder, running flat-out for five miles with soldiers after him, wanting his blood. . . .

He'll get over it. He's always been strong.

Doria gave her rucksack a final pat, then raised an eyebrow in an unvoiced question. There would be a bit of time until the others were ready to leave; Ahira had assigned loads based on physical strength, and the only one with less to carry than Doria was Aristobulus. Less to carry; less time to pack.

He gave her a nod and the warmest smile he could come up with. "Go ahead." Even if she was almost out of healing spells, maybe she could do some good.

As Doria crouched beside Hakim, Ahira beckoned the others to him.

"You almost ready?" Ahira kept his voice low. No need to distract Doria or Hakim.

Andrea nodded. She was keeping her distance from Barak. That was strange, considering the way she'd behaved the previous morning. Then she had clung to him like a leech. "Just a couple more minutes."

Barak frowned, rubbing fingertips against the bloodstained tear on the arm of his jerkin. The blood had dried, and Doria had healed the wound, so it couldn't be hurting him.

Then again, not all wounds are to the body.

Barak shrugged. "I'll be done shortly. I can take more, if necessary. No need to have the rest put out a lot of effort carrying what I can haul easily." He flexed his shoulders, threatening to split the seams of his jerkin.

Ahira smiled. Barak was getting damn cocky, after the way he'd almost gotten himself killed. Then again, that was better than his Karl-self exercising his guts about a few local soldiers who had been trying to kill Hakim and him when they died.

"You too, Ari? Good. Just as soon as Doria's done talking to Hakim, we head down to Lundeport, and see if we can book passage to Pandathaway." He stooped to pick up Hakim's knife and stuck it diagonally under his belt, the cutting edge up, then bent carefully at the waist to make certain it was secure, and that it wouldn't cut him. A quick check on the straps binding his battleaxe to his chest showed that they were tight, too, although it would take only two quick tugs to undo the loops and free the axe.

"Pandathaway? Andrea's forehead wrinkled. "God, that sounds familiar." She turned to Barak. "Doesn't it, Karl?"

He shook his head. "No. First I've heard of it. Maybe you overheard something, when Hakim was telling Ahira what happened down there." He glared down at the dwarf. "Not that he's seen fit to share it with the rest of us."

The warrior had all the sensitivity of a stone. "He didn't want to have a bunch of people around," Ahira said, not bothering to keep the scorn out of his voice. "How would you feel if you'd been cut up like he was?"

"Listen—"

"*Karl*." Andrea took a careful step closer to him. "Didn't you tell me once, quite a while back, about another character of yours? Something of Pan-something . . . ?"

Barak nodded, quizzically, stroking at his beard just the way Karl Cullinane used to stroke at the stubble on his face. "Sure. Lucius of Pandathaway—*Pandathaway*." His face lit up; he dropped his sword, grabbed her by the arms, whirling her around. "Pandathaway! Of *course*. I know where we are, we—"

"Put me *down!*" As he did, she rubbed at her shoulders, arms crossed defensively across her chest. "You practically pulled my arms off, you clumsy—"

"Quiet." Ahira turned to the big man, who was still grinning like an idiot. "Two things: First, what do you mean, you know where we are? Second: Why the *hell* didn't you mention it before?"

"It was a . . . character Deighton and I rolled up, once. I never got a chance to use him, but he filled me in on the background—where he came from, like that." He rubbed his fists against his temples. "I . . . I don't know why I didn't think of it before. It's like there's too much inside my head, too much to manage."

"I understand." Ahira had been wrong to give him trouble for not remembering. Things in James Michael Finnegan's life seemed like something distant; it took a bit of effort to *be* James Michael, sometimes, to think like him.

But that didn't cure his impatience. "Would you please tell us what you know about Pandathaway? It could be—"

"*Damn* important." Barak nodded, still smiling. "And it's all good. Pandathaway's a port city, on the Cirric—"

"The Cirric?"

"It's a huge freshwater sea, sort of like one of the Great Lakes, only big—" He caught himself, pointed an eager finger at the vast expanse of water spreading out over the horizon. "That's the Cirric!"

"Almost certainly. You were talking about Pandathaway?"

"You're going to like it. Nice place. No government—well, not much of one. The city's run by a council of guilds. Lot of them are merchants, so they like to keep the city open and safe, to keep the customers coming. Doc said that you can buy most anything there. There's a saying: Tola crgat et Pandathaway ta." *Everything comes to Pandathaway,* in Erendra. Barak shook his head, puzzled. "But he didn't say it in Erendra, he said it in—"

"It translated." Aristobulus nodded wisely. "As we did. It makes sense, if you think about it."

"Not to me," Barak said, shrugging. "But I was saying—you can get anything there: jewels, silks, spices, slaves, horses— Lucius owns a Pandathaway-bred mare; keeps a quarter horse's pace for a full two miles—anything." He beamed. "And I haven't even given you the best."

Ahira returned his smile. The swordsman's enthusiasm was positively contagious. "Do I have three guesses?"

"No. You wouldn't guess right, anyway. In the city—right smack in the *middle* of the city—is the Great Library of Pandathaway. Doc said, and I quote, 'The Great Library of Pandathaway is to the Great Library of Alexandria as a broadsword is to a paring knife.' "

Andrea chuckled. "You mean that it's big and awkward, no good for paring an apple?"

"Get off my—"

"Shut up." Ahira couldn't help joining in the laughter. "What he's trying to say is that there might be a map there, to show us where the Gate is."

"Might? If it's known, it's there. It seemed kind of strange, then, how he kept going on about it. I thought Doc was patting himself on the back."

Aristobulus had been listening quietly, his lined face somber, his head cocked to one side. "And there might be something else there. Something we need, badly." His gesture included both Andrea and himself. "Spell books. Give me sufficient time, and I'll make two copies of—"

Ahira shook his head. "I hope we have time for that. But we might not. Consider—"

"I will consider *nothing*. Do you have any idea what it is like for a wizard to be without spell books? It's like being a, a . . ."

"Being a cripple?" Ahira kept his voice low, as his hands balled themselves into fists at his side. "I . . . have some idea of what that feels like." He forced himself to open his hands. "Believe that. But tell me: How long does it take to write a spell? Just one spell, a simple one."

Aristobulus shrugged, indifferent. "Given the right materials and enough quiet . . . ten days, perhaps. But I don't see—"

"Precisely. You *don't* see. And if you don't have everything you need on hand? How long would it take?"

"That depends, of course. For the Lightning spell, the ink must contain soot from a lightning-struck tree—preferably oak, of course. And then the pen has to be made. . . ." The wizard spread his hands. "But it doesn't *matter*. I *have* to have spell books. So does she."

Ahira shook his head. Didn't the old fool see that anything—*everything*—had to take a back seat to getting to the Gate? This world was dangerous. It had already cost the life of one of them. They had to get home.

And me? Am I going to exchange security for the ability to be a full person? Here, I'm not a cripple. "Just listen—"

Barak stepped between them. "Let's leave this alone for the time being. We should have enough time to argue about it on our trip, no?" He frowned.

Ahira nodded, accepting the implied criticism. Barak was right, of course: The leader had no business getting involved in an argument, not when there were things to be done. Maybe Barak should take over—no, he hadn't acted very intelligently during the fight. An excess of bravado was bad enough in a team member.

And besides, I took on the obligation. It's mine, not his.
"Correct, Barak. My fault. —You haven't packed your armor, have you?"

"Huh? What does that have to do with anything? I haven't, but I don't see what—"

"Take off your clothes—I need your jerkin, but you can keep your leggings. You can put your armor on over your bare hide."

"*What?*"

Ahira smiled. "I said, take your clothes off." Not a good time to bring it up, but he didn't want Barak musing on the leader's shortcomings. Best to keep him off-guard. He sobered. "I don't intend to make a habit of explaining myself, but . . . what do you think the chances are that they're looking for Hakim, down there? A big man, dressed only in pants, no shirt? That can't be too common around here, not from what we've seen and heard of the locals. So we make sure he isn't dressed only in pants, go for more standard clothing. You're the only one bigger than he is, so you get to provide the clothes." Ahira extended a palm. "It'll be a bit scratchy for you—the inside of boiled leather isn't too smooth—but that's the way it goes." He tapped a thumb against his axe. "Come to think of it, give me your leggings, too. You can switch pants with him; they won't look so loose on you."

"Now? Here?"

"Now."

Aristobulus snickered; Andrea giggled.

Glaring at all three of them, Barak began unlacing the front of his jerkin, then shook his head. He chuckled. "You little *bastard.*"

"Right." Ahira returned his smile. "But hurry up; I want another chance to talk to Hakim before we get going. The sooner I get finished with that, the less time you have to wander around in your bare skin."

Ahira seated himself in front of Doria and Hakim, dropping the pile of clothing to the grass. He jerked his head at Doria. "Go put your pack on. We're leaving in a few minutes."

She nodded and walked away, shaking her head when she got behind Hakim. Clearly, she hadn't gotten anywhere with him; he was sitting against one of the now-empty boxes, running stiff fingers over the thin pink scar that was all that remained of his wound, staring blankly off into space.

"I want you to put those clothes on, before we leave. You can give your trousers to Barak. And you'd better stash your scimitar in your pack—I'll give you my crossbow, so you don't feel naked."

"Fine." He made no move to pick up the jerkin and leggings; he just sat there, rubbing the small scar as though he were trying to rub it away.

"And you'll be glad to know that Barak knows quite a lot about Pandathaway. Sounds like a nice place." Ahira crabbed himself sideways, into Hakim's line of sight. "No lords."

"That's nice."

The best thing to do would be to try—gently, gently—to get him to talk it out. But there just wasn't time. The area around Lundeyll was probably not a healthy place for any of them. The graves of the dead soldiers were shallow, and nearby; it was only a matter of time until the bodies were discovered. And that would be one hell of a problem.

Quite possibly a fatal one. They could all end up like Jason Parker.

But why don't I feel anything for Jason? Granted, I never liked him—but I should feel something for him, now that he's dead.

Ahira shook his head. Introspection could come later; for now, he had to get Hakim up and moving. *One more try the nice way.* "I thought I could count on you. You disappointed me."

The thief's head snapped up. "*What?* How the hell was I supposed to know that he was going to pick Lund's pouch, get himself killed? You told him not to take chances, *I* told him not to . . ."

Good. Anger was better than shocked numbness. "That's not what I meant. We've got to get going. But you're just sitting there, feeling sorry for yourself—I expected better of you."

Hakim spat. "What do you know about it? You ever have to run a few miles with a knife in you, a bunch of people behind you, wanting your goddam blood?"

"No." Ahira shrugged, then started to rise. "I had better go give Doria a talking-to. Looks to me like she did a pretty poor job of healing you, if it still hurts you like this."

"Wait." Hakim held up a palm; Ahira lowered himself back to the grass. "It's not that. The time I played in the . . . game against Cornell—the time I played a half with a torn triceps . . ."

"I remember." He nodded. "That must have hurt almost as much as this did."

"It hurt *more*. But that was different. We won, that time."

"We won this time."

"But *I* didn't." Hakim slammed a fist against the ground. "I was supposed to get back intact—with Jason, with information."

"One out of three isn't bad, considering the situation."

"You don't understand, do you? I've never *failed* at anything before. I'm big, I'm strong, and I'm smart. I've always just assumed that was enough. This time, it wasn't." His eyes bored into Ahira's, as though daring him to deny it. "If you and Karl had been just a few seconds slower, I'd be dead. Like Jason." He shuddered. "*God*, James, you should have heard him screaming. I could have been next. I was lucky."

And you're terrified that you won't be lucky next time. I don't blame you for that.

Once, he had envied Walter Slovotsky. His attitude, his perfect faith and complete confidence that he was firmly at the center of the universe, and that all was well with him and his universe—that didn't seem so enviable. Not now. A self-image cast in stone could shatter. "Of course I never failed at anything." That was easy, as long as you didn't run into a situation you couldn't handle; that was fine, until you had to stagger down a road, armed men chasing you, knowing that if you fall, you die.

But when that self-image shatters, where do you go from there?

He clapped a hand to the thief's shoulder. "I don't know about next time. No promises." He shrugged. "But I'll be there, if you need me." He rose to his feet. "And for right now, I need *you* to get back on top of things. We had better get down to Lundeport and book passage the hell out of here. There could be trouble, if anyone recognizes you. On top of that, Barak is giving speeches when he should be fighting, Aristobulus is objecting to anything and everything, Doria can't get her spells back—and I'm waiting for Andrea to give me a problem; so far, she's the only one who hasn't." He held out a hand. "So I need your help."

Hakim sat motionless, then nodded weakly. "I'll do my best. I . . . I can't promise that that'll be good enough." He accepted the hand, and let the dwarf pull him to his feet.

"Welcome to the real world." Ahira found himself smiling. Almost. "Now, get the hell out of your clothes and into Karl's." He raised his voice. "*Everybody*—we're moving out."

Aristobulus, standing sweatily in his robes, bent to lower his rucksack to the sunheated wood of the pier. There was no need to keep it on his back while Ahira and Hakim negotiated with Avair Ganness, captain of the *Ganness' Pride*—it looked to be a long bargaining session, and Aristobulus' muscles were already complaining from the strain.

He rubbed a fist against the small of his back and closed his eyes, trying to ignore the constant babble from merchants arguing over the price of grain, the squawking of the gulls overhead, the foul stench of rotting fish.

Eyes closed, he could see his own power wrapped about him, a strong crimson aura that warmed him—and pleasantly, despite the heat of the day. He raised his hand in front of his face, working his fingers, enjoying the way the redness outlined his unseen hand, even as it moved.

It was magic, of course. Which meant that it was good. And which meant that it was power—something Lou Riccetti had always wanted, but never known.

Off to his side, another source blazed—but less intensely, much less so. Andrea simply wasn't in his league. Was that just because her character had been of a lower class than his? Or was it that she just hadn't *wanted* this as badly as he had?

He shrugged. It really didn't matter. The only thing that did matter was that he had been reprieved by Deighton. Life had condemned Lou Riccetti to be an inconsequential little man; at best, a second-rate civil engineer in an age when damn close to nothing important was being built. No more great suspension bridges to span mighty rivers, few if any dams; the future of American engineering was in electronics—diddling with little circuit diagrams, not *building* things, not making magic.

And if you couldn't make magic with stone and steel, all that was left was to dream about real magic. All that *had* been left. . . .

He let his remaining spells cycle through his brain, making sure each one was ready and complete. Not that that was necessary; an incomplete spell wouldn't make his mind pulse, wouldn't push at him night and day to release it, as though it were some sort of huge sneeze, backed up in his nostrils. He could live with that, easily, in exchange for the power.

He could even live with the knowledge of his best friend's death. His *only* friend's death. Probably he should be mourning Jason; perhaps Lou Riccetti would be going over all his contacts with Jason, dredging up pleasure and pain from their friendship, regretting that Jason was gone.

But he couldn't do it. Not with his power wrapping him, keeping him warm. The death of one powerless human just didn't seem significant. Now, the loss of the spell books, *that* hurt.

Which makes me a small person, perhaps?

If that was so, then so be it. He—

"Are you falling asleep?" Andrea asked, nudging him. "Standing up?"

He opened his eyes regretfully, the warm glow of his power overwhelmed by the bright sunlight. "No."

"Well, Ahira says to keep an eye out for anybody who looks official—since the soldiers chasing Hakim didn't come back, the locals may be looking for him. And I don't think that would be very healthy for the rest of us."

"Very well." Although Aristobulus didn't see why *he* had to be the lookout—probably there was something interesting going on at the boat. Keeping an eye on the shoreside crowd, he moved closer to where Hakim was haggling with the captain.

Avair Ganness tapped bare toes on the wood, his heavy calluses clicking like dice. "Well then, make up your mind. It hardly matters to me. I can make a profit of five, perhaps six gold by carrying good Lundess wine, instead of you." He spoke Erendra in a pleasant rhythm, his r's rolling melodiously. Huge shoulders shrugged inside his sweat-stained sailcloth tunic, belted at the waist with a length of rope. The tunic stopped abruptly at midthigh; below, his thick legs projected like treestumps.

Hakim smiled, raising an eyebrow. "There would be advantages to carrying us, instead."

Ganness nodded. "That is so." He sighed. "I do have this problem—happens to many a man my age. It would cost me much to have it cured in Pandathaway. Perhaps even more than your passages will cost me, all things considered. But only perhaps."

Problem? He looked healthy enough.

96

"That wasn't what I meant." Hakim gestured at the crewmen swarming around the sloop, checking lines, stowing cargo, pausing occasionally to leer at Doria and Andrea. "I have been watching the way they check their bows, their arrows. There are few spots on deck that don't have a weapon within reach. You are concerned about pirates, no?"

"Not concerned. Properly cautious. I've sailed the Cirric for . . . forty years, man and boy. Only run into pirates seven, eight times." He grinned, a gap-toothed smile that was not at all friendly. "And I have managed to give a good account of myself, those few times." He tossed his head, his waist-length pigtail curling around his torso like a snake. "So I have no need of wizards or warriors to protect me. But"—he extended his arm toward Doria, frowning as Hakim moved between them—"I do require a cleric's help." His face went blank. "But that can wait until we dock in Pandathaway. I won't need . . . I won't have any use for it until then. I don't bugger my seamen." He smiled at Doria.

Well, that explained what his "problem" was—a case of impotence, eh? And just perhaps Avair Ganness was a bit more eager to have her cure it than he appeared to be—otherwise, he might well have set his price for passage at enough money to overcompensate the loss of cargo space.

Aristobulus nodded to himself. Yes, that made sense—but best to whisper it quietly to Ahira or Hakim, rather than confront Ganness. The trouble with most people was that they weren't rational; the captain might refuse to carry them, just out of stubbornness.

He took a few steps closer, and called to the dwarf.

"What is it?" Ahira snapped. "We're talking, here—and I thought you were told to—" He cut himself off, his eyes going wide, as he looked past Aristobulus' shoulder.

The wizard turned. A troop of ten—no, twelve soldiers were working their way toward the pier, stopping and questioning passersby as they came. He moved toward the end of the pier, trying to carry his rucksack casually.

"We had best conclude this quickly, no?" he said, careful to speak in English rather than Erendra.

Ahira turned to the thief. "Hakim?"

Hakim shrugged in the loose tunic. "I don't think they'll

recognize me, not unless—cancel that. The one with the long-bow is Marik—he'll know me, if he sees me. Maybe.''

"Then turn *around*."

Ganness frowned. "What tongue was that?"

Barak took a step toward him, smiling faintly. "I don't think that is any of your concern, is it?" He switched to English. "Better agree to *something*, folks—other than her Heal Disease spell, the only decent one she's got left is for Minor Wounds. And she's only got one of those left. If we get in a fight . . .''

Doria spoke up. "I don't remember anyone asking me if I wanted to cure him, and then . . . prove that I have."

Aristobulus sneaked a glance over his shoulder. The soldiers were still working their way toward the end of the pier, where the *Ganness' Pride* was tied up. But unless the one that knew Hakim recognized him at a distance, they still had a few minutes; the soldiers were a few hundred yards away on the crowded pier.

Barak shrugged. "I don't see what your problem is. After all, you've always been willing to make it with practically any—''

Her hand struck Barak's face with a loud *whack!* It probably wasn't the force of the blow that staggered him, it was the surprise.

Aristobulus sighed. It was starting to look like he'd have to waste a spell or two. *The stupid, overmuscled, underbrained—*

"That is *it*," Ahira snapped, then switched back to Erendra as he turned to Ganness. "We have been trying to reach an accommodation with you, captain, but clearly you're unwilling to talk business," And in English: "I'm a lot of things, but I'm not a pimp. Hakim, keep your head turned away; everybody, up packs and move quietly down the pier. And I do mean quietly." He fiddled with the straps holding his battleaxe to his chest. "We just might be able to get out of this without—''

Doria raised a palm as she shot a look back at the approaching soldiers. "Wait. I . . . I agree to your terms, Avair Ganness," she said in Erendra to the captain. "Free passage for all, in return for . . . in return for . . .''

"Agreed." Ganness smiled gently, then spoke to the others. "Your cabins are forward, belowdecks. A bit cramped, perhaps, but I do keep a clean ship. And my cook is of the best; I bought him in Pandathaway." Ganness vaulted over the railing, landing lightly on the deck. "And you, Lady, I will see in my cabin, as soon as we clear the harbor"—he ran blunt fingers across his

stubbled cheeks—"and I shave myself. I'll be gentle, I swear."
He smiled. "You might even enjoy it."

Her knuckles whitened as she clutched the railing. "This is a
business affair, Ganness. And I'm only agreeing for reasons—"

"—that are nobody else's concern," Ahira interrupted.
"Captain, you were about to show us our cabins?"

"*That's him!*" A rough voice shouted, from down the pier.
The twelve soldiers broke into a trot. Aristobulus sucked air into
his lungs. "I'll slow them down—yes?"

Ahira nodded, unstrapping his axe. "Everybody else—get on
board. Captain, you're about to be in the same trouble we are, if
you don't get this ship moving quickly." Idly, he tore through
the leather strap that slung his crossbow across his shoulders and
tossed the bow and his quiver to Hakim. "Use it."

Ganness stood motionless for a long moment, then shrugged.
"It seems I have little choice. All hands! Cast off!"

Asristobulus turned, raising his arms. *Now, let the power
flow.* . . . It would have to be the flame spell; nothing else would
slow down the charging soldiers.

So I'll give you fire. He let the spell click to the forefront of
his mind, his chest tightening, straining as though he had drawn in
twice as much air as his lungs could handle. The red glow
brightened, a hot envelope enshrouding him, tingling his skin, so
intense it blanketed his vision.

And the urgency grew; the spell had been pushing constantly
at the back of his mind—but pushing gently. Now it roared,
demanding use, painfully growing in his skull until he thought
his head would explode from the pressure and heat.

Aristobulus released it, the rush of sound so loud he couldn't
begin to hear or understand the words issuing from his own
mouth.

The charging soldiers were a scant hundred feet away; halfway
between the two men at the head of the group, the pier exploded
into fire. The wood glowed with white heat for a moment before
it could start to flame.

The wall of fire grew, tongues of flame licking easily two
hundred feet into the sky, roaring, crackling.

Aristobulus dropped his hands. It was done.

"You stupid—" Ahira grabbed the collar of his robes; the pier
dropped away under his feet as the dwarf threw him over the

rail. He landed on his shoulder on the deck of the *Ganness' Pride,* sliding until he banged into a mast.

Pain lanced through him; he staggered to his feet.

And then he understood: He had cast the spell too far away; the lead soldiers had been able to get past the wall of fire before it blocked the way for the rest.

Ahira waited for them, his battleaxe held easily in his hands.

"*Cast off, damn you all!*" Ganness shouted at his crew, following his own orders as he raced to the front of the boat to slash through the bow line. "*Get those sails up—a hard hand on the tiller, there.*"

The first soldier glanced at the boat as seamen pushed it from the pier, then moved toward the dwarf, only his outline visible against the wall of fire.

Aristobulus had known that the dwarf was strong, but he had never realized just *how* strong; Ahira ducked under the swing of the soldier's sword, planted the stock of his axe against the man's chest, and *pushed.*

The soldier tumbled back, head over heels, a full fifty feet into the leading edge of the fire. He jerked to his feet, gibbering and flaming, and twitched himself over the side of the pier, splashing into the water.

Ahira turned to the other soldier.

A crossbow bolt *spanged!* into the pier at Ahira's feet. Aristobulus turned to see Hakim, swearing, pull back the bowstring, then reach for another bolt.

The dwarf moved smoothly toward the remaining soldier, feinted with the blade of his axe, caught the soldier's swordthrust on the haft of his axe, and swung, once.

Once was more than enough. The soldier, chainlink armor and all, dropped to the pier, his torso twitching itself a few feet away from his legs before it stopped. Ahira had sliced the man neatly in half.

Raising his bloody axe over his head, Ahira threw it at Aristobulus. It thunked into the deck beside him, only a yard from his sandaled feet. The dwarf took a running start and jumped across the ten feet separating the boat and the pier.

"Not too bad, though," he smiled. "*Captain,* let's get out of here."

Ganness swore under his breath as he bounded across the deck to the tiller.

PART THREE:

Pandathaway

CHAPTER SEVEN: *In the Midst of the Sea*

The entire land sets out to work,
All beasts browse on their herbs,
Trees, herbs are sprouting,
Birds fly from their nests . . .
Ships fare north, fare south as well,
Roads lie open when you rise;
· The fish in the river dart before you,
Your rays are in the midst of the sea.

—*The Great Hymn to the Aten,* Stanza Three

Barak stood by himself at the bow, leaning on the rail. Starlight shimmered on the flat black water ahead; an occasional wash of cool spray tingled his face.

He unhitched a small waterskin from the railing, taking a small swig of the leathery water to wash out his mouth. Which didn't do much good; his tongue still tasted like vomit. At least he was adjusting, thank whatever. The first two days aboard the *Ganness' Pride* had been a continual bout with nausea—of all of them, why the *hell* did he have to be the only seasick one?

It was getting better, a little. His feet had picked up the rhythm of the pitching deck and his gut had unknotted; while he had no urge to let anything but water past his lips, he could keep from throwing up, as long as he kept his eyes on the horizon. Sleep was impossible, except for a few brief snatches—a nap

103

was an almost certain invitation to another battle with the dry heaves.

He rubbed at the back of his neck. It could be worse; he could be dead. At least he was alone for a while, or as close to that as possible; the bow of the boat was long and slender. He could ignore the scurrying of feet on the deck, and just watch starlight.

Footsteps sounded behind him. Sandaled feet, walking over-heavily.

"Come to push me overboard, Walter?"

The thief chuckled. "As I understand it, that might have been a favor, yesterday, or the day before—to more people than you. On the other hand, I owe you my life. You think that letting your stupidity pass is a fair trade, Karl?"

There was just a touch of emphasis on the name; he let it pass. "At least you're talking to me. The only other words I've heard from any of you during the two days we've been on this garbage scow were to the effect of 'Don't throw up on me.' " He found himself shivering, so he picked up the blanket from between his feet, gathering it around his shoulders. Another night sleeping on deck—or not sleeping . . . well, that was better than putting up with the stony silence of his so-called friends.

Walter took a position at his side, joining in his staring campaign at the Cirric. He was back in his normal clothing—or lack of it—but the chill air coming across the water didn't seem to affect him. "You're getting off easy, Karl. You did a dumb thing—two, actually, if Ahira wasn't exaggerating about your trying to strike up a conversation during the fight."

"He wasn't. And I did know better. It was just that—"

"It was just that you were acting like Karl Cullinane, when you should have been busy *being* Barak. If that makes any sense to you." Walter shrugged. "Which I hope it does. I think that's what killed . . . Jason."

He raised an eyebrow. "You're sure he's dead?"

"Yeah. I heard his screams as I was running away." Walter shuddered. "Which makes me hope to God he's dead. We'll be lucky if he's the only one of us to die before we reach the Gate."

"If we reach the Gate."

"Right." Walter produced a piece of jerky, tore it in half. "Chew on it slowly, eh?" He stuck the other half in his own mouth.

"Thanks." It wasn't bad, actually. As tough as a piece of old leather, but the flavor was rich and strangely sweet, reminiscent of hickory. Hardly salty at all—he suppressed *that* thought; just the notion of salt made him gag. "But you didn't ask the right question."

"I didn't ask any question—but what do you think the right one is?"

"Try this: *Should* we try to find the Gate?" He felt Walter's gaze, turned to see the smaller man staring quizzically. "Or hasn't that occurred to you?"

A shrug. "It has—particularly an hour or so back—but never mind that. Tell me: How do your teeth feel?"

Barak started at the non sequitur. "Huh?"

"Your teeth, your teeth. You know, the things you chew with? How do they feel?"

"Well, fine, but—oh." He nodded.

"Right. The only dentistry they've got here is clerical spells. And that gets to be expensive; magic isn't that common. I spent a bit of time pumping some of the sailors; there's one—*one*—cleric in Lundeport, and he sounds to be about B-Class, from their description. Pandathaway's going to be different, so I hear, but clerics and wizards will hardly be growing on trees even there." He sighed. "So if you decide to stay, you can say goodbye to medicine and dentistry, among other things. Bet your teeth rot right out of your head within a few years."

" 'Among other things'? Like football, for example?" He chuckled. "You that eager to stomp more quarterbacks?"

"Yes, football, too. As well as reasonably safe homes and streets—you can forget that, if you stay here. And you can give up on any profession other than cutting people up. And you can probably count on not making it to old age." He cocked his head. "You may be a heavy-duty swordsman, m'friend, but you're going to run up against somebody better—or luckier—if you stay in the profession."

Barak sighed. Walter was right, of course; he was just being contrary, still burning because the others were shunning him for talking that way to Doria. Not that she—

Don't get off the track. Remember the smell of that soldier's burning flesh? He wrinkled his nose. "I didn't exactly have much of a profession, back there. Andy-Andy was right; I've always been a dilettante." He stopped talking to chew on the jerky, keeping it slow, ignoring his stomach's protestations. "She isn't speaking to me, either. I think she blames me for getting her into this."

"You could be right." Walter took a final nibble and tossed his stub of jerky forward. "And I don't think Doria's exactly thrilled with you. She doesn't understand."

He snorted. "And you do?"

"I think so. I'm not sure your stupidity is your fault. Though it damn well is your responsibility." Walter shook his head slowly. "When you talk about a woman's sexual habits, Karl, it's not exactly nice to make her sound like a . . . public utility. You wouldn't have done that, say, a week ago, back on the other side. Hope you get over it soon."

"What the hell are you talking about?" He didn't bother to keep the irritation out of his voice. Maybe being ignored was better than being nagged at. Nagged at by a thief who didn't have the slightest notion what it was like to be a warrior. The stupid . . .

"Remind me to gamble with you some time. I wish I could have read Doc's letter as easily as I can read your face." He scuffed a sandal against the deck. "Trouble with you, Karl, is that you spend too much time thinking like a warrior. 'To a warrior, everything is either a challenge, or a reward'—right?"

"That's right."

"Including, say, a woman?"

"Now, wait—"

"You wait. Hear me out. If a woman is supposed to be one or the other, it would stand to reason that one who sleeps around a lot isn't much of a challenge, no? And if anybody can have her—that isn't true for any woman I know, but let it pass—then she isn't much of a reward, either. Eh? I didn't hear you."

"Why don't you just leave me alone?" If he didn't, Barak could break him like a twig. Idly, he glanced down at the other's waist. Walter wasn't even wearing his knives.

Which reminds me—he turned to make sure his sword was still lashed to the forward mast. It hung there reassuringly.

Walter went on as though he hadn't interrupted. "I'm not talking about Doria, now. She's got some problems. Which are none of your business—although you might have known about them if you'd *talked* to her, that time, instead of grabbing your pants and—"

"*Shut up.*" The time Karl made it with Doria wasn't exactly one of his favorite memories. "Sounds like somebody talks too much. As well as—"

"*You keep your mouth closed* when you don't know what you're talking about. Okay?" Walter glared up at him. "Now, as I was saying, consider this: Maybe, just maybe, there's nothing wrong with a woman—or a man, for that matter—having sex with somebody she likes, for her own damn reasons, not yours. And not because it's a reward, but just because she wants to."

"So?" He rubbed at his eyes. It was . . . confusing. To his Karl-self, that sounded reasonable, even obvious. But to Barak, it was absurd. Worse—immoral, and—

"So if you try thinking of Doria as a person, instead of a . . . community facility, maybe you won't make such an ass of yourself again." Walter smiled. "Or not over that, anyway."

"Thanks a lot." He put all the sarcasm he could muster into his voice. "But I don't remember asking you to come over and tell me what a jerk I am. Why the hell are you bothering me?"

The thief considered it for a moment. "Two reasons. I'll reserve one, for the time being, but the other . . . is kind of complicated. Part of it is that I owe you. I kept slipping in and out of consciousness, the other night, but I do remember you stopping one of those bastards who was after my blood." Walter toyed with the spot on his shoulder where the knife had been. Even the scar was gone now. "But mainly it's that it seems to me you've got one hell of a lot of potential. You use it right, and you can be one fine human being, Karl Cullinane."

Barak smiled. "And if I don't?"

"Depends on the situation." Walter's smile was icy. "I care about Doria. Maybe I couldn't take you in a fair fight, but you hurt her like that again, you *damn* well better make sure you never turn your back to me. Ever. Understood, my friend?" There was no trace of sarcasm in that last.

Barak shook his head. He didn't understand Walter; he never had. Football hero Walter Slovotsky could have had practically any woman on campus—and frequently did. But why Doria?

"Why Doria?" Walter echoed his thoughts. "I tell you, we've *got* to get up a poker game, once we get back." He chuckled, then sobered. "Because I know more about her than you do—

remind me to tell you about it, the next time I'm into breaking confidences.''

"How about right now?''

"Well . . . '' Walter shrugged. "As long as you understand you have to keep your big mouth—''

"There you are. Walter, I—oh.'' Andy-Andy's voice cut off as if someone had thrown a switch. Possibly her eyes hadn't adjusted from the lighted cabins below, spotting Hakim's light skin and white trousers before she had been able to see Barak, wrapped in a dark blanket, concealed in shadow.

Walter waved her away. "I'll be back down in a minute.''

"Then you told him—you *didn't.*''

"He didn't tell me what?'' Barak turned.

She was barefoot, wearing only a loosely belted silken robe, probably borrowed from Ganness. Her long hair was mussed, as though she had been sleeping. Or *not* sleeping. "What were you going to tell me, Walter?''

The thief answered calmly, "I've got nothing to tell you, Karl.'' He backed off a step. "Just take it easy.''

"I said, *what is it you were going to tell me?*''

She glared at him. "You don't own me, Karl. I can—''

"*Shut your mouth.*'' Walter jerked a thumb at Barak. "You don't have to rub his nose in it. Now get back belowdecks, *please.*''

Barak moved away from the railing, his weight transferred to the balls of his feet. Plenty of room . . . "Yes, please do,'' he said, never taking his eyes from the thief. *Watch his navel—the center of gravity is always there. He can't fake you out if you don't let him.* "So, you were going to reserve telling me you'd slept with her, eh? This whole thing wasn't about Doria, was it? You were just taking out a bit of insurance.''

"I thought you might take it wrong.'' Walter balanced himself lightly on his feet, his eyes flicking from side to side. He moved away slowly, the soles of his sandals *whisking* on the deck.

"Bad choice. Much better to keep bare feet on deck. This way, you're liable to slip, fall overboard.'' He circled around, the traces of nausea vanishing. The only weapons nearby were the stacked crossbows, the boltbins, and Barak's sword, all lashed to the forward mast. And they were at Barak's back—if Walter didn't want to take him on barehanded, he'd have to go through him in order to lay his hands on a weapon.

"I doubt it, Karl." Walter held out both palms. "Just take it easy, and we'll talk about—"

"Don't stall. She's gone. And if I hear anybody behind me, I'll break your neck before I send you on your way. You don't have much of a chance at best. Want to try for none?"

"No. I don't want to fight at all." Walter shifted to a fighting stance, his body angled slightly away from Barak, his hands held chest-high. "Because I'm under a handicap. I don't want to hurt you—"

"That's too bad." Barak smiled, mirroring Walter's position, keeping his hands open, relaxed, ready to form fists, or parry a kick with an openhanded block. "Take your best shot." *He's liable to try a feint toward the head, then actually go for the body. Or vice versa. But it's going to be something tricky.*

Walter smiled. "Fine. Then, think about this. If you—"

"I meant to try to hit me, little man. Not talk."

"Doesn't the condemned man get a last speech? If you kill me now, it's because you think I've violated your property rights. And that would mean that Andrea's your property, Karl. You go around owning people, do you?"

Barak moved in, kicked out sideways. Walter blocked it with a forearm, but the force of the kick sent him crashing up against the rail.

He sprang off the rail at Barak. The thief extended a hand, reaching for Barak's throat—

Barak clubbed it aside with a heavy fist, then brought both fists down on Walter's rising knee. A backhanded slap sent the thief skittering toward the bow, half stunned.

It would be easy, now. All he'd have to do is flip Walter up and over. He took a step forward—

You go around owning people, do you?

Why not? said Barak.   *Of course not, said Karl.*
What's wrong with that?   *You don't own people.*
                               It's wrong.

—grabbed the thief's upper arms, lifted him—

He slept with my woman. I   *If she's ever going to be my woman,*
have to kill him. Honor demands   *it's going to be in the same sense as*
.   *my friend, not my dog.*

* * *

—and set him on his feet. Karl Cullinane glared down at him. "You manipulating *bastard*."

"Karl?" Walter shook his head to clear it. "I'm sorry—"

"Don't press your luck. I'm not going to kill you, but don't expect me to—"

Footsteps thundered on the deck behind him. He turned; Andy-Andy, Aristobulus, Doria, and Ahira stopped a few feet away, sleepy-eyed seamen crowding the deck behind them.

Ahira hefted his axe. "*What the hell is going on here?*"

Walter rubbed at the side of his neck. "Can't a couple of people have a quiet discussion without drawing a crowd?"

Karl sighed, letting his adrenaline high fade into a deep weariness. Ignoring raised eyebrows and half-voiced questions, he shouldered his way through the crowd, toward the forward hatch. "Wake me when we get to Pandathaway. I've got some sleep to catch up on."

Walter nodded, unfastening Karl's sword from the mast. He tossed it to him. "Don't lose it."

"Thanks." He started down the ladder.

Andy-Andy grabbed at his arm. "Karl, wait. I . . . I want to talk to you, explain—"

He pried her fingers from his sleeve. "There's nothing I want to hear from you." *I am Karl Cullinane. Karl, not Barak. I'll learn from my Barak-self, but I won't be* him.

Ever.

But damned *if I'm going to be the same Karl Cullinane you've been leading on as long as I've known you.* "I don't want you to talk to me, except when it's in the line of duty. Is that clear?" He didn't wait for an answer before turning to Doria. "I owe you an apology, Dore. And I pay my debts—do you want it long and flowery, or is the intention good enough?"

Doria nodded gently, her face studiously blank, but her eyes smiling. "Long and flowery, I think. Since I have a choice."

A tightness in his chest grew, as though steel bands were being clamped on his heart. He forced a chuckle. "Later, then. You deserve to have it when I'm completely awake." He pursed his lips. "But for now—you've always played fair with me. I had no business passing judgment on you. I promise it won't ever happen again." He exhaled deeply. "And now, goodnight."

Doria cocked her head to one side, her expression becoming infinitely tender. "Are you sure you want to sleep alone? Just sleep."

If I accept the invitation, it'd hurt Andy just as much as she hurt— "I think I'd better be by myself." *No, it wouldn't.*

Besides, playing people off against each other isn't the sort of thing that Karl Cullinane is going to do.

He gripped the pommel of his sword tightly, so tightly that his white knuckles stood out in broad relief.

But I would *have. Last week, last month—even yesterday. What is happening to me?*

He shrugged, and walked slowly to the nearest cabin, ignoring the rush of sound on deck.

I guess I must be growing up.

It must be that. He sat on a bunk and buried his face in his hands. *Nothing else could hurt this much.*

CHAPTER EIGHT: *"Welcome to Pandathaway . . ."*

That is no country for old men. The young
In one another's arms, birds in the trees
—Those dying generations—at their song,
The salmon-falls, the mackerel-crowded seas,
Fish, flesh, or fowl, commend all summer long
Whatever is begotten, born, and dies.
Caught in that sensual music all neglect
Monuments of unaging intellect.

—William Butler Yeats

Ahira frowned up at Doria as she clung to the rigging a couple of yards above his head, the wind whipping her hair, rippling her robes.

"You should see this, Ahira. Pandathaway is . . . beautiful."

He shrugged. "I'll wait until we see it close up. Probably has warts, just like everything else." Besides, while his night vision was much better than any human's, a dwarf's eyes were not built for looking across a sun-spattered sea.

She stiffened. "There's a ship—it's coming toward us, fast—"

"Shi-ip," the lookout at the top of the forward mast called out. "Just a hair off starboard, captain."

Avair Ganness chuckled. "Nothing to fear, Lady. It's just the guideboat." He raised his voice. "Drop all sails. Helmsman, bring us about. Secure all weapons—we've made it again." He glared at the dwarf. "Although I'd want more than a few bows and swords before I'd sail into Lundeport again." He considered it for a moment. "Perhaps you'd care to reimburse me for that?"

Ahira let his hands rest on his battleaxe's hilt.

Ganness shrugged. "Then again, perhaps not. Do you always leave such friends behind you as you did in Lund's territory?"

Ahira scowled at him. "Shouldn't you be doing something nautical?"

Ganness laughed, reaching out a hand, then thought better of it, letting his arm drop by his side. "It would waste my time and effort. That's what the guideboat is for, to bring us in."

"You can't do it?" Doria asked, lowering herself carefully to the slowly rolling deck.

"I wouldn't want to try. Can you see—no, you'd have to know what to look for." With an easy familiarity, he put an arm around her shoulder, a blunt finger pointing shoreward. "See that . . . darkening in the water . . . right . . ." his finger wavered, then stiffened—"*there*."

"Yes?"

"It's a sparling, metal-tipped, it is—lead, I think—sunk solidly into the bottom, canted outward. There's thousands of them in the harbor; they'd gut the *Pride* and sink us, were I foolish enough to try to dock without a guideboat." He leaned against the forward mast, idly twirling the end of his pigtail around his fingers. "Can you imagine what a prize Pandathaway would be for pirates? Not that it'd be easy to take, but the Guilds' Council doesn't like to take chances. Particularly the wizards—they want Pandathaway to be absolutely safe for them. Anyone trying to sail into the harbor without a guideboat is asking to die." A crooked grin flickered across his dark face. "Besides, it's another way for the Council to make a few extra gold. Not that they need it."

Ahira looked up. "What are you talking about?"

Ganness chuckled. "Oh—this is your first time in Pandathaway. You'll see." He walked over to the railing as the guideboat braked smoothly, then swung around so that its high, broad stern was a scant few yards from the port side of the *Ganness' Pride*.

Hakim coughed discreetly behind him. Ahira turned.

"How the hell is that thing moving?" The thief's brow wrinkled as he looked at the smaller, stubby craft. "I don't see any oarports—and if there's a mast and sail, they're both invisible."

As crewmen slid a gangplank from the guideboat to the *Pride*, Ahira moved to the rail. Under the water, dark shapes crowded around the guideboat's tubby hull. He blinked twice, then squinted, trying to make out their forms; could they be—

"Silkies," Hakim breathed. "They've got silkies chained to the hull."

Joining them at the rail, Andrea frowned. "Silkies?"

Ahira nodded. "Silkies—sort of were-seals. Except in seal form, they're big—about the size of sea lions. In our world, they're mythical; probably the myth came about the same way dugongs were thought of as mermaids." Or maybe not. And maybe mermaids weren't as mythical as he'd always thought. Slippage between the universe wasn't limited to humans; and it could happen in both directions.

Both ends of the plank were made fast, as the guideboat's crew gathered on deck: fifty or so humans in heavy, center-ridged breastplates, their bows strung and arrows nocked, although the bowstrings weren't drawn, and the arrows weren't quite pointed at the *Ganness' Pride*. From the stern of the guideboat, a tall, slender man in a silvery tunic stepped lightly across the gangplank, not bothering to touch its low rails as he made his way quickly to the rail of the *Pride*, then dropped lightly to the deck. He was followed by two hulking swordsmen, who made their way across more carefully, walking in a half-stoop, hands clinging to the gangplank's railing.

Ganness walked up to the slim man and bowed deeply.

Andrea shook her head. "I wouldn't want to just bounce across, not while wearing that much metal. If he'd missed, he would have sunk like a stone."

Barak—no, he said to call him Karl—*Karl* snorted. "He's an elf. See the ears? There's as much chance of his missing a jump as there is of you—"

Ahira cut him off. "Enough." He turned to Hakim. "How do they manage to keep the silkies chained? Seems to me all they'd have to do is revert to human, and slip out of the collar, no?"

Hakim nodded knowledgeably, as though to say, *Anything to keep those two from going at each other, eh?* "I can think of a couple of ways. For one thing, say the transformation takes a few minutes—any of those archers could put enough bolts into it, when it's in human form, to be a fine example to the others."

"A couple of ways, you said?"

He nodded. "Yeah. Maybe some of the silkies have wives, husbands, or children. Don't think I'm going to like these people a whole lot."

Particularly if they find out what your specialty really is.

Karl's fingers whitened on the hilt of his sword, as a slick black shape broke the surface and gasped a lungful of air. Then it dove sharply, its chain whipping behind it.

Ahira tried to seem casual as he put a hand on Karl's arm. "What's bothering you?"

"This." He pointed his chin at the guideboat. "I've half a mind—"

"Exactly." *At best.* "We don't buck local customs." Ahira forced a chuckle. "What were you thinking of, diving overboard, sword in hand? This your week to play Abe Lincoln?"

Karl cracked a weak smile. "More like a human pincushion."

"Right." He jerked a thumb at Ganness and the elf, who were quietly examining a series of parchment sheets, almost certainly cargo manifests. "I read this as a customs inspection. You?"

A nod. "And it looks like he's done."

The elf favored Ganness with a brief smile, clapped him condescendingly on the shoulder, and walked aft toward where Ahira and the others stood near their rucksacks.

"Greetings," he said airily in Erendra, then tossed his head, the tips of his ears momentarily peeking out of his neck-length blond hair. He was strangely thin, as though he were a normal man—except for the ears—who had been stretched, or distorted in a funhouse mirror. "I am Airvhan ip Melhrood, the delegate of the Guilds' Council of glorious Pandathway." His words came quickly, as though this were a set speech, down to the adjective. "I will need your names and occupations, so that I may assess your entry tariffs. You may, of course, decline to state your business here, in which case the maximum tariff will be levied." He sneered at Karl. "You needn't bother; you're a warrior, no?"

Karl took a step forward. "You have something against warriors?"

The elf's two guards moved quickly; they took up positions

behind Airvhan, hands on their swordhilts. Over on the guideboat, fifty bows swung into line.

"Stand easy, Karl," Ahira snapped.

Karl stepped back. The elf chuckled, shaking his head, then leaned against the railing, supporting himself on spread-fingered hands. He nodded lightly; the guards and bowmen relaxed. "Personally, or professionally?" Airvhan responded to Karl's question as though there had been no interruption. "Not that it matters; it is the policy of the Council to allow free entry to warriors, provided they agree to participate in the Games." He shrugged. "Not that we need to enforce that; you professional killers seem eager enough to win large purses at little risk." Raising a slim eyebrow, he smiled. "I take it you claim to be a swordsman. A true *master* of the blade, no doubt."

Ahira never saw Karl move. One moment, the big man was just standing there, his scabbarded sword in his hand.

And the next, the tip of his blade had *snicked* out a chip of wood from the railing, from between the middle and ring fingers of the elf's left hand.

As the guards went for their own weapons, Karl slapped their hands with the flat of his sword, then returned it to its scabbard, all in one smooth motion. He leaned it against the mast, then folded his arms across his chest.

"So I claim." He stroked at his beard. "Hakim, here, is even better. He taught me everything I know. He would have gotten both fingers, instead of missing, as I did. Try him?"

Airvhan glared at his two guards, as they stood sheepishly, swords half drawn. He held up a shaky hand. "No need. No need at all, friend . . . ?"

"Karl. And yes, I know of the Games. Hakim, Ahira, and I will be happy to attend."

The elf nodded, fidgeting. Ahira suppressed a chuckle, as Airvhan moved away from the rail; it seemed that the elf was eager to finish.

But it didn't take much to suppress laughter; Ahira followed the elf's gaze sideways, to the deck of the guideboat. Had Karl been just a touch slower, they might all well have found themselves filled with arrows.

Airvhan spoke quickly. "And I take it that the others of you are two wizards and a cleric? That-will-be-a-total-of-three-gold-pieces-and-seven-silver-if-you-please." Clearly, the elf had no desire to spend any more time than necessary standing next to a human crazy enough to risk becoming a pincushion in order to make a point.

But Karl's action hadn't been wise. Not at all. A bit of discipline was in order. "Pay the nice elf, Karl."

"You sure, Ahira?"

"Certain." The dwarf kept his face serious. "I'm sure that *friend* Airvhan is eager to get back to his boat." And antagonizing a customs official further didn't make any sense. "And I, for one, have no desire to spend any more time in the hot sun. I take it we will find good taverns near the docks?"

Airvhan nodded quickly. "Quite good. *All* the inns in Pandathaway are superb, friend Ahira. Much wine. Good wine." Cautiously, he held out a palm, keeping it near his body.

Karl lumbered over to him, smiled at the guards . . . and paid.

Karl and the rest followed Ahira into a sidestreet off the docks. The street opened into a cobblestone courtyard, surrounded by two-story buildings, white marble houses curved to accommodate the courtyard, and the fountain in its center.

The stones were hard under Karl's sandals, and his legs had grown used to the rolling of the *Pride;* he was glad when Ahira called a halt.

Karl dropped his rucksack and leaned his sword against the fountain's rim, taking a moment to smile at the two dolphin sculptures spouting water into the breeze. He smiled as he wiped the spray from his face; the dolphins seemed to smile back as they stood, frozen in midleap. "I like that."

The dwarf scowled. "Business first. Then, if there's time, you can rubberneck all you want."

Doria spoke up. "That's unfair, Ahira. We've got time." She smiled at Karl. "Plenty of time."

Walter took a knife from the sheaths at his hip and flipped it end over end, catching it absently as its hilt thunked into his palm. "Matter of fact, I think *friend* Karl is owed a thank-you." His mouth quirked into a smile; he took two more, juggling all three knives in a steady, effortless flickering of steel. "Without that diversion, I wouldn't have been able to pass as a warrior. A juggler, maybe," he said, picking the knives one by one out of the air and replacing them in their sheaths, "but not a swordsman." He patted at his scimitar. "I can't use this damn thing worth shit." He stood. "But you're right. Let's find ourselves a place to stay, then go exploring."

"*Exploring?*" Aristobulus hissed. "What we have to do is find the Great Library, and—"

"How about getting something to eat?"

Karl quashed his own resentment at the way the dwarf had snapped at him. "Everybody, *shut up*. Ahira's in charge, and he's talking."

Ahira rewarded him with a puzzled nod. "Fine. But first of all, what is this about games? I don't remember you telling me anything about it. Them."

"Whatever." But the dwarf was right. He hadn't said anything about the Games. Karl scratched at his ribs. But why think about all that now?—what he really needed was a bath and some sleep, on safe, dry, unmoving land.

No, don't let yourself get lazy now. He hadn't remembered, not until the elf had mentioned the Games. It was the same problem he'd been having, ever since they landed on this side. Memories of things he'd known back home were irregular, elusive. When he could remember something, it was reliable; but it was much easier to think like Barak, be the swordsman—

No. "Sorry . . . I didn't remember."

"Wonderful." Andy-Andy glared at him. "And what else don't you remember?"

He forced himself to ignore her and spoke to Ahira. "If it's as Deighton said, then the Council likes to encourage the best warriors to stay around, to stay in Pandathaway. Some are hired for the local . . . police force; helps to keep the city a nice place to be. As for the rest, well, having the best around keeps up Pandathaway's reputation as *the* place to buy or hire anything, anybody.

"For wizards or clerics, there's no problem: There's always good-paying work. Besides, there's a bunch of churches and magical guilds, who pretty much run the city—so guild members get a stipend from the Council when they're out of work. It's easy to do that—*hey!* I forgot all about the prices." Information, images crowded his mind. Deighton had shown him a listing. A night's stay in a relatively low-cost tavern would run more than two pieces of gold. A good bottle of wine would cost ten, twelve silvers. And it was a full— "It'll cost us at least a gold piece—

each—just to get into the Library. And that won't include . . ." He curled his fists in frustration. What wouldn't it include? It was just on the edge of his mind.

But he couldn't think of it. That was—

"Easy, Karl." Andy-Andy held his arm, then visibly remembered she wasn't speaking to him. She turned away.

"Relax." Walter smiled at him. "You were telling us how they manage to keep mercenaries around."

"Right. Since there isn't much work here, they put on Games. If you're good enough, you can support yourself in the once-a-tenday ones, if only just barely. But in the Seasonals, you can make a killing." He smiled. "So to speak. You can't get much more than bruised; the contact events use blunt, wooden weapons."

"Wonderful." Ahira spat on the cobblestones. "Do you think we have to waste our time on these Games, or can we just hit the Library, buy what we need, and get out?"

"I don't know." Karl shrugged. "What's our total worth?"

Ahira turned to Aristobulus. "Give me your best guess."

The wizard's eyes went vague. "Assuming standard rates of exchange . . . maybe two thousand gold." He shook his head slowly. "And from what Hakim—"

"Walter."

"—said about Lundeyll, that would have been almost enough to have bought the whole town, back there."

"So what?" Ahira turned to Walter. "We're here now. How far away do you guess the Gate is?"

"Mmmm, it's got to be some distance; Frann only knew that it was east of Pandathaway, and he's from here. I don't know; maybe we have enough, if we don't spend too much money on room and board while we're here."

Karl snorted. "Two thousand? That isn't a lot; Lucius paid five hundred just for one horse. We need six."

"Five and a pony," Ahira snapped. "Fine. Here's what we have to do." He extended a blunt finger. "One, find a place to stay, at least for the night. Two"—another finger—"get to the Great Library, find out where the Gate is, figure out how we'll need to equip ourselves in order to get there."

"Which wouldn't be a problem," Karl said thoughtfully, looking at Aristobulus, "if somebody hadn't blown up the box with all the goodies."

"Shut up. Three, we need to know what the situation is here, find out how to raise the money we'll need. Which also means we'll need to know when the next Games are—is.''

"Whatever." Karl nodded. "We might be able to do well enough in the tendays, if we're good enough." He fondled the hilt of his sword. *I bet I am.*

"Don't." Walter didn't look at him.

"Don't *what?*"

"Don't be sure you're good enough."

"Damn you, just because I got a bit sloppy, that first time—"

"It isn't that. Think it out." The thief's expression proclaimed that Karl wasn't going to like it. "We're all G-Class or so, right?"

"Right, but if that corresponds to the way things work—"

"As it seems to, then you think we're pretty much up there, right?"

Karl thought as hard as he could, *If you don't stop reading my mind, I'm going to break some bones,* making sure that his face showed what he was thinking.

"Well," Walter went on, "we aren't pretty much up there if they've got the best warriors in this world in Pandathaway, are we? We might be big fishes in—"

Karl smiled and held up a hand. It had been a long time since he'd been able to outthink Walter. "*You* think it out. Look, what would a really high-level fighter do? Go around looking for work? Hell, no. They gather followers, claim some land—either dragging in peasants to farm it, or using locals. There's not going to be a whole lot of folks as good as we are—as good as *I* am—who are still wandering around, trying to build a name. Maybe we'll have to deal with a local champion or two, but not more than that. Right?"

"Not bad, Karl. Not bad at all."

Ahira rapped his axehilt on the fountain's rim. "Enough. I came up with three things we have to do; anybody else have a fourth?"

"No."

"Uh-uh."

"I don't."

"I want to see about finding myself a tavern girl. It's been . . ." Walter trailed off at Karl's glare. "Sorry."

"As I was saying," Ahira went on, "there are three things to do. Since this is a safe city, we'll split up into three groups. I'll take the Library, but I want one of you literate types with me. Andrea?''

''Wait,'' Aristobulus snapped. ''I need to—''

''Fine. You, instead, since she hasn't used a spell, yet.''

Andrea smiled. ''I've only got three; I haven't wanted to waste them. But if you need somebody put to sleep, or charmed, or want me to disappear . . .''

Right now, Karl thought, *there isn't much I'd like better*. ''That last could be useful, if we need a bit of extra money, no?''

''True.'' Ahira raised an eyebrow. ''Your charm spell—think you can get us a decent rate for lodging with it?''

''Maybe. You want me to see to the rooms?''

''Fine. You take the thief with you.''

I won't be jealous. I won't. I'm just going to—

Walter shook his head. ''I'd rather go look around; I'll keep an eye on Karl and Doria—Andrea should be able to handle the innkeeper by herself, no?''

''Okay. Why don't you get going, meet the rest of us back here, say, at sundown?''

She nodded and left, her sandals slapping against the cobblestones.

Ahira turned to Karl. ''You three are to stay out of trouble, understood? I just want you to find out when the Games are, get an idea of the prices of things like horses and supplies, then meet us back here. No fights, *and make damn sure that there's no stealing*. We won't have another Jason. Yes?''

Good. While Walter was his best friend, Ahira was too smart to leave the responsibility of seeing that he didn't steal with him. ''I'll watch him.''

''And he'll watch you to make sure you don't pull another stunt like the one you did with the elf.'' He picked up his two rucksacks and beckoned to Aristobulus. ''See the rest of you at sundown—in case somebody misses it, everybody else stays put.'' The dwarf beckoned to Aristobulus, and both of them walked away.

Walter waited until they had vanished into an alleyway beyond the fountain before turning to Karl. ''Beer?'' He smiled. ''Just one or two.''

Of all the irresponsible—

No. No more kneejerk reactions. ''I guess one beer wouldn't hurt any." Karl shrugged. "And I could use a drink, at that. Doria?"

She looked up at him sadly. "You never asked me out for a drink before, Karl." Her hand stole toward Walter's. "I couldn't turn you down, even if I wanted to." She gripped Walter's much larger hand, with shaking, white-knuckled fingers.

Great. Maybe I'd better have that talk with Walter, and soon. This is getting too damn complicated.

The three armored guardsmen at the top of the broad stone steps nodded in unison at Aristobulus, then glared suspiciously down at Ahira.

The dwarf forced himself to keep his hands at his sides, although his palms itched to feel the smoothness of his axe's handle. Probably this was just the guards' professional demeanor, but perhaps there was more to it: Dwarves were not renowned as scholars, and Ahira's presence might have excited their professional suspicions. If he didn't keep cool, that could lead to a fight.

And three-on-one would not be something Ahira would look forward to, not even after going berserk. Besides, it wouldn't be just *three*-on-one; these guards were wearing the same center-ridged breastplates that Airvhan's guards had worn; patently, they were part of the Pandathaway police force, or whatever passed for such. They had seen similarly equipped men on their way toward the Library—there would be, easily, half a dozen within shouting distance.

The largest of the three, a pale-skinned man with a heavy brow and a small sharp nose, gestured with his spear. "What are you doing here?"

Aristobulus raised an eyebrow; the guard lowered his spear, and touched his free hand to his forehead. "Your pardon—I was addressing the dwarf, sir."

At the wizard's sideways glance, Ahira nodded slightly. Best to keep the guards thinking that Aristobulus was in charge, since they were treating him respectfully.

"The dwarf," Aristobulus said, "would like to use the Library, as would I. Is his coin not good?" The wizard smiled thinly.

A chuckle. "It had better be. Sir. The last one trying to get counterfeit coin past the Librarians found himself full of arrows." He turned to the guard at his left. "Challa, take the dwarf's packs and weapons—everything except his pouch.'' Through yellow teeth, he grinned at Ahira. "That, you are going to need." The guard bowed slightly at Aristobulus. "If you and your . . . companion will come this way?''

"What do you want with my pack and—''

"We can't have you taking anything out of the Library, now can we?''

Ahira lowered his two rucksacks to the broad stone steps, then handed his crossbow, flail, and battleaxe to Challa, holding back a grin as the man staggered under the load. "You will make certain that nothing of mine . . . walks away?''

"You must be new to Pandathaway,'' Challa panted through gritted teeth, as he led the two of them through the entrance, past the open oak doors. The doors were massive, towering easily ten times Ahira's height, inlaid with gold and silver tracings. "We're under oath to the Library. An accusation, even, would put us out on the streets—at least until it was decided on.'' He set Ahira's gear down on top of a pile of other goods: swords and bows, sealed boxes and mesh bags. "But don't get any notions, *dwarf*. A suspension would give us *plenty* of time to find whoever accused us, and take our pay out of his small hide. Do you get my meaning?''

The entrance foyer of the Great Library of Pandathaway was a large, bare room, illuminated only by spears of golden light from tiny, fist-sized windows high above, only a few feet below the juncture of the stone walls and the ceiling. Below the windows, a wooden walkway ran the length of the front wall. No—*not* windows; those were arrowports. Whoever had designed the Library had provided for its defense.

Their sandals scuffed against the floor as Challa led them toward the rear of the room, with its two exits.

One was a small archway, leading into a lamplit corridor. Ahira started toward it, stopped by Aristobulus' tug on his sleeve.

"That is my entrance,'' the wizard whispered. "Glyphs over the doorway—they say, roughly: 'If you can read this, pass in safety.' I'll see to my needs, then locate you.''

Without waiting for an answer, Aristobulus stepped briskly toward the archway and walked through. As he did, a bare glimmer of red outlined his body, then faded as the wizard walked quickly out of sight, not looking back.

I'll have to discuss this sort of thing with him later, Ahira thought, idly toying with images of bashing Aristobulus' head against a wall. Until they reached the other side, they were all in danger. Walking away without consulting him was not going to be repeated. By anyone.

Challa brushed Ahira toward the other exit, where a bored, white-bearded human sat behind a door made of thick steel bars, reading a leather-bound book. With a deep sigh, he closed the book and raised his head. "What is it?"

Challa jerked himself to a semblance of attention. "The dwarf is here to use the Library, sir. At least, that's what his friend said."

"A dwarf? And what friend?"

"A wizard, sir."

"You're certain about that?" The old man raised a skeptical eyebrow. "With the likes of this?"

"Certain, Librarian. He walked right through Wizard's Arch. There isn't any other possibility, is there?"

A shrug. "Well, if there is, it's no concern of ours. Wizards Guildmasters built it; it's their responsibility." He extended a palm through the bars. "That will be two gold."

Ahira reached into his pouch and drew out a single gold coin. "I thought that it was one?"

"Two." The Librarian pointed at a plaque set into the wall next to the door. "Can't you read?"

"No." Ahira shrugged, drawing out another coin.

"Then what are you doing here? Never mind, it's no concern of mine. Just an old man's curiosity. We don't get many dwarves here."

And at these prices, you're not going to get many more. Ahira dropped the coins into a withered palm.

The Librarian sighed, slipping the coins into the slot of a stone box, its lid secured by a steel strap and heavy padlock. "Enter-and-be-welcome," he said. "And guard, you can hurry back to your post. If you would care to keep your position." The door creaked open; the Librarian hurried Ahira inside with a quick gesture. "Come along, now. I don't have all day."

Ahira stepped through. The room was small, but tightly packed with bookshelves and scrollracks, labeled and unlabeled tomes exuding the pleasant reek of old paper and aged parchment.

Beyond the farthest stack, an open doorway gave him a glimpse of a marble-floored corridor.

The Librarian seated himself on his highbacked chair and folded his hands on his lap. "Well, now, why are you here? You can't read, and—"

"That is none of your business." An explanation was out of the question; Ahira wasn't sure how they treated the supposedly insane here, but he was damn sure that he didn't want to find out firsthand.

"Very well." The old man sighed. "But your insolence is going to cost you. Another gold, please."

Ahira took a half-step forward. "I could break you with—"

Wheeet! The man gave out a piercing, pursed-lips whistle, rewarded instantly by the thumping of feet in the corridor. Within seconds, Ahira found himself at the focus of an arc of five crossbowmen, weapons cocked and aimed at his head.

"And that will be enough of *that*," the Librarian said. "I am Callutius, Junior Librarian. You will address me either by my title, or simply as 'sir'—and always, *always* with respect. Is that understood?"

"Yes. Sir."

Callutius gave him a sour smile. "One gold for insolence plus another for the information is two, please."

"Information?"

Callutius didn't seem to hear him.

"—sir?"

"My name and title, fool." He held out his palm and accepted Ahira's gold, dropping one coin into the box, the other into a fold of the yellow sash at his waist. Callutius steepled his hands in front of his chin. "And now, what can the Great Library of Pandathaway do to serve you?"

Ahira scowled. "I'm afraid to say. How much will the answer to that question cost me, Librarian?"

"Junior Librarian—which is why I'm on greeting duty." He turned in his chair to face the bowmen. "You may go now; I think our customer is learning proper deportment."

As the bowmen shuffled off, he turned back to the dwarf. "How much it costs depends on what you wish to know. I assume that you'll need an apprentice to read for you? That will be three gold, for his services until the close of the Library today." He raised a warning finger. "And don't think to pump

126

him for location information; there are severe penalties for that."
Callutius smiled. "And as to how much the location of whatever
it is that you wish to know will cost you, that is negotiable with
me. Quite a lot, probably—nobody except a wizard comes to the
Library unless he needs to know something very badly." He
snickered. "Of course, you could just look around with the
apprentice, and try to find out whatever it is that you need to
know."

Ahira nodded. "That sounds good to me."

"Don't be silly!" Callutius was shocked. "There are four
hundred fifty-three rooms in the Library, with an average of five
thousand three hundred twelve books or scrolls in each.
Conceivably, you could cover one room each day—it could
easily take you better than a year to find out what you want. At
two gold each day." The Librarian leaned back and closed his
eyes. "I'll wait until you've made your decision."

Ahira thought it over. He could just wait there for Aristobulus,
but that might be a while—and spending time around Callutius
was not a pleasant prospect. Or he could hire an apprentice—no.
A compromise was in order. "I won't need an apprentice, but I
do want to find directions to the Gate Between Worlds. A map,
if there is such a thing."

Callutius chuckled. "A treasure hunter, eh? You choose an
expensive form of suicide—sixty goldpieces for directions."

"One."

"Fifty."

"One."

"Forty-five."

"*One.*"

"Really? Is that all you're willing to pay?" Callutius shrugged.
"Well, it's none of my concern. Look around; you've already
paid for that." He raised a finger in admonition. "But if you
damage one *page*, its replacement will be the skin of your back,
suitably tanned and cured." Callutius closed his eyes again.

"Ten gold. And that's all."

"Done!" Callutius smile was genuinely friendly as he took
the proffered coins in his cupped palms, tucking all of them into
his sash. "And a well-struck bargain, little one."

"Meaning that I gave in too easily?"

"Not at all." The Librarian's grin made his words a lie. He
whistled again, this time a complex four-tone theme that was

picked up down the corridor, then echoed off into the distance. Callutius picked up his book, then gestured at the doorway leading deeper into the Library. "Go on—an apprentice will meet you, to guide you," he said, ushering Ahira along. "And it has been a true pleasure aiding you in your search for knowledge." He patted at his sash.

"An enriching experience?"

"Quite. I take it this is your first time in Pandathaway?"

"Yes."

"Welcome to Pandathaway, then. And if you hurt anything, I'll see your head on a pole."

CHAPTER NINE:
Maps and Dragons

Wilt thou seal up avenues of ill?
Pay every debt, as though God wrote the bill.

—Ralph Waldo Emerson

Karl enjoyed himself as the three of them wandered through the open-air markets of Pandathaway. The markets were a rainbow of sights, sounds, and smells: dwarf blacksmiths hawking mailshirts and steelplate greaves; jewelers selling rubies and sapphires in settings both plain and ornate; foodsellers displaying spits of garlic-laden meat and glass bowls of tangy fruitices; bakers calling all to sample golden, fist-sized loaves of bread, dripping butter and fresh from stone ovens.

The prices were high for most things, although a beerseller let them drink three huge tankards for a copper; it occurred to Karl that bread and circuses might have translated into beer and games, here.

At an armorer's canopied stall, they stopped to haggle with a dwarf blacksmith over the price for charming a blade—Walter had suggested that Andrea's and Aristobulus' spells might earn some extra money if needed.

"Well," Karl finally said, quickly bored with the bargaining that the smith seemed to enjoy, "if it's only worth one gold for two swords to you, it's probably not worth bothering our friends. But we might take you up on it later."

The dwarf spat, muttering in some tongue that Karl couldn't follow. "No promises that my offer will stay open. Many wizards in Pandathaway."

Walter looked at him, raising an eyebrow. His unvoiced question: Maybe it would be worth it to nail down the deal now?

"*Out* of my way," Doria snapped, shoving her way between Karl and Walter. "You two have the bargaining sense of—never mind." She slammed her palm down on the weathered counter. "*Look, you,*" she said in Erendra, "we don't have the patience for that sort of nonsense. Understood?"

The dwarf spread his hands. "I don't know—"

"*None of that.* A charmed sword has to be worth, easily, a hundred, hundred-fifty gold if it has any kind of edge—that would be about twice standard—and you're trying to get these two poor fools to agree to half a gold, *each?* Don't bother keeping *that* offer open; we don't need it."

The dwarf chuckled deeply. "Well, it was worth trying for a fast bargain. They look new. You're a Hand cleric, aren't you?"

"Yes."

"It figures. No offense intended, but I don't care for your sect. I'm just an honest armorer and smith, trying to turn a bit of profit, and—"

Karl took a step forward. "And cheat us just a little?"

"Well," the dwarf shrugged, "maybe take a bit of advantage. From the way you three keep spinning your heads around, I figured you might be new to Pandathaway." He eyed Karl's sword. "You any good with that thing?"

Karl slipped his right hand to his swordhilt. "I manage."

The dwarf held up both palms. "Be easy, friend. I'm not threatening. It's just that I have a few spare coins, just now. Since you're new here, the oddsmakers probably will undervalue you; I might be persuaded to put a bet down."

Doria nodded. "*And* give us a good price on a spell or two."

The dwarf dismissed that with an airy wave. "I don't see the need—"

Doria reached out and grabbed him by the collar, pushing her face close to his. "You're familiar with healing spells?"

The dwarf could have pushed her away with ease. Instead, eyeing Karl and Walter, he nodded slightly.

"And," she continued, "have you ever seen one work in reverse?" She ran a fingertip lightly across the dwarf's throat.

He shook his head.

"Then," she said as she released him, "if you don't want to, maybe you'll stop trying to take advantage of my friends, no?"

The dwarf looked curiously at Karl and Walter. "Where did you get this one? I thought that Hand clerics were nonviolent."

And I didn't know Doria was capable of this sort of thing. Karl eyed her curiously. "She's a new kind."

"I'll go along with that—I'll make you a deal. Put *her* in the Games, and we'll all bet on her and get rich as elves. The stupid swordsmen will never know what hit them, eh?" The dwarf laughed, a deep-throated roar that came across as sincere, not just a bargaining technique. "But seriously, if you'll cover half my losses if you don't place, I'll give you, say, twenty gold for glowing a sword, thirty for charming one. Agreed?"

"No," Doria said. "You'll give us those prices anyway—and your wagers are your own profit or loss. Agreed?"

The dwarf's mouth quirked into a frown. "Can't get away with anything around you, eh?" He picked up his hammer and turned back to his forge, pumping his bellows with a muscular arm. "Go on, now—find somebody else to persecute. If you win, come back and I'll do well by you." As they started to walk away, he called out, *"And don't bring her with you next time."*

Karl chuckled. "It seems you gained some skills during the transfer that we didn't know about, Doria."

"Not quite." She smiled up at him. "I spent a summer in Tel Aviv, back at the end of high school. That little dwarf has nothing on the Arab merchants in the Jaffa flea market—you've got to take the first offer as an insult, threaten a bit of violence . . . *then,* you can get down to business. Otherwise, you can end up spending the rent money on a pair of sandals—or take the whole afternoon just picking up lunch." She glared at both him and Walter, but there was a bit of pride mixed in. "It seems as though the two of you are going to need a keeper—or at least a teacher. Watch." She paused in front of a fruit vendor's stall and picked out three ripe, red apples from the slanted bin, examining the back sides of the fruits—"you've got to check for worm holes"—before pulling a copper coin from her pouch, holding it out to the vendor in offer of payment.

The vendor, a frowzy, overweight woman, brushed away the

two dirty children clinging to her tattered skirts, nodded, and walked over to take the coin.

As they walked on, she handed Karl the reddest of the apples, Walter another, and took a bite out of the last. "Good. See," she said around a mouthful, "if you look like you know what you're doing, you'll save a bit of money, and a lot of time."

Karl crunched a bite out of his apple. It had been too long since his last meal, aboard the *Pride;* the cool, sweet fruit tasted almost *too* good. "We've still got to find out when the next Games are." He eyed the afternoon sun. "And then get back to the fountain—I make it about three hours till sundown."

Walter took a last bite out of his apple and threw the shreds of stem and core away. "I could use another beer."

"No." That was a rule he'd learned back when he was a freshman: always set your limits *before* you have your first drink. "Let's walk this way."

Ahira found the Librarian in charge of the Room of Gold and Gray to be an unlikely occupant of the post: The man was tall and well muscled, his shoulders straining at the seams of his gold-trimmed gray woolen tunic as he bustled over to the door to greet the dwarf and dismiss Ahira's escort.

"Welcome, welcome to the Room of Gold and Gray," he boomed. His voice was a deep baritone, his handclasp firm and friendly. "I am Oreen; I am the Specializing Librarian in charge of"—he interrupted himself to chuckle—"all that you now survey. And you are . . . ?"

"Ahira." *And I am also confused.* This Librarian's manner was diametrically opposite to Callutius'.

"Ahira," the Librarian repeated, drawing up two three-legged stools, seating himself on the shorter one and gesturing Ahira to the other. "This will let us have our eyes on the same level, or close to it. Please, make yourself comfortable. You are both my first patron of the day, and my first dwarvish patron ever—let us enjoy the moment, shall we?"

"Do I get charged extra for the friendly treatment?"

Oreen's brow furrowed under a shock of brown hair. "Friendly? —oh. Callutius is on greeting duty today, isn't he? I haven't seen the old bastard for months. Does he still look as though he'd just discovered half a maggot in his meat?"

Ahira chuckled. "Quite."

Oreen shrugged. "Well, it's his own fault. He never specialized, you see—instead of trying to learn one room, he went in for indexing, trying to learn *what* is kept *where*." Oreen punctuated the words by thumping himself on the knee. "He wants to be Chief Librarian someday. Which he may be, though I doubt it. And, in any case, he is certain to be unhappy in the interim." Oreen gestured at the shelves and racks lining the small, bright room. "As for me, I know every page of every book, every section of every scroll here. Vellum maps and hand-copied books; printed scrolls and explorers' notes—I know them all." Oreen folded his thick arms across his chest. "Which makes me the master of all I see, and a happy man. Now, what is it that we're looking for today?"

"I'm trying to find a map that will show me where the Gate Between Worlds is, if you've ever heard—"

"There's no such map." Oreen held up a hand. "But please, let me show you . . ." He stood, sucking air through his teeth, and walked over to a scrollrack, flipping aside several scrolls before selecting one. "Hmmm . . . I think that this will give you the best overview of the situation." Oreen beckoned Ahira over to a wide table and rolled the scroll open, carefully pinning his selected panel open with four springy clamps. "My own design, these clamps—they keep the scroll firmly open, without hurting it at all. —You see, here we are: Pandathaway." The Librarian held his finger over the designated spot, not touching the yellowed parchment. "I could show you the floor plans of most of the structures here. Do you follow me, so far?"

"Yes, but—"

"Be patient for a moment, friend Ahira, be patient. We now move north and east . . ." His finger traced a path through a scattering of upside-down V's. ". . . where we reach the Aershtyl Mountains, and Aeryk, there. This is the trade route into the mountains; we have much contact with the Aerir. So, I could show you maps of the landholding around Aeryk—contour maps, if you're familiar with them; much of the land is on its side." His finger went farther north. "Now, here's a problem: the Waste of Elrood. Do you know of it?"

"No." Oreen's friendliness tempted Ahira to be more complete—but it was better to be safe. "I'm new to this area."

"Oh?" Oreen's lifted eyebrow invited him to go on.

"I believe you were saying something about a Waste?"

Oreen nodded. "It was almost a thousand years ago—I don't have the date on the tip of my tongue, but I could get if for you if you want me to—it was a thousand years ago, that two powerful wizards dueled on the plain of Elrood. It was a lush farmland, back then. They destroyed everything around them, for a great distance. Now, it's devastated. Nothing grows." He shook himself. "But . . . you pass through just the edge of the Waste, and—"

"Wait." Ahira indicated a patch of green in the large brown circle that marked the Waste. "What's this? I thought you said that it was all destroyed. That's farmland or forest, isn't it?"

"Very good." Oreen's smile held no trace of condescension. "That's the forest surrounding the home tabernacle of the Society of the Healing Hand—oh, you know the Society?"

"Slightly," Ahira admitted. "I have a friend who is a member." *In a manner of speaking, that is.*

Oreen stood back, impressed. "Really. They're powerful healers. Their Grand Matriarch is said to be able to raise the dead, although I couldn't swear to the truth of that. I've never heard of a Hand cleric's talking about it, though." He snorted. "On the other hand, the damn Spidersect clerics claim *they* can do anything, and they lie. But, as I was saying, the Matriarch is *most* powerful; she fully protected the tabernacle and its grounds from the battle."

Ahira frowned. "I thought you said it was a long time ago— hundreds of years, no?"

Oreen's face wrinkled. "Where are you from, friend Ahira?"

"What do you mean?" There was a challenge in Oreen's voice that made Ahira's hands itch for the handle of his battleaxe.

The Librarian sighed, and shook his head. "My apologies; it's not my place to pry. But it must be a strange land, where powerful clerics can't maintain their own life functions."

The James Michael part of him welled up with an image of old Father Mendoza, his parish priest, who had collapsed with a heart attack while celebrating Mass, and died a few hours later. It *was* strange, come to think of it: Why couldn't the gods—God take care of his own?

He shook his head. That was beside the point; the problem was how to deal with Oreen. Possibly the best thing to do would be to lay his situation before the Librarian, and ask his advice.

But how could he put it? *I used to be a cripple on another world, until a would-be wizard sent me here, to clear the way for him?*

No. That wouldn't do. Just because magic worked here didn't mean that there was nothing that the locals wouldn't consider insane.

And how do they treat the insane here? Beat them, to drive the demons out? And might that even work here?

It might, at that. But the cure could easily be worse than the disease. "You were showing me the route, I believe."

Oreen looked at him for a long moment before shrugging. "Very well. As I was saying, I can't show you detailed maps of the Waste, simply because nobody has ever made one. At least, not to my knowledge—anyone going through there would be more interested in getting out than they would be in mapmaking." He smiled. "And to every rule, an exception: I could show you a map of the road from Metreyll to the tabernacle of the Healing Hand." His finger hovered over a line from a lake to the green spot that marked the forest preserve of the Society. "But that would take you out of your way. Far out of your way, if you're going to Bremon."

"Bremon?"

"Bremon." Oreen tapped at a lone inverted V, near the Waste. "That's where the Gate Between Worlds is supposed to be. I have a description—no map, just some notes—of an entrance into the mountain. A hundred years back, someone gave up on finding the Gate when he was just outside of the mountain. So, I can show you where *that* is. But I can't show you a map of the inside of the mountain, simply because—"

"Nobody who has ever gone in has ever come out again, to tell the tale."

"Of course." Oreen was puzzled. "What do you think I've been getting at?"

An easterly wind brought a stink to Karl's nostrils, as the three of them walked along a quiet cobblestone street. It was a stench of dung, and sweat, and fear. He was about to pick up the pace, to urge the others along, when Walter plucked at Karl's sleeve.

"I think there's a slave market over that way—I can just barely hear an auction. You two want to go look?" The thief shrugged. "I know we can't spend any serious money right now, but it might be worth our while to find out how much some

135

bearers cost. Could be cheaper—'' He was interrupted by the crack of a distant whip, immediately followed by a scream of pain. Walter winced. ''. . . than buying horses and such.''

Karl shook his head. ''We won't own people. It's wrong.''

Doria frowned at Walter. ''How could you even *think* of such a thing? That's—''

''Thinking it through. Which you two aren't. Look, what would we do with a bunch of slaves, after we reach the Gate? We'll let them go, no? In effect, it'd be more like a temporary indenture than real chattel slavery; they'd trade a bit of service for their freedom.''

''*No.*'' Karl clutched his sword more tightly. ''That's out. Just forget about it. One of the few virtues our world has is—''

''Don't be silly. In our world, it's been the norm for most of history. Even in our time, chattel slavery isn't unknown. It's still legal in half a dozen places I can think of—Saudi Arabia, f'rinstance. You—''

''I won't stand for it.'' *You don't own people. It's wrong.*

Doria interposed herself between the two of them. ''Just let it be. We're supposed to be seeing the sights, no?''

''Fine.''

The street sloped gradually downward as it narrowed, the one- and two-story stone houses that lined it becoming progressively more ill-kept. Through latticed windows, Karl could see an occasional head, peering out at him, ducking aside when he returned the occupant's gaze. Idly, he let his free hand rest on the hilt of his sword, loosening it in its scabbard. Probably that was an unnecessary precaution, but that was the trouble with precautions: You couldn't know which one was necessary until it was too late.

Ahead of them, where the now narrow street opened into some sort of plaza, there was a distant roaring, as though of a fire.

Fire? Karl sniffed the air. No good; the wind was at his back. ''You two hear that?''

Doria and Walter nodded, stepping up their pace to keep abreast of him. ''Sounds like a fire,'' Doria said. ''A fire? This whole place is built out of stone. There can't be a fire.''

''Bets?''

They reached the end of the street. What had seemed to be a plaza was more of a large, railed balcony, overlooking a vast pit, easily two thousand feet across, a hundred feet deep at its center.

And in the center of the pit, chained by the neck to a massive boulder, was an only slightly less massive dragon.

It was a huge brown beast, easily twice Karl's height at its front shoulder, only slightly shorter at the hips. Two leathery wings sprouted from behind its shoulders, curling and uncurling constantly as the dragon flamed patches of brown muck into ash and steam, its tail flicking nervously from side to side.

The head was a horror. It was shaped much like an alligator's head, but it was massive, teeth easily the size of daggers, wicked red eyes that bore into Karl's, sending him reeling away from the pit's edge.

A gout of flame issued from its mouth, roaring as it touched the stream of sludge that poured out of one of the pipes feeding into the pit.

Go away, sounded in his head, accompanied by waves of nausea.

Karl fell to his knees, gagging, his tearing eyes jammed shut.

"Karl?" Walter knelt beside him. "What happened to you?"

"Karl—are you all right?" Doria's face went ashen as she crouched in front of him.

Another burst of flame sent up a cloud of steam from a sludge pipe.

Karl forced his eyes open. No, there was nobody else there— all of the buildings that circled the pit presented it with only blank walls.

After all, no one would want to look out on a sewer, would he?

This time, the voice was unaccompanied by nausea; Karl staggered to his feet, wiping his mouth on the back of his hand. "You're talking, in my head."

Very clever, swordsman. The dragon's directionless voice dripped with sarcasm. *And you are talking with your mouth. And the mixed-up little healer and the smug thief beside you are standing mute. Have you any more subtle observations to make? If not, please taunt me in my captivity, and then be on your way.* The dragon's forepaw idly clawed at the coils of chain around its neck—no, it wasn't chain, exactly; more like cable. And in spots where the filth that covered it had flaked away, specks of gold showed through.

That is so I can't flame myself free, fool. Were I so foolish as to try, I would only burn myself. It had tried that, more than

137

once. The gold plating on the steel cable conducted the heat away. To the dragon's neck.

Karl's hands flew to his burning neck, circled by a ring of fire.

But the fire wasn't there; the pain faded instantly, until it was only a memory, as distant as a half-forgotten pain from a childhood fall.

How do you like the feeling, human? Your kind—

"No, not me."

"Karl, would you—"

"Shut up." *You're not hearing my voice, are you?*

Why would I be interested in your voice?

I . . . don't know. But . . . how can your own flame burn you? And why are you angry at—

A magical creature the dragon is, but not immune to flame, to heat, to burning. I control my own flame, of course, but the . . . indirect effects, no. And I hate you because . . . wait. Who are you?

"My name is Karl Cullinane. This is Doria and Walter." *And I don't know why you're angry at me. I never did anything to you.*

I am Ellegon. The disposer of wastes.

I . . . don't understand.

Wait until the wind changes, Karl Cullinane. This pit is where the sewers of Pandathaway empty, so as not to foul their precious harbor. I must flame the wastes into ash, or sit here buried in human filth. They captured me, when I was only half a century out of the egg, and chained me here, dumping their excrement on me for these three centuries.

You're more than three hundred years old?

The dragon had been chained in sewage for three centuries; it let Karl feel what that was like.

For just a moment.

As he lay retching on the stones, Walter pulled at his shoulders. "C'mon, we've got to get him out of here. It's killing him."

Yes, I'm only a child. Do you think it's right, to treat a child like this? Do you?

Nausea.

Karl shrugged their hands away, closing his eyes, trying to close his mind. *Please. Don't do that again.*

138

You wouldn't have done it? No, I see that you wouldn't, not even to a dragon.

The nausea ceased. "Take it easy, you two. Everything's okay." *No, I wouldn't do it to a dragon.*

Karl would *kill* a dragon, if it endangered him. If he could. But this was wrong. Karl had felt just a trace of Ellegon's suffering, and that was more than enough. Unless the dragon wasn't as sensitive to—

Do you want to feel it again?

No. This was wrong, but it didn't look as though there was anything that Karl could do about it: The dragon looked hungry, and the cable was thick.

I am hungry, and I haven't asked you to cut the cable. Not that I need to eat; dragons are magical, don't you know. We like to eat—the satisfaction of crunching a cow, eating it in two bites, sent the last traces of nausea away—*but we don't have to.*

I didn't know. I didn't know anything about dragons.

A mental shrug. *Are you stupid, or merely ignorant?*

Just ignorant, I hope.

Hmmm. I have a proposition for you. If I do two things for you, would you do one thing for me?

That depends. You can't—

I can't reach your mind from much farther away, yes. You could run away, and I wouldn't be able to talk to you, or do thi—

DON'T. I don't want you to make me vomit again. But you were offering me a proposition? I . . . I'm not sure I trust you enough to go down there, and try to free you.

Flame roared. *Fool. I wasn't asking for that. Not from a filthy human. But if you could see your way to bringing me something to eat? A sheep, maybe? I'll do something for you, I'll start by telling you something you need to know, if you are going to find the Gate Between Worlds, Karl Cullinane.*

How—how do you know?

Blistering scorn. *I read minds, remember?* Ellegon roared.

Sorry. —And yes, if I can afford a sheep, if you do something for me that makes it worthwhile, I'll bring you one. Or something else to eat, if I can't manage to buy a sheep.

Agreed. First: You will find the Gate deep under the mountain Bremon, just north and west of the Waste of Elrood. And—

I thank you, but maybe Ahira—

*—I know. Your companion may already have found that out. I wasn't finished. I was going to tell you something else, something that he could *not* have found out. Something that I know, simply because I am a dragon, and know where all of my kind are.*

"Karl, what is—"

"Shut *up*. I'm talking to the dragon."

"You're talking to a dragon?"

Yes, he's talking to a dragon.

Walter and Doria both jumped, as Ellegon included them.

But it's easier to talk to only one.

You were telling me that there's a dragon there, at the Gate. That was bad. But maybe, if they were lucky, the dragon wouldn't be as large as Ellegon.

No, He won't. He will be much larger. He has lain there long enough for the mountain Bremon to grow up around him, as He sleeps there, guarding the Gate.

"Wonderful." He turned to the others. "Ellegon just told me that there's a dragon at the Gate, guarding it."

"Karl," Doria shrilled, "would you tell me what is going *on*?"

Tell them to go away. Their minds are even narrower and more cramped than yours. Although the woman's holds more. Strange. And the other's is built differently, as though it's not quite the same kind. I . . . don't understand.

"Ask him," Walter said, "what the other dragon's name is. Maybe Ari can put together a name-spell, and—"

Fool.

"I heard that." Walter glared.

And fool you are. He was the first dragon, created before all the rest of us.

"So?"

So, in the old days, when there was but one thing of His kind in all the world, why would He have need of a name? Just so, billions of years later, some stupid human could cast a spell using it? No. He is The Dragon, oldest of us all, and has no need of a name.

So what can we do to protect ourselves against him?

Don't wake Him. He is older than the mountain, and you could break the mountain more easily that you could dent the smallest of His scales. Karl Cullinane?

Yes?

I have done one thing for you, no? Will you bring me my sheep now, or must I do the other?

You make that sound like a threat. And I don't like threats, Ellegon.

Very well. Ellegon sighed mentally. *Then, I will let you understand.*

Understand wha—

The universe fell apart.

He was fifteen, and a nice Jewish girl. Or, at least, she was supposed to be. But there were things she wasn't supposed to be, and things she wasn't supposed to do. Like grope in the dark with Jonathan Dolan, and slip out of—

Enough? Or do you really want to understand Doria?

You're letting me into her memories? Why?

So you'll understand.

No, wai—

And she couldn't tell Daddy, of course. He called her his one-and-only, and Mommy thought she was still a virgin. That was one of the rules: You don't talk about it. But it wasn't only that she was late, there was this burning—and that damn Jonny Dolan was telling everybody that *she'd* given *him* the clap. And that couldn't be true. It couldn't. He was the first, and the only one, so far.

And it hadn't even been any fun. Just a sticky mess. He lied. They all lied. It wasn't any fun at all.

You still don't see it.

But I can't tell anybody. Besides, it's probably not *that*. Maybe, if I just forget about it, it'll go away?

I think, perhaps, just a bit more.

"She's a sick little girl, Mr. Perlstein, but with a bit of luck we'll have the fever down in a few hours." She lay panting beneath the plastic, no longer able to paw at the tubes in her nose and arms—they'd fastened her hands down.

"But it can't be gonorrhea. Not my little—"

"You know, Mr. Perlstein, you make me sick."

"Doctor, I—"

"If she'd been able to tell anybody—if she'd felt able to tell anybody . . . if there'd been *one goddam person* for her to talk to, maybe she wouldn't be lying there now. We could have treated it easily, if we had gotten to it. Before."

"Before?"

"Before it grew into one hell of a raging pelvic infection that'll leave her sterile, if it doesn't kill her."

"Sterile? My little—"

"Sterile. Unable to conceive. Ever. If we're lucky. Nurse." A cold hand felt at her forehead. "I want a temp and BP every five minutes. If her temp doesn't start to drop within the hour . . ."

And the last portion of the payment.

And I guess it doesn't matter anymore and besides in a lot of ways I'm perfect because nobody ever has to worry about getting Doria Perlstein pregnant ever which means that every cloud has a silver lining because now I can have any boy I want to but they all treat me like I was a cigarette they pass around but I guess that doesn't matter because that's what I deserve isn't it because becausebecausebecausebe—

Enough.

"Karl, are you okay?"

"I don't care what he said, Walter, we've got to get him out of here."

"No—*wait*. I think he's coming around."

Karl pried an eye open. Doria and Walter bent over him, concern creasing their faces. "It's okay," he said, not surprised to hear his voice coming out as a harsh croak. "Help me up."

"What did he do to you?" Doria asked. "He hurt you again. That—"

"Shh." *Understanding, eh?*

Understanding. It's not always easy to understand things, Karl Cullinane. Even I know that.

She doesn't know?

No, of course not. Why would I want to hurt—

You would have killed us, a few minutes ago. If you could have reached us.

A different thing entirely, no?

A different thing entirely.

Will you get me my sheep now? Ellegon asked plaintively.

Karl walked slowly to the railing and stared out at the dragon. "You two keep watch. I've got a debt to pay."

"What did it do to—"

"Shh."

Then I get my sheep!

No. He slipped out of his sandals, using their thongs to lash his scabbard to his shoulders.

No? Then you are like all the rest, you—

Shh. Just be quiet for a moment.

Karl Cullinane pays his debts. That was the rule. And even if the debt came out of a window into Doria's mind, a window that he wouldn't have wanted to look through . . .

And to think I treated her like—

You didn't know. What are you doing?

Karl levered himself over the railing. Good—the rockface below was rough and cracked; there would be many finger- and toe-holds. *I took up rock climbing one summer—hey! why are you asking? I thought you could read my mind, even what I'm not consciously thinking about.*

Not now. There's an intensity—

Shh. I've got to pay attention to what I'm doing.

He picked his way carefully down the face, ignoring Doria's and Walter's shouted questions from above. *You can't turn off my sense of smell for me, can you?* he thought, as he lowered himself into the ankle-deep foul muck.

No—you're really going to do it? Thankyouthankyouthankyou—I'll leave, I'll fly away, I will. Please, Karl, please don't change your mind. Pleaseplease—

Shh. Stumbling and gagging at the stench, he started to walk toward Ellegon.

Never mind, Karl. He's been in this for three hundred years.

As he got closer, it became shallower; a harder surface beneath the ooze supported his bare feet.

The dragon loomed above him, its breath coming in short gasps, its wings curled protectively by its sides. *Lower your neck, will you? If there's a weak point in this cable, it'll probably be there, where you can't see it.*

Ellegon knelt in the filth, his huge head just inches away from Karl. His mental voice was strangely silent as he presented his barrellike throat.

It was a cable, and like all cables, made up of smaller strands. It took a moment for Karl's swordtip to snick through the first strand, and a moment longer for the next.

Easy, my friend, easy. Just a few dozen more. He had to stop to quell his gagging reflex; wading through this . . . sewer was something he'd try to forget.

And—he cut through the last strand—*done!*

Ellegon's massive head tilted at him. *Thankyouthankyouthankyou—*

Shh. Better get going. He slipped his sword back in its sheath.

Grab my neck, the dragon said, its mind muttering a background of *Free. Free. I'm Free.*

Karl reached out, and as he did so, the creature's wings flapped, blurring with speed as it eased into the air, then whirred over to the balcony, Karl dangling for a moment, then dropping to the tiles. *Free.*

One more thing, Ellegon said, landing.

"Look out, Karl, he's going to—"

The dragon's mouth opened, and a gout of flame rushed out, enveloping Karl. Just flame; no heat, although the reeking muck covering much of his body burst into fire, sparkling and burning away. *My flame couldn't hurt you, Karl Cullinane. Not you. Not now.* It tingled pleasantly, that was all. He turned in the firestream, letting it wash over him like a shower.

Free. The flame stopped.

Better get going.

With a snap of his wings, the dragon jumped skyward, his wings just a blur as he left the balcony and the pit behind him.

Free.

Fly away, my friend.

Three times the dragon circled overhead, gaining height as he flew.

Free.

"Karl," Doria said, shaking her head, "would you mind telling us just what's going *on?*"

"I think we'd all better get out of here, folks," Walter said, moving them along. "When the authorities find out about this, they aren't going to be all that pleased."

Ellegon flew off toward the north, now so high he was only a dark speck against the blue sky.

Free.

"Karl, why?" Doria asked.

He slipped one arm around her waist, the other around Walter's as they walked away. "Because I never felt this good in my Whole. Damn. Life."

Free.

That was faint now; did he hear it, or just imagine it?

It really didn't matter.

Not at all.

Free.

CHAPTER TEN: *The Inn of Quiet Repose*

> *We may live without poetry, music and art;*
> *We may live without conscience, and live without heart;*
> *We may live without friends, we may live without*
> *   books;*
> *But civilized man cannot live without cooks.*

—Edward Bulwer-Lytton, Earl of Lytton

Walter Slovotsky suppressed a chuckle at Andrea's bubbly enthusiasm as she led the group down a broad street toward the Inn of Quiet Repose.

"You should see it," she said, hurrying them along. "And I got a *fine* deal for the suite—it's going to cost us just one hundred gold for the next ten days."

A hundred gold? By local prices, that wasn't much at all. Walter shrugged. Either she had landed them in some horrid hovel, or her Charm spell had been awfully effective.

Apparently, Ahira had the same idea. "If you charmed whoever's running it, won't—"

"Nope." She took a smug, prancing step. "The owner has an amulet around his neck, one he thinks wards that kind of spell away." She spread her hands. "But it doesn't have any kind of aura at all—either it's dead, or it's a phony. But here we are."

The inn was a three-storied edifice, a marble mansion like a stone version of something out of *Gone with the Wind*. Tall fluted pillars guarded the broad staircase; the foyer was a vast, soundless room, with deep, blood-red carpets that seemed to suck the weariness out of Walter's legs. He smiled as he tilted his head back to enjoy the mural that spanned the high ceiling: chubby nymphs chasing unicorns through a green glade.

He started to lower his pack to the floor, but six young women in filmy white kimonos descended on them, relieving them all of their burdens as others arrived bearing silver trays laden with steaming cloths to bathe their hands, feet, and faces, and yet others carrying thick towels to pat them dry, and tall, frosty glasses of ice and wine.

And all this when they were barely inside the door. Walter nodded. *I think I'm going to like this.*

And then, for a moment, he had his doubts. A huge man, yards of yellow silk caftan barely containing his oversize belly, stepped from behind a curtain. "Well, it seems as though you were correct, my little friend." He scowled down at Andrea, easily half again her height. Walter tried to guess his weight; three-fifty, four hundred perhaps? "I wouldn't have believed that there was so scruffy a group if—but never mind, pay no attention, Tommallo is but ranting, again. And these are guests; their way has been pai—" He stopped himself, rubbing a finger against his almost impossibly aquiline nose, then shook his head. "My guests: Will you go to your suite now, or would you care to dine first?"

Ahira spoke up. "Is there a bath—"

"You insult me!" The owner stood back, his hands on his hips. "This, my dear sir, is the Inn of Quiet Repose. Nowhere, I say, nowhere in glorious Pandathaway will you find an establishment so well kept, so replete with every facility necessary to provide a guest ease or comfort. *Every* comfort."

Walter looked the nearest of the serving girls up and down. Quite a difference from the ugly, unbathed serving girls of Lundeyll. Then he glanced at Karl. On the other hand, maybe the stupid swordsman would give him trouble over that—couldn't he see that there was a difference between here and home? When in Pandathaway . . .

The owner was still talking. ". . . you will even discover—perhaps I should save this? No, no—you will find that your suite's bath is complete with running water, requiring only the merest turn of a valve for its use." He stamped his bare foot soundlessly on the carpet. "And you will find your rooms to be quiet; your sleep will be deep and sound and filled only with light, pleasant dreams. Our table is the finest, with food—" He smacked himself on the forehead. "But I forget my manners! I am Tommallo, your host for the next ten days—and at an unusually low fee." Again, his forehead wrinkled, as though he were trying to figure out why he had agreed to such a relatively small charge. He glanced at Andrea and Aristobulus, in their gray robes. "It's as though—but no," he murmured. "I've a token to ward that away. But perhaps its potency has fled? No, no; pay attention, Tommallo, for you have guests, and yet to find out what their pleasure is, you old fool. Letting your mouth run free when—"

Ahira held up a hand. "I'm for the bath, first. I suppose everybody else is, too."

"Not me." Those were the first words out of Karl since they'd left the sewage pit. *The stupid—but never mind. I've got to help Jimmy contain the damage. Not sure what kind of police force they have here, not really—but whatever kind they have is going to be looking for Karl. And they'll be bloody unlikely to overlook his accomplices.*

"I managed," Karl went on, "to get myself cleaned up earlier. Right now, I could use some food. Anyone else?"

Well, that might have been true for Karl, but Walter hadn't been cleansed by fire—and had no desire whatsoever to try it out. He scratched at his arm; the itching from lack of bathing had subsided into a dull background of irritation, but now there wasn't anything he wanted more than a bath.

Except survival. And that means I'd better keep an eye on Mr. Cullinane. "I need some food, too." Walter patted at his stomach. "Been a long time since breakfast. Tommallo?"

"Yes?" The innkeeper beamed at him. "Snacks—I have a fresh, pungent beetlepaste—or would you prefer something more substantial?"

"Beef?"

"Ah . . . the cooks have a wonderful roast in the pit. Hindleg of a virgin heifer, marinated in wine and herbs for a week, then cooked in a vat with—"

"Enough." Aristobulus held up a hand. "Let us get to it, shall we?"

Andrea nodded, as did Doria.

Ahira shook his head. "The rest of you go along—I'll head up to our suite, and get myself a bath and a nap."

Tommallo snapped his fingers. A buxom blonde led the dwarf away. "And for the rest of you—would you care to dine in the common room, or—"

Walter shook his head. "We need some privacy."

The innkeeper tilted his head, smiling knowingly. "Ah—and will you require an additional wench or—" .

"We're fine the way we are."

Tommallo nodded, and conducted the five of them down a hallway, to a staircase, then up two flights to another hallway, and finally to a room at the corner of the building, two walls composed mainly of open windows and bead-curtained exits to the veranda outside. He bowed them in, waiting until everyone was seated on a bench at the massive oak table before clapping his hands together. "Wine for my guests!" he commanded the air.

As though they had been waiting behind the curtains, three women stepped out, bottles in hand, along with heavily laden trays. Bowls and small sharp knives were set in front of them, along with serving dishes of buttery corn, served on the cob with a tangy brown sauce, small fowl—squab, perhaps?—the skin broiled to a perfect golden crispness, a purple paste that was somehow sour and hot and sweet, all at the same time, and delightfully so.

Tommallo bowed. "Enjoy yourselves, my guests. If you have any desire at all, you need merely snap your fingers, or when in your room, pull a bellrope." He left, but the servitors kept bringing platters of food, setting them down, and leaving.

Walter sampled a knobby sheet of bread. The bulges turned out to be a cheesy orange filling. A strange combination of flavors, but a delightful one; he debated for a moment whether to reach for another helping or sample the steaming slices of beef and lamb or the silver tureen of leeks floating in a clear broth before deciding to take all three, *and* more of the bread.

There was no sound for minutes, except for the noises of chewing and frequent oohs and ahhs as all sampled the fare. *Do we talk here or—stupid!*

"Everybody," he said in English, "no Erendra—just keep the talk in English, understood?"

Aristobulus shook his head. "No," he said around a mouthful of fowl, "I don't understand—we've got nothing to hide."

"We do now." Walter jerked his thumb at Karl, who was silently chewing on an ear of corn, careless of the way the sauce was dripping on the tabletop. "Genius, here, decided to ruin the city's sewage system." He looked over at Andrea. "And besides, we don't want the staff here to overhear how we got the cut-rate price on the lodgings, do we?"

Andrea shook her head. "I wouldn't worry about it. As I said, Tommallo isn't the sort to talk things over with his employees, and—"

"*Not* employees," Karl growled. "Let's at least keep it honest."

"They are *so* employees, stupid. Slephmelrad, to be precise."

Slephmelrad. Fealty servants. Walter shrugged. It had taken a while to get used to the way that oddities of the Erendra language awakened knowledge that he hadn't known he'd had, but it had become a frequent phenomenon. *And, come to think of it, when I get some spare time it'd be worthwhile to run through every Erendra word I know, and try to integrate all that.*

"Oh." Karl shrugged, smiling awkwardly at a slender girl who looked to be about thirteen; she deposited another clay bottle of wine on the table before leaving. "Just women?"

"No." Andrea smiled broadly. "Male servants, too. And one of them—"

"Enough." Walter rubbed at his temples. Granted, the two of them had had a good time together aboard the *Ganness' Pride,* but it hadn't been *that* good. And the way she rubbed Karl's nose in her right to—something had to be done about that.

You're a fine one to talk, Walter Slovotsky. You've never made any pretense with Doria that she was your one-and-only. "We'll talk about it later." Then again, that was different. For one thing, unless he was totally misreading Karl, *and* Andrea was a liar, those two had never gotten together. And, dammit, he didn't rub Doria's nose in it. Ever.

Complications . . . everything's got complications. And Jimmy was probably at the heart of one of the worst of them. Why hadn't he made a play for Doria? It was as clear as anything that the little guy wanted her—and here, it might work. Or would that be some sort of perversion, come to think of it? What would you call it, humanity?

He shook his head. It'd probably take Jimmy a while to work

things out. If he slept with Doria, was he, Ahira, being queer for humans? And if he made it with a female dwarf, was James Michael—

The trouble with me is that, way down deep, I'm shallow. My best friend is finally in a situation where he can be a whole person, and all I worry about is whether that's a perversion of some sort.

And whether I have to sleep alone tonight. He caught Doria's eye, tilting and raising his chin in an unvoiced question. She glanced at Karl, then at Andrea, frowned, and nodded. *Well, at least that's taken care of. That's the trouble with me, though—I'm just a slave to my hormones and digestive juices.* He reached out and speared another slice of red, rare beef.

"Sewage system?" Aristobulus looked over. "You mean that little dragon?"

"How'd you hear about it?"

"I spent some time in the wizards' section of the Library, chatted with a few guild members taking a break from doing some research. Found out some . . . interesting things, between my reading and talking."

"Well?"

"Hmmm, I think I'll save it for later. There are some calculations I want to recheck. But for now . . . did you realize that this whole Guilds' Council thing is a sham?"

Karl frowned. "Wait a minute. I—"

"You didn't spend the afternoon with some of the people who really run Pandathaway, Karl. It's the wizards—the rest are just window dressing. Which is why we don't have to worry about To—about our host's getting angry, even if he does find out what Andrea did." Aristobulus smiled smugly. "Assaulting any wizard is a capital crime—ditto an authorized cleric, member of any of the five recognized sects. Including"—he nodded to Doria—"the Hand, by the way." The wizard frowned and shook his head. "I'd leave you all right now, if it wasn't . . ."

Damn me. I've got a mind like a sieve. Ever since he had learned about the Great Library, Walter had worried that Aristobulus might choose to leave the group in Pandathaway. He hadn't said anything; nothing could be done about it. If Aristobulus wanted to go, he could. "And why won't you?"

Aristobulus took a long swig of wine before answering. "It's the damn spell books again." He drained the mug and slammed it down on the table. "I may be good, but I'm not a Wizards' Guild member."

"So?"

"So, if and when I apply for membership, I'll be better off having a set of books of my own. Otherwise, I've got to *apprentice*, of all things."

Walter chuckled. The notion of Aristobulus apprenticing to some other wizard was almost absurd. Ari was pretty far along as a wizard; it was unlikely that there were many others in Pandathaway as powerful as he was. But it was a certainty that there were plenty of wizards who could gang up on him and make him toe the line. "How long an apprenticeship?"

He scowled. "Until my—get this—my *master* decides that I'm worthy." He shook his head. "And that's not the worst of it. All apprentices in the guild have to submit to being put under geas."

Now that was bad for Aristobulus, but good for the rest of them. A geas would rob him of his ability to disobey his master's orders. And it was unlikely that any master wizard would want to dispense with the services of someone with skills as developed as Ari's. Normally, the tradeoff between master and apprentice—in any profession—was that of training in the craft for doing all the trivial gruntwork. But Ari was capable of doing much more than preparing a potion under supervision; whatever guild wizard he'd be apprenticed to would quickly find his services indispensable.

But it was good for the group, at least. With a lifetime of apprenticeship to look forward to if he stayed in Pandathaway, Aristobulus was certain to stay with the group. At least until they reached the Gate, and Deighton. "You're assuming that Doc'll furnish you with another spell book or two."

"*Very* good." The wizard popped a ball of deep-fried prawns and garlic into his mouth. "And then I'll come back here, apply to the guildmaster, and live off my earnings and the stipend guild members get, just like all the others." He chuckled. "Including the extra earnings from selling phony charms, like the one that Tommallo has. The fool—why would the wizards bother to sell him a real protection when he can't tell the difference?"

As Karl reached for his third helping of beef, the wizard

cocked his head. "I thought you're supposed to go light on food, before?"

"Before *what?*"

"The Games, stupid—the every-ten-days ones are tomorrow, aren't they? I thought that's what—" Aristobulus wrinkled his brow. "You mean you didn't bother asking anyone about them? I thought—"

Walter held up a hand. "We got distracted." *And it's just as well that the Games are tomorrow, at that. The cops are going to be looking for Karl, Aristobulus is probably trying to figure out a way to swipe a set of books from a local, and—*

And the simple fact is that I'm scared. He rubbed a thumb against the spot where Lund's henchman had cut him. *I know I won't stop being scared until we get home. But will it stop, even then?*

He stood. Somehow, the food didn't taste so good anymore.

Rubbing at his hair with a thick flannel cloth that served as a towel, Ahira decided that Tommallo hadn't been bragging. Their suite in the Inn of Quiet Repose was broad and spacious, oozing comfort from the deep crimson carpet that tickled his ankles, all the way to the chandeliers overhead, scores of candles burning almost smokelessly, dripping only a sweet fragrance into the common room. Beeswax, perhaps?

He sighed. And there was even half-decent plumbing—superior, by local standards. Granted, the hot water for his bath had been taken, bucket by bucket, from a copper kettle, but at least it had been hot.

He dropped to the floor next to his weapons and stretched out on his back, pillowing his head on his hands, letting his eyes sag shut. With a bit of luck, he could catch a nap before the others returned from dinner.

And it was good to be alone, without having to worry about where the others were, what the others were doing. . . .

The world slowly faded away into the warm twilight of oncoming sleep.

"Shh." Hakim's whisper boomed. "Don't wake him; he needs his rest."

Ahira opened his eyes. "Thanks for the thought, anyway."

As the others filed into the room, he shrugged, deciding against slipping away to one of the sleeping rooms. There was much to talk about; they had to figure out what the next move was.

Karl stretched out on a fur-covered couch and patted at his belly. "Sorry. Hey, you missed one hell of a good meal, though. I don't think I'll be able to eat for hours. How was your bath?"

"Restful." Ahira forced himself to sit up. "Very restful. You all should try it, a bit later."

Doria sat beside him, hugging her knees. "Why not now? You go get some sleep. We've got a long day tomorrow, what with the Games and all."

"Tomorrow? Then never mind." He rubbed at his eyes. "All right, everyone, gather around. Let's get this over with."

Hakim sat down next to Doria, followed by Karl, then Aristobulus, then Andrea. Ahira could almost see bands of tension flowing between her and Karl; it was evident in the way he avoided looking at her, and in the curious little pursed-lips headshake that she would give every time she looked at him. Probably there was some intelligent thing to do, to get the two of them to agree to better than a coldly hostile coexistence.

Trouble is, I don't have a single idea what that intelligent thing to do is. Oh well—what cannot be cured, must be endured. "I'll go first," he said. "I know where the Gate is; I've got it right here"—he tapped a finger against his temple—"and I'll sketch out a map sometime tomorrow. Somebody pull a pencil and some paper from their pack. I don't have any."

"I do." Andrea nodded. "But how far is it?"

"Looks to be a fairly long haul from here—a month of traveling, easily."

Karl cocked his head to one side, a faint smile playing across his lips. "And once we get to Bremon, it'll be tougher, maybe. Almost certainly."

"What do you mean?" Ahira hadn't mentioned Bremon; he hadn't said anything about it since they'd all met at the fountain.

Karl rubbed his hand across his face. "I . . . had a talk with a friend. He says there's a big mother of a dragon under the mountain, guarding the Gate. Sleeping."

"A *friend?*" Andrea snapped. "What sort of friend?"

Hakim raised a palm. "Best not to talk about it—he's talking about the baby dragon that is—that used to be a part of Pandathaway's sewage system. But it's best to keep quiet about it. We'd just better get ourselves together and get out of here. Could be the authorities are looking for us, even now."

Karl shook his head. "I don't think so. We were down in the slums. The folks who live there probably won't be eager to talk to the . . . cops. Even if they saw us."

Walter sneered. "You ever live in the slums, genius? Sometimes you *have* to talk to the cops, even when you don't want to."

Aristobulus nodded his agreement. "And when the sewage starts rising around their ankles? You *know* who's going to have to take care of it, and they won't like it. Not at all."

Ahira didn't know what they were talking about, but the fact that Karl knew about Bremon—apparently knew more about Bremon than he did—was something that had to be explained. The best way, probably, would be to wait, to escape the worry of being overheard if they spoke in Erendra, or being labeled as strange if they talked in an unknown language like English. But too many precautions, too much paranoia, was in itself a chancy thing. "Just talk, Karl. Keep your voice low, by all means, but please tell me *what the hell you're talking about*."

Karl nodded slowly. "Fine. They have a funny sort of sewer system here. It dumps out into a pit, where the sewage used to be flamed into ash by a dragon, a young one."

"Used to be?" Andrea arched an eyebrow. "I take it it—"

"Doesn't anymore." Karl smiled. "They had the dragon chained there. I didn't like that, so I set him loose. End of story." He shrugged. "Probably not a big deal; all they'll have to do is get some high-ranking wizards down there, every now and then, to Fire the slop into ash."

Ahira shook his head. *The brainless*— "How long ago?"

"An hour or so before we met at the fountain. Why?"

Andrea spoke up. "Because probably the news is all over Pandathaway by now, and somebody is going to be looking for whoever did it, stupid. I thought that Walter was just joking before. Tell me, Karl, have you *ever* thought about the consequences of—"

"Shut up." That was from Doria, oddly enough. Her defending Karl made little sense. "Tell me, Karl: Did you think about the consequences?"

Karl didn't answer for a moment; he sat there tailor-fashion, his body relaxed and loose, his eyes misty like an absurdly overmuscled Buddha. "To be honest, I didn't. It . . . it was

156

important enough that . . . consequences just didn't matter. I'm sorry if you're upset—"

"*Upset?*" Andrea was almost hysterical. "If they find out who did this, we all could get *killed*."

Doria's face clouded over. "He said that it was important enough, didn't he? I don't understand why—but maybe I don't have to. We all—"

Andrea threw up her hands. "That's the trouble with you," she shrilled at Karl, ignoring Doria, "you're always so damn *intense* about everything. That's why—never mind." She shook her head slowly, rubbing at her eyes. "It's done."

Ahira picked up on that. "Right. It's done." He turned to Karl. "Did anyone see you three?"

"No." Karl chewed on his lower lip. "And besides, around here, the three of us aren't all that unusual-looking. Maybe even if someone did see us, and somebody else links that to Ellegon getting away—"

"—it might not matter," Ahira finished. Well, that wasn't likely, but at least it was a possibility. "But let's not take chances. I don't want you three to be seen together in public until we're gone from Pandathaway. And we'd better arrange to get out of here soon. Soon as possible. And that means that you and I'd better do well enough in the Games tomorrow so that we can buy what we need *quickly*, and get out of here." He considered that for a moment. "Better: We buy just what we need to get to Aeryk, and finish outfitting ourselves there."

Aristobulus cocked his head to one side. "I'll still need another two days in the Library, at least. I've gotten one of my spells back, but I need the Fire spell. and I think, with a bit of effort, I could puzzle out the spell that would let me bring writing materials past the Glyph—"

"No." Ahira made that as final as possible. "We don't have time for all that. You and Andrea each have one spell to relearn— you do that tomorrow morning while we get ready to leave after the Games."

Hakim lifted his head. "I've got a better idea. We could have Ari Glow a blade or two—we ran into a smith who might pay nicely for it, if Doria handles the negotiations. And then he can relearn both that and his Lightning spell. That way . . ."

"Good." Ahira nodded. "And that's the way we do it. Where are these Games taking place?"

"Mmmm." The thief spread his arms, embarrassed. "To be perfectly honest, we got kind of dis—"

"At the Coliseum," Aristobulus snorted. "North side of the city. The oddsmakers set up their tables at dawn; contestants have to be there by midmorning. Anything else you need to know? It's fortunate that at least one of us spent some time asking questions—"

"Enough." Ahira cut him off. "Spilled milk. Doria?"

"Yes?"

"You and Walter take care of placing the bets on us. Don't go deep into our money, but if Karl and I are as good as I think we are, we shouldn't have any problem winning. And since we're new here, I bet—"

Doria nodded. "—that you'll be undervalued. Fine. How much should we put down?"

Karl spoke up. "That's not the way you gamble. Not if you know what you're doing. Figure out what we need, find out what the odds are, and *then* you'll know how much to bet."

Andrea stood and stretched. "Well, unless you've got something for me to do, I'm going to wash up"—she put her hand over her mouth to stifle a yawn—"and then get some sleep. That meal's going to my head." She started to walk away, then stopped and turned. "One thing—what if you and Karl don't win?"

Ahira shook his head. "You're looking at it the wrong way. —Now, Doria and Hakim, I want to go over what you've got to buy tomorrow, just at a minimum. That way, you can price it out, and know what you'll have to bet in order to make the kind of money we need."

Andrea scowled down at him. "What do you mean, I'm looking at it the wrong way?"

He sighed. She still hadn't worked it out? "Karl, tell her."

The big man shrugged. "Look at at it this way: We don't have enough money to buy what we need to get out of Pandathaway, and this is the only way I can see of making it in a hurry. And whoever's in charge of this place is probably looking for me right now, and isn't likely to think all that highly of the rest of you. So . . ."

"So?"

"So we'd damn well *better* win, hadn't we?"

CHAPTER ELEVEN: *The Games*

A man cannot be too careful in his choice of enemies.

—Oscar Wilde

Karl frowned. The place felt normal, but the chatter was strange. The swordsmen's pit beneath the right-hand limb of the Coliseum was a large bare room of gray stone, lit only by a few flickering oil lamps that dangled from the ceiling. The air was cold and damp; the reeking sawdust that covered the dirt floor should have been changed long ago.

But the conversation was positively merry.

"Bet I get past the second round without two marks on my hide, and you—"

"You serious? I put down a couple of silver on myself, but I only got thirty-to-one I make it to the finals. Who you betting with? I've been going to Antrius, that slimy son of a dungfly—"

"Well, of course Ohlmin's going to grab first. Nobody else can move near that fast. So I'm not holding back anything in the early rounds; I'll be satisfied if I can just get into the finals—"

"You're *dreaming*, friend. Or crazy. Dwarves are no damn good with longbows; they're just too short. Although the little buggers—"

A pinch-faced elf waved the hundred or so swordsmen—humans, elves, dwarves, and curious mixes that Karl couldn't quite identify—to a semblance of silence. Standing on a waist-high

159

stone block in the center of the high-ceilinged room, he wore a light-blue tunic with matching leggings, a gold headband that marked him as an official of the Games, and a bored expression that proclaimed that being around a bunch of ill-washed swordsmen was not his ultimate pleasure in life.

"I am," he intoned, "Khoralt ip Therranj, Wineseller's Delegate to the Guilds' Council—"

"So bring us some wine!" a mocking voice called out from the crowd.

The elf sighed. "If you will all keep silent for a few moments, just a few moments, this will be over, and you can proceed to the winning of some money." He made as though to step down, but moved back toward the center of his pedestal as the rush of noise diminished somewhat. He went on: "I will be the chief official of the swords competition. The top prize will be two hundred pieces of gold; lesser prizes in the usual ratios."

The same voice called out, "If it's as usual, then why are you wasting our time telling us?"

Karl looked over at him. He was a thin, dark man, dressed—like all the other contestants—only in sandals, leggings, and tunic; armor was not allowed in Pandathaway's Games. Karl had a flash of dislike; the swordsman's crossed-arms slouch, his thin smirk, his whole manner suggested that he was slumming, that he was too good to be here, with ordinary warriors.

Khoralt sighed. "Perhaps not everyone here is a veteran of the Games, Ohlmin. I see some new faces; perhaps there are some men who would not even recognize you."

The thin man—Ohlmin—shook his head. "If they don't now, they will soon." He smiled thinly. "Business has been slow, lately—I've an order to fill in Aeryk, and if I don't win today, I won't have enough coin to make my purchases."

The elf shook his head. "Your business concerns are not germane, but . . ." He shrugged, raising his head to address the crowd. "Ohlmin, here, has won the swords competition every time that he has entered it, whenever his selection of slaves has dipped low enough that he's needed the extra coin." He turned back to Ohlmin. "Now, is that sufficient acknowledgment?"

Ohlmin paused. "For now." He smiled.

In another setting, Karl would have wanted to wipe the smirk off Ohlmin's face, but drawing attention to himself for no profit hardly seemed to be a good idea.

"Before I begin," Khoralt continued, "an announcement. Our sewer dragon, as most of you know, escaped yesterday. It is not known if he managed to free himself, or if he was aided. If necessary, the Wizards' Guild will discover which. But in any case, there is a standing reward of three thousand pieces of gold for the capture of the one or ones responsible, if any."

"Dead or alive?" someone called out.

"Alive. Two hundred fifty for the body or bodies, with proof." The elf pursed his lips together. "We want the culprit for a Coliseum execution. Now, as to the rules of this competition: This will be a single-elimination event, and will begin just as soon as the axe-and-hammer contest is over. You can choose your weapons just as soon as I finish; we have a broad selection; there is no reason to push. Two critical hits constitute a win, and there will be *no* arguments as to whether a blow on a non-sword arm is a critical hit: It is *not*. Decisions of the judges will be just short of final. Any dispute of the judges' decisions will be settled by bowmen in the stands, at the judges' discretion." He smiled thinly. "And that *will* be final. Are there any questions? If not, then let—"

"Wait!" A new voice called out. "Who won the bows? I had a bit of coin riding on it, and the damn armsmen say if I leave to find out, I can't get back in."

Khoralt sighed, examining a slip of parchment which he drew from his sleeve. "I will give you all the winners. Wrestling: Gronnee of the Endell Warrens. Crossbows: Edryncik, Pandathaway's Chief Man-at-Arms—" A ragged cheer went up. Clearly, a few of the swordsmen had bet on Edryncik as a local favorite. "And the axe-and-hammer is down to the last two: Wyhnnhyr of Aeryk, and a dwarf—umm, Ahira of the . . ." He paused to work out the next words. ". . . Len-kahn Tunnels. And no, I don't know where those are, either."

Karl smiled. Good. Ahira had made it to the finals, at least. And with a bit of luck . . .

The elf cocked his head to one side, considering the volume of the muted roar from the crowd outside. "From the level of noise, I would hazard a guess that the newcomer has won."

Karl sighed. *And now, the rest of it is up to me.* It was a long way to Bremon; getting there safely could depend on how well they were equipped. And that would depend on his winning the purse and the bets that Walter and Doria had placed on him by now.

The elf bowed quickly. "And now, it is time for you to select your weapons, and get out there. Good fortune to you all. Anyone who makes trouble gets an arrow through his liver."

Karl joined the ragged column shuffling toward the exit, stopping in his turn at the armory to turn in his sword and pick out one that was roughly the same size and heft.

Although, it *wasn't* a sword, not really: The weapon was made of wood, except for the wrought-iron crosspiece that served as a guard. But it hefted well; probably it was lead-filled. He fitted his fingers to the hilt and took a few cautious swings. The sword didn't balance too badly, but he was a bit nervous about the black tar that coated the "blade."

"Your first time in this nonsense?" The swordsman to his right let his own sword dangle, keeping it from touching his leg with an easy three-fingered grip.

Karl nodded. "Yes. This thing feels . . . adequate, I guess, but—"

The other, a short, stocky man with an easy, gap-toothed smile, interrupted him with a nod. "But you're worried about marking yourself with your own stick." He shook his head. "Don't worry about it, as long as you can keep from marring yourself before the first round; they send out slaves to rub the gunk off between rounds." He cocked his head to one side. "Are you willing to do me a favor?" he asked, as they stepped out of the tunnel, into the brightness of the Coliseum.

Karl sucked in air. He hadn't seen the Coliseum from the inside before, and it was a sight. Pandathaway's Coliseum was a huge curve, two gray stone arms reaching out toward the plains beyond the city, lined by rows and rows of cheering, shouting spectators in the stands. Near to the base of the curve, the cup of the Coliseum where the swordsmen stood, the stone of the Coliseum was dark, stained with age; beyond, toward the open mouth of the structure, the stones lightened, as though they were newer, added on.

And in the distance, the Aershtyl Mountains loomed, a massive backdrop that covered the horizon. From this distance, they seemed blue, wreathed with feathery clouds that clung to their peaks like cottony halos. The highest peaks were touched with snow, and glistening threads that twinkled on the mountainsides, combining into larger streams and rivers.

"Gives the actors one *hell* of a time," Karl's companion said.

Karl tore his eyes from the mountains. "What?"

A smile. "You *must* be new here—the Classics Festival just finished last month." He gestured at the plain, and the blue mountains beyond. "How would you like to play *Iranys* with that as your competition? It either breaks an actor, or pulls out the performance of his life."

"It would." Just a few weeks ago, just a few eons ago, Karl had been an acting student, paying less attention than he should have to memorizing his lines in *The Glass Menagerie*. But that was to be played on a proscenium stage; flats and lighting to aid the players. He shook his head. To act, to compete with that as a background, was a challenge that would frighten Alec Guinness.

"Now, how about that favor?"

Frowning at the smaller man's persistence, Karl turned back to him. "What favor?"

"Look, friend, this is your first time here; odds are, you're not going to make it past the first round." He jerked his chin toward the slaves raking the sands. "As soon as they finish, we have to square off—for the first round, it's pick-your-opponent. You have any objection to taking me on? I could use an easy first round."

Karl smiled. "I just might win, you know."

The other gave a slight shrug and a doubting grin. "I'll take my chances. Let's move out, now—I want to get a spot well away from the stands; sometimes they throw things."

Karl followed him out to a playing area near the center of the field. Like the fifty or so others, it was square, the corners marked by four iron poles. There would be two ways to lose a round, and any chance of advancing in the competition: either be hit by two blows that the judges deemed critical, or leave during play the five-yard-square area marked by the poles.

As the other swordsmen settled into their places, sound in the playing areas died down, except for bitter grumbling from several swordsmen, unhappy that they had not snagged weaker opponents.

Karl put that out of his mind, trying as well to tune out the increasingly loud roar of the crowd. He had to win; there was too much riding on it to let himself be distracted.

And if he was going to win the event, he would need to conserve his energy for the later rounds. He hadn't counted the contestants, but it was vanishingly unlikely that their number was exactly a power of two—and that meant that some would be awarded byes, now or in the later rounds. Likely the byes would go to contestants with winning records; in order to be ready for the last rounds, Karl would have to win the early ones quickly and easily so that he wouldn't be winded in the later ones.

From behind him and to his left, Khoralt's voice boomed, *"Prepare to fight!"*

Karl gripped his sword carefully.

And then, *"Fight!"*

Karl's opponent moved in cautiously, his sword weaving, ready to block or strike. The smaller man lunged—

Karl dropped flat on his back, his right foot kicking up toward the other's hands. The sole of his sandal connected with his opponent's wrists; Karl was rewarded by a cry of pain and the sight of the other's sword flipping end over end out of their playing area.

As he bounced to his feet, Karl's own sword lashed out, drawing a big, black X across the front of his opponent's tunic.

The other sighed, raising his hands in mock surrender. "Damn *me!*" He shook his head. "Not as clumsy as you look, big man—that should teach me to try and take advantage of a tyro." As Karl accepted his extended hand, he brightened. "Although, now that I'm out of it, I might put down a coin or two on you. Think you can make it to the final round?"

Karl shrugged. "I think I might manage to do that."

"It gets harder from here on, you know." He walked away.

Karl counted the remaining contestants, as the losers walked off the field. Sixty-two were left. One of the judges beckoned to Ohlmin and a beetle-browed dwarf, giving them byes, as Karl squared off with his assigned opponent, a tall elf, almost half again Karl's height. He was light-skinned and blond, almost an albino. But not nearly as frail as he appeared; it took several tiring minutes of sparring for Karl to work his way inside the other's guard and smack the sword out of his opponent's hands.

Thirty-two left. Karl was paired off with the dwarf who had been given a bye the previous round. The dwarf fought with a sword longer than Karl's, and with physical strength much greater.

Fortunately, he was just a bit slower, and a sucker for a false opening.

Karl came out of that match limping. Before he'd been able to mark the dwarf twice, the little bastard had connected with a wicked slash to Karl's right knee.

Sixteen left. Karl favored his injured knee as he limped over to the playing area a judge indicated. This time, his opponent was a human, a long-haired, smooth-shaven man who fought in a bizarre two-swords style. It took a bit of time for Karl to weave his sword in between the long slashing sword and the short parrying one—and it cost him another blow to his knee.

He ended that round with a stroke to the other's temple; the man dropped as though he had been a puppet, his strings slashed.

As the harried slaves ran out to daub the remaining contestants off, Karl forced himself to breathe slowly, shallowly. With a bit of luck, he would have three rounds left—and that goddamn Ohlmin hadn't even worked up a sweat. Karl snatched the slave's rag, wiping the dripping sweat from his forehead. He set his sword down for a moment and rubbed at his swollen knee. It would support his weight, but just barely.

Eight contestants left. His opponent was a hulking creature, seemingly a dwarf-human hybrid: He had the heavy brows, huge jaw, and oversize joints of a dwarf, but he stood almost six feet tall, grinning with yellowed teeth as he raised his sword in a mocking salute.

Too tired. I'm just too tired. At the command to begin, Karl swept up sand with his bad leg; his opponent ducked under the spray—

—right into Karl's stroke. The blow to the hybrid's jaw knocked him out of the playing area, out of consciousness, and out of the competition.

Four. Facing an elf, Karl staggered under a preemptive slash, then barely connected with a backhanded stroke that had been aimed at the elf's midsection, but connected with his throat. Gasping for breath, the elf stumbled into a pole, and then into Karl's winning stroke.

Karl turned to see Ohlmin grinning at him, from a playing area only a few yards away. "Nicely done," Ohlmin called out. "But you're up against me, now. Care to concede, or don't you believe in accepting fate?"

Easy—he's just trying to bait you, to get you angry. Possibly that was how the smaller man had won all of his matches without working up a sweat? He certainly didn't look sturdy enough to wear his opponents down. Could he be that good? "No," Karl said, forcing himself not to pant. He drew himself up straight, not moving from his spot. No need to show Ohlmin how badly he'd limp. "Why don't you come over here and persuade me, *little man?*"

A slave ran up with a dirty cloth; Karl snatched it to scrub at his knee, making sure that he rubbed more of the oily tar on it. Best to try to hide from Ohlmin just how much the battered joint was swelling.

Karl dropped the rag to the sand. "I don't see you moving. Maybe you're not so good with that stick after all."

Anger creased the other's dark face for a moment. "I wouldn't, if I were you." Superior smile back in place, Ohlmin walked over to Karl's playing area, taking up a position at the far corner of the square.

"Wouldn't what?" Karl moved back a step, wincing at the pain shooting through his leg. As it kept swelling, the pain got worse.

Damn.

"Wouldn't make it personal." Ohlmin's face grew somber; he shook his head slowly. "The last one to make it a personal thing, well, he's chained to a mill in Sciforth." He pinched his nostrils with the fingers of his free hand. "By the nose." Ohlmin dropped his hand and smiled. "After I beat him on the field." He stretched out his tar-covered wooden sword, the point almost touching Karl's chest. "So don't make it personal."

Karl pushed the point away with his own sword. "Just—"

Ohlmin slashed at Karl's right knee. Fiery pain shot through it, and Karl's leg buckled beneath him. He fell to the sand.

"Foul!" Khoralt shouted, running up. "That is a foul!"

Ohlmin eyed him slyly, while Karl struggled back to his feet, his knee burning as though it were on fire.

"My apologies." Ohlmin gave a quick bow. "I thought I had heard your command to begin."

Khoralt hesitated for a moment, then shook his head and pointed toward the exit. The crowd responded with a wave of hissing and shouting. The elf crossed his arms across his chest. "As I was about to say"—he gave Karl a sheepish half-smile, probably the only apology Karl would get—"I am tempted to disqualify you. But that would be too harsh, since you made only a simple mistake," he added quickly. "Instead, your penalty will be that it will take three hits for you to win, Ohlmin; your opponent will need but the usual two."

Karl opened his mouth to protest, then shut it. It wouldn't do any good. The crowd wanted to see the final match, and the elf wasn't going to deny the crowd. *So let's try to buy a bit of time, give my knee a chance to stop throbbing.* "I'll need a little time, to wipe this mark off."

Khoralt shook his head sadly. "No, we must let the match go on. We will remember that there is a false mark on your leggings." He backed out of the square. "Prepare to fight."

Karl flexed his knee. If he didn't put too much weight on it, it would support him. Probably.

"And . . . *fight!*"

Ohlmin smiled, and moved in.

In the first few seconds of the match, Karl saw that he was hopelessly outclassed—and would have been even if his knee weren't swollen. Ohlmin's weaving sword deflected Karl's swings effortlessly, and forced him back, back—if Karl hadn't backed into one of the poles marking the playing area, he would have stumbled out of the square.

The tip of Ohlmin's sword slithered in and drew a light line across Karl's chest; Karl batted the sword out of the way, slashed—

Stepping back, Ohlmin parried easily. "Try again, big man." He spat. "I have time."

Khoralt called out: "One point for Ohlmin, none for the challenger. Both require two to win."

Ohlmin paused for a moment. Karl lunged; Ohlmin dodged to one side.

I can't beat him. I'm good with a sword, but he's faster and better.

But damned *if I'm going to let him walk all over me.*

Ohlmin moved in. "Give up. You're not good enough; nobody is." He launched an attack that brought the two of them together, *corps-à-corps.* Karl tried to push him back, but the smaller man was stronger than he looked.

With a sneer, Ohlmin spat in Karl's face, then whirled away. "I'd be more frightened of a novice than I am of you. A novice might get in a lucky shot," he sneered. "You won't."

"Shut up and fight." Although the other was right; a novice might throw his sword or something, or accidentally bounce Ohlmin out of the—

Got it! Karl threw his sword at the smaller man, flipping it end over end.

Ohlmin stepped smoothly to one side. The sword bounced off a pole and out of the playing area. "And that is—"

Karl lunged at him barehanded, receiving a wicked slash to the temple before he was able to fasten his left hand on Ohlmin's sword arm, just at the wrist.

Karl *squeezed*. Ohlmin screamed.

Bones crackled beneath his palm; Karl seized the front of Ohlmin's tunic with his free hand and lifted him off the ground, and—

"*—two points for Ohlmin, none—*"

—wobbling on his good leg, Karl raised the twitching form of the other man above his head and threw him as far as he could, out of the playing area. Ohlmin landed with a thump and a strangled moan.

Khoralt smiled at Karl. "*Ohlmin is disqualified, for leaving the playing area. The winner of the swords competition is—*what *is* your name?"

Karl stood up straight. "My name is Cullinane. Karl Cullinane."

"*The winner of the swords competition is Karl Cullinane.*" The elf leaned over. "And if you want some advice, Karl Cullinane, I would suggest you get yourself and your winnings out of Pandathaway."

Karl smiled. "Just what I had in mind."

Whistling to himself, Ahira bounded up the stairs to their suite in the Inn of Quiet Repose, his battleaxe strapped to his chest, and a leather sack well weighted down with gold slung over his shoulder. Between his winnings, Karl's winnings, and what Doria and Hakim would have from having bet on them, it wouldn't be a problem to equip themselves right. And with a bit of luck, the others would soon be through the Gate, and home.

As he pushed through the curtains and into the common room of the suite, he saw Hakim, Aristobulus, and Doria sitting on the rug, coins, jewels, and finger-size bars of gold bullion scattered in front of them.

"Where are the other two?"

Hakim shrugged, a strangely sheepish smile creasing his face. "Karl hasn't gotten back yet, and Andrea's still in the Library, working on her spell." He looked from the wizard to the cleric, then shook his head.

Aristobulus nodded; Doria frowned, then snorted.

What was this? From the looks passing between the three, it seemed as though they were sharing some private joke. "Want to let me in on it?"

Aristobulus considered it for a moment. "I might as well. I didn't go into this last night; I wanted to recheck my calculations first." He pursed his lips, rubbing withered fingers against his temples. "Unless I'm sadly mistaken, the Gate Between Worlds won't work quite the way Deighton thought—*thinks* it does."

"It's not going to get us home?" Ahira almost staggered. *You mean that all this has been for nothing?*

"No, no—not that. It's just that magic doesn't work the same way in . . . our native universe. A Gate on this side won't create a . . . doorway between worlds, but more of a trapdoor. We can go through—belongingness will bring us back there—but we can't get back here through it."

For Ahira, that was no problem. He flexed his shoulders and tensed his thigh muscles—going back to being James Michael Finnegan was something that had no appeal, be it permanent or temporary.

But for the wizard, it was different. And if Aristobulus couldn't get back, he wouldn't go to the Gate—no, better: If Aristobulus didn't *think* that he could get back to this side, *with* spell books, he wouldn't go.

"I wouldn't worry about it," Ahira said, unfastening his axe, then seating himself with the other three. He cupped a pile of gemstones in his hands, then let the rubies, opals, and round-cut diamonds trickle through his fingers and bounce on the rug.

Responsibilities, responsibilities—we never would have translated across, if it weren't for me. None of the others wanted it as badly. Not even Aristobulus. I've got to get Hakim, Karl, Doria, and Andrea home. "Deighton sent us all across once; I'm sure we can persuade him to do the same for you. With spell books."

"Persuade? Even though it won't help him any? I don't remember you having so *persuasive* a manner about you, back on the other side." The wizard snorted. "And you hardly had the physique—"

"I have," Hakim said. "Maybe I'm not quite as strong back home as Karl is here, but . . ."

"You'll help?" The wizard looked hopefully at Hakim.

"I promise." The thief smiled. "If he doesn't send you back—fully equipped—then I'll break a finger at a time until he does. And in the meantime, you'll keep your mouth shut in front of K—"

"*What* is going on?" Ahira spread his hands. "I thought you two had settled that, back on the *Pride*."

"Not that." Hakim picked up a diamond that was almost the size of his eye, and held it up to the light. "This one has a small flaw, dammit." He dropped it, and smiled. "But we still have enough, what with yours and Karl's winnings, and—"

"And your winnings, betting on us—we should be able to outfit ourselves more than well enough. Matter of fact, I want the two of you to take some of this gold, go out, and pick up all the healing draughts you can. We just may—"

"Not quite *winnings*," Doria interrupted, holding up three gold bars and a small leather sack. "This is what we won by betting on you. We got good odds—it averaged out to be about eighty to one."

"And the rest from betting on Karl? What were they, a hundred to one?"

"*Two* hundred." Hakim shook his head. "Everybody thought that Ohlmin was such a sure winner that you couldn't even bet on him—the little bugger's won every single time he's entered. So . . ."

"So?"

"*So I didn't bet on Karl.* I thought it'd be just throwing money away, dammit." Hakim threw up his hands. "And you saw what he had to go through to win that competition—he was sweating, and limping, and—"

"So how did you?—you *didn't*."

Hakim smiled sheepishly. "Actually, I did. I spent most of the morning and a good part of the afternoon picking pockets. Lots of money in Pandathaway."

Ahira sighed. If Karl found out that he'd worked that hard to win, but the others hadn't had enough faith in him to bet on him at those odds . . . "He'll break your neck."

"Only if one of you tells."

"We won't. But if it happens to slip out . . ."

Hakim nodded. "I'd better work on my sprinting."

Ahira shook his head. "No, make that long-distance running." He stood. "Well, let's get to it—I want us to outfit ourselves and be out of Pandathaway by sundown. Doria—you, Hakim, and I are going shopping; Ari, you wait here for the other two."

Out of Pandathaway by sundown—that had a nice ring to it. Then up the road through the Aershtyl Mountains, pass through Aeryk, skirt the edge of the Waste to Bremon.

And the Gate. And no more responsibilities for the rest. No more worries about the others getting themselves killed.

He sighed.

Hakim nodded knowingly. "It's hard on you, isn't it, m'friend?"

"At best."

PART FOUR:

Bremon

CHAPTER TWELVE: *The Waste of Elrood*

A heap of broken images, where the sun beats,
And the dead tree gives no shelter, the cricket no relief,
And the dry stone no water. Only
There is shadow under this red rock,
(Come in under the shadow of this red rock),
And I will show you something different from either
Your shadow at morning striding behind you
Or your shadow at evening rising to meet you;
I will show you fear in a handful of dust.

—T.S. Eliot

Ahira called a halt at midmorning, easing himself painfully out of his fore-and-aft peaked saddle, then turning the horses and his pony loose under a spreading elm. He squatted on the ground, rubbing at his aching thighs. *Someday, I'd like to get my hands on whoever invented the horse. For five minutes, that's all. Just five minutes.*

"Ahira?" Hakim called out, from his perch on the bench of the flatbed wagon. "You want me to turn these critters loose, too?" He jerked his thumb at the two scraggly mules hitched to the wagon.

Ahira shook his head. "No. I'm tired enough of fighting them back into harness every morning. Set the brake, twist on the hobbles, and slip their bits—you can feed and water them where they are."

Climbing down from his gray mare's saddle, Aristobulus shook his head. "You wouldn't have so much trouble with them," he said, "if we had decent harnesses. Those stupid straps half-choke—"

"Enough." Ahira waved the wizard to silence. Granted, the strap harnesses they had bought in Pandathaway weren't nearly as good as even medieval horsecollars. Given, under Ari's direction—or, more accurately, Lou Riccetti's direction—putting together an efficient horsecollar was a trivial feat of design and engineering, but—

—But do I have to put up with his constant whining about it? "No," he said, "we're not going to turn the mules loose. They might run off again, and we don't want to waste the time chasing after them." Maybe Hakim got along well with the two snorting creatures—Ahira chuckled; even *mules* got along with him—but there was no sense in taking chances.

Not when you didn't have to. Take the caravan behind them, for example. In the twenty days it had taken them to get from Pandathaway to Aeryk, and the week since they had stopped overnight in Aeryk to finish outfitting themselves and stock up on food and water, the caravan hadn't been more than a couple of days behind; Ahira could see them moving, even at night.

They could be reasonable people; quite possibly it would be in both parties' interests to travel together as long as they were headed in the same direction. But—

Ahira sighed, seating himself on a gnarled root. He propped his back against the tree's rough bark. —But that was only probably, only possibly. Best not to take chances. Best to keep a distance.

Andrea walked over and stretched out on her side on the ankle-high grass. "Nice." She unslung a small waterbag, took a sip, then offered it to Ahira. "I don't guess that it'll be this easy from here on in."

He took a sip and recorked the bag. "Thanks." He gestured at the long slope below them. Perhaps ten miles away, the lush grassland gave way to the Waste, the line of demarcation between dark, water-rich greenery and brown, sun-baked earth as sharp as a knife. Why hadn't the Waste claimed part of the grassland, or vice versa? Or had it—no, that couldn't be: The boundary between Waste and grass curved smoothly away in the distance; a curve as even as that had to be artificial, not natural.

It could be involved with the aftereffects of the wizards' battle that had created the Waste of Elrood, but—

—but there's no way of knowing. And it really doesn't matter.

"No, it probably won't be this easy." He handed her the water-bag. "And we'd better start going easy on this; I'm a bit nervous about the water supply."

Her brow wrinkled. "But we bought the two extra barrels in Aeryk. That should be enough, even at the rate Karl and the horses swill it, no?"

He gave her a nod. "It *should* be. But should isn't always enough." Ahira chuckled, dismissing the subject with a wave of his hand. "Don't pay any attention; I'm just getting cynical." For the thousandth time, he took a mental inventory of their supplies. Twelve healing draughts, sealed in gray metal bottles. Karl had wanted to use one, back in Pandathaway, to fix his sprained knee. But Ahira had overruled him; best to save the potions for emergencies, and rely on natural healing whenever possible. A sprain wasn't like a cut; it couldn't be a path for infection.

There was a score of white woolen blankets, along with the makings of an iron framework, so that they could rig a canopy over the bed of the wagon for travel in the heat of the Waste. The blankets would keep them cool during the day, and warm at night.

And then the food: dried meat and fruit, sweets for variety and quick energy, oats for the animals, a head-sized cube of gritty salt—plenty, surely, for both people and animals. No problems there.

Miscellany: a sewing kit, seven oil lanterns with twenty forearm-sized flasks of evil-smelling green oil, a flint-and-steel kit for every member of the party. A spare crossbow, with a lighter pull than Ahira's; fourscore extra quarrels for that—if Ahira didn't need it, Hakim could handle it without much difficulty. And without much accuracy, for that matter.

And then there was the one magical implement he'd bought: a clump of dragonbane, packed carefully in a soft leather pouch. If they couldn't sneak by The Dragon, perhaps the creature's allergy to the mossy stuff would give them time enough to use the Gate.

What else? Spare knives for everyone; several hundred yards of deceptively light rope—a knife could barely cut it; a few

177

pounds of charcoal cubes, just in case they needed a fire when there was no wood available; hammers and spikes to use as pitons, if necessary. And thinking of wood . . . he raised his head. "Karl, Hakim—we're a bit short of firewood, and we're not going to find any in the Waste. Go cut some."

Hakim nodded, getting slowly to his feet; Karl stood quickly and spun around to face Ahira.

"What do we need more wood for?" There was only a trace of challenge in his tone.

Ahira cursed himself silently. Karl wouldn't have raised any objection if Andrea hadn't been nearby. Something had to be done about the relationship—whatever it was—between those two.

But now wasn't the time. Ahira forced a smile and started to raise himself painfully to his feet. "Fine—if you don't think we need it, I'll cut it myself." He unstrapped his axe and propped it carefully against the root he'd just vacated. The battleaxe was a weapon, not a tool. "Who saw where the woodaxe is?"

Doria trotted over, her robes flapping. "Some problem?"

Ahira shrugged. "It's nothing—don't worry about it."

Karl looked sheepish as he raised his palms, shaking his head. "I'm sorry. My fault—I forgot that you and your pony don't get along. I'll cut the wood." He retrieved the woodaxe from the bed of the wagon and followed Hakim out into the woods, away from the road.

Ahira rubbed gently at his thighs. Nice of Karl to remind him. Dammit, dwarves weren't built for riding horses, and that alleged pony was a dappled demon, camouflaged. Just barely camouflaged.

On the other hand, Cullinane had been getting more considerate, ever since that first day in Pandathaway. *Which reminds me—* "Doria, why don't you and Aristobulus take a waterbag and go see if there's a spring around here. You do the walking through the brush, and let him—"

Doria's brow furrowed. "I doubt that there's a spring. And why me?"

Because I think I'd better have a private talk with Andrea, and this is a convenient excuse to get you out of the way for a minute, and do I have to be argued with about every damn thing? No, he sighed, that wouldn't do. "Because of your robes." He picked up a pebble and fingerflicked it at her sleeve; it bounced off as

178

though it had struck a solid wall. "We don't have to worry about you getting scratched by brush."

She gave him a nod and a half-shrug, then walked away.

Ahira turned back to Andrea.

She smiled knowingly, brushing hair away from her face. "Alone at last, eh? Although"—she reached out and patted him on the shoulder—"I think you're a touch too short for me. No offense."

The way she put it, it was impossible to be offended. "None taken. But that's not what I wanted to talk to you about." He hesitated. The personal relations among the group really weren't any of his concern, not unless they affected their chances of surviving, of reaching the Gate.

Then again, anything could affect their chances. "What's the problem between you and Karl? *He* isn't too short for you, is he?"

She gave him a clearly *pro forma* grin. "No."

"Well, you don't blame him for our being here, do you? If wanting this has anything to do with that transfer's working, it's my fault, not Karl's." To Cullinane, it had always been a game, no more. And from the way Karl's demeanor kept improving, as they got closer to Bremon, it was likely he'd be happier when it was just a game once again.

"No." She looked away. "I'm not that stupid."

Ahira snorted. "You're not stupid at all. You've been treating him like a leper. I'm sure you've got your reasons; I'd like to know what they are." *Andrea, I don't care who you sleep with, or who you don't sleep with. But Cullinane's all bent out of shape over you, and that could blunt him as a warrior. I want him thinking about our survival, not about you.* "Maybe there's something I could do?"

"No." She shook her head slowly. "There's not a whole lot that can be done about it." Her fingers grasped the air clumsily. "He's kind of . . . I don't know—how well did you know him, back on the other side?"

"Not all that well. I don't think I saw him more than three, four times outside of the games." Ahira smiled. "And we didn't take any of the same classes—I don't think Karl's gotten around to majoring in computer sciences, yet."

"Not yet." She sighed. "But give him time. He keeps getting involved in different things."

179

"A dilettante. Can't stick to one interest."

"No. Well, yes, but it's more than that. He's . . . sort of a monomaniac, gets completely, *intensely* into whatever he's interested in. . . ." She rubbed at her temples with stiffened fingers. "And he kind of extracts whatever he got into it for, then drops it and goes on to something else." She let her hands drop into her lap, then raised her eyes to meet his. "I know I'm not expressing myself well, but do you understand?"

"It sounds like you're scared of being, err, seduced and abandoned. No?"

"I knew I wasn't explaining it well—it's not like that at all." Her pursed lips spread into a broad, self-assured smile. "Do you think I'm the sort of woman who gets seduced and abandoned, Ahira?" Extending a finger, she waved it under his nose. "Do you?"

Her tone was light and playful, but he sensed a serious undercurrent. "No, I don't. I think you can handle any sort of relationship, whether it's whatever you've got going with Hakim or"—he chuckled—"something a bit more distant with a neurotic dwarf."

She laughed. "Thank you. But you and Walter aren't the problem. It's Karl and his goddam—"

"*Ahira!*" Doria ran toward them, her robes flapping, breathlessly waving a dripping scrap of cloth, and—

Dripping? He jumped to his feet. "What is tha—"

"We found it!" She stopped in front of him, taking a few moments to catch her breath. "Aristobulus and I—we found the spring, back in the brush." She shook her head. "It's amazing—it just burbles out of a crack in the rock, and then drains back into another one. We couldn't even see it until we were practically on top of it. How in the world did you know that there'd be one?"

Andrea hid a chuckle behind her hand. Sending Doria and Aristobulus off to find a spring had been a distraction.

Ahira looked at her and shrugged. "Serendipity, Doria." Well, there'd be a chance to try to straighten out Andrea later. "Simple serendipity."

"What?"

"It's when you dig for worms, and strike gold." He raised his voice. "Hakim, Karl—they found a spring. It's water this morning, soup for lunch, and baths for dessert." No need to worry about the water supply, not anymore. With seven full barrels, all people and animals well watered, the week-long trek across the Waste should be easy.

Well, relatively easy.

Doria shook his head. "I don't understand."

"Don't worry about it." He looked at Andrea, spreading his hands as though to say that they'd finish the discussion later, when they again had a little privacy; she nodded. Ahira turned back to Doria and pulled a trick from Hakim's repertoire: He breathed on his fingernails and buffed them lightly across his chest. "Sometimes I'm so clever I don't even understand myself."

Karl and his horse were the first to reach the Waste; Ahira had let him range ahead a bit, and he liked that. He was relaxed, even comfortable on his large, reddish-brown mare; the fore-and-aft peaked saddle supported him well. But it wasn't just the saddle. Karl was taking full advantage of having his Barak persona to draw on: His thigh muscles held him firmly to the seat, his hips shifted automatically to keep him firmly astride, instead of bouncing on his tailbone, the way that the rest had been for most of the trip, until they gradually learned how to ride.

Except for Walter, of course. Karl turned to give a nod to the thief, who was basking comfortably in the late-afternoon sun on the blankets he had used to pad the cart's seat, guiding the mules with only an occasional twitch of his lazy fingers. Probably some of Walter's avowed affection for the mules was honest; certainly he'd staked out the cart at least partly from concern for his own tender buttocks, leaving his swayback gelding hitched behind with little to no regret. "Enjoying the ride?"

Walter responded with a nod and a wink. No, no doubt about it at all.

Aristobulus' whine drifted forward. Complaining, as usual. Karl urged his mare farther forward. A good horse; she needed only a touch of his heels to break into a canter, and then a light flick on the reins to slow her back down to a walk.

He stroked her reddish-brown neck, solid and dry under his palm. "Good girl—you don't even mind hauling my weight, do you?" She raised her head a bit higher, and snorted.

Ahead the Waste of Elrood stretched out across the horizon; a flat brown ocean of sunbaked mud, random cracks in the hard surface covering as if it were a fine netting that had been woven by a mad giant.

Ahira's voice boomed from behind him. "Karl—wait a moment."

Shrugging, Karl let the dwarf, bouncing on the back of his little pony, catch up. "Problem?"

Ahira shook his head. "No, I need some advice. The rest of these . . . animals seem to be kind of spooked by the terrain. Do you think we ought to walk them a while? Maybe that way they can get used to it?"

Karl turned to look behind. The others' horses were twitchy, all right; what with the snorting and skittish steps they were taking, it could easily tire the animals out much sooner than it should.

"I don't think so," he said. "Look at them. Hell, look at you. You're the worst."

The dwarf scowled. "What about me?"

"The purpose of riding isn't to keep as much air as possible between your backside and your saddle, you know—the reason you have to spend so much time walking your pony is that you don't have the slightest idea of how to ride him. Same for the rest, although they're not as bad."

Aristobulus' mount stepped to one side to avoid a rut; as usual, the wizard tried to overcontrol the little mare, frustrating the horse almost as much as himself.

Ahira's right hand slipped to the hilt of his axe. That was probably unconscious; Karl resisted the urge to loosen his sword from its saddle-bound scabbard. *Easy, you're among friends.*

"Dammit, Karl, have a bit of sympathy. How long did it take you to learn how to ride?"

Karl shrugged. "I just seemed to pick it up."

"Came with the territory, right? Sort of like Hakim's ability to move silently and—and my darksight, no?"

"So?"

The dwarf threw up his hands, startling his pony. "Easy, you damned little—easy, I said. *So,* it didn't come naturally to me. Or Andrea, Hakim, Doria, or Ari. Don't put on airs because you ride better than we can; it's just a lucky break. For you. It's not a virtue." Ahira reached behind himself, rubbing vigorously.

"Don't."

"Don't *what?*"

182

Karl sighed. "Don't twitch in the saddle like that. Your pony doesn't know what you're doing, and he doesn't like it."

Ahira opened his mouth as though to say something to the effect that he really couldn't care less what his animal liked or didn't, then shrugged. "You still didn't answer my question."

Karl thought it over for a moment. At least Ahira's idea would give the riders some time off their mounts, give them a chance to work out some stiffness. "Actually, I've got a better idea."

Ahira's mouth quirked. "Let me guess: We get the critters used to the different surface by galloping them for a few miles, right?"

"Wrong. A horse isn't an automobile; you can kill it if you push it too hard. No, how about this? We pitch camp here until dark, then travel at night. At least for tonight—we can pitch those blankets as tarps, keep the sun off. I know you don't think that water's a problem anymore, but we might as well save all we can. And this way the horses, at least the ones who need it"—he patted his mare's neck—"can take some time to get used to this surface, just by standing around on it."

"Done!" The dwarf jerked his pony to a halt and bounced to the ground. "Everybody, time for a break."

Andrea slumped in the saddle. "Thank goodness."

"About time." Aristobulus slid off his horse.

"Fine with me." Doria levered herself out of her saddle and dropped lightly to the ground.

Walter reined in the mules, shrugging. "I don't see what the problem is. But I'm easy." He tied the reins to the back of his seat and vaulted to the sunbaked earth. "What's the plan? We've got another couple of hours until sundown—shouldn't we get some traveling done?"

Now free of his pony and any necessity of following Karl's advice not to spook the animal, Ahira rubbed viciously at the base of his spine as though trying to scour the pain away. "This surface is so flat that it won't be dangerous to travel at night. So that's what we'll do, at least for tonight. We'll pitch the tarps for shade, catch some sleep, then start up again around midnight, when the ground's cooled off enough."

Doria nodded. "You're still worried about the water."

"Not worried. Just cautious." Ahira stretched broadly. "Once we hit the far side of the Waste, I want to have as much left as possible. We don't know how deep in Bremon the Gate is, and we may need all we can carry.''

Karl nodded. A good point, and one he hadn't thought of. Then again, knowing how to deal with tunnels probably came naturally to the dwarf in the same way that riding came easily to Karl.

Ahira pulled the thin white blankets out of the back of the wagon. ''Hakim and I can pitch these as puptents. Do we have any volunteers for first watch?''

Andrea smiled. ''You sure do.'' She walked over to Karl and tapped him on the chest with an extended finger. ''I think Karl's had an easy enough time in the saddle; time to put him to work.''

The dwarf nodded. ''Fine. The *two* of you are on watch until it's been dark for at least a couple of hours. Walter and Ari replace you then.''

''Now wait a minute—'' she started.

''The two of you.''

Karl's forehead wrinkled, almost painfully. Now that was strange. Ahira *had* been keeping Andrea and him away from each other. Which made sense. But—*never mind. If I understood people, I'd have stayed in psych.*

He cast an eye at the setting sun. Well, he'd already put up with worse than a few hours of stony silence.

Andrea stared out at the Waste of Elrood. By starlight, it reminded her of the pictures the Apollo astronauts had brought back from the moon, the ones from the Mare what's-its-name, the Sea of something-or-other.

She sighed. *I was supposed to have that quiz the morning after that night at the Student Union, and that probably would have been on it.*

Stars twinkled over a scarred wasteland. Just flat, cracked ground, gray in the dark. The sorcerers who fought here must have been very powerful, and more than a bit mad; what sane person would want to turn greenery into *this*?

She turned around to look at the others. Under the bed of the wagon, Walter snored quietly. She couldn't make out his features, but she knew that his broad face would be creased with a light smile. *Still maintaining the image, eh?* The fight back in Lundeyll had scared him badly, but Walter Slovotsky wouldn't reveal that, not even in his sleep.

Doria curled next to him, tossing fitfully. *Look,* Andrea wanted to say, *I don't know what's gone on with you and Karl, but . . .*

But what? That was the problem.

Under their respective puptents, Aristobulus and Ahira slept quietly. There was something similar about the two of them. Maybe it was that they were both so one-directional. Ari just wanted to get some spell books, and this trip across the Waste seemed to him to be a way to do that. Period.

Ahira was different, though. He was just pushing to get them home. *Just the rest of us, James Michael Finnegan. And who do you think you're fooling?* The dwarf had never said so, but anyone could see that he was just along to get the rest of them through the Gate; once that was done, Ahira would turn and run. *You don't really expect any of us to believe that you're going back to being a cripple, do you?* Not when he could be healthy and strong here.

She nodded in admiration. Not for the first time. A sense of responsibility, that's what Ahira had. Ahira felt guilty about the rest of them being here. No, not guilt; she was right the first time. Responsible, that was it.

She turned back. Karl was still looking at her out of the corner of his eye, pretending to be ignoring her. Maybe that was for the best, at least for the time being.

At least, that's what I keep telling myself.

He got up from his seat on a stack of blankets and walked over. "Enough games, Andy. We've got to talk."

She jerked her chin at the plain. "Then let's move away a bit. No need to wake the others."

He smiled thinly as he followed her. "I wasn't planning on yelling and screaming. Were you?"

She shook her head. "Not really. I think this is far enough. Do you want to sit down?"

He snickered. "I'd better be sitting for this? Okay." They sat tailor-fashion on the cracked ground, Karl balancing his sword across his lap.

"Do you have to have that with you? I don't think anyone's going to steal it, out in the middle of nowhere."

He shrugged, and pulled the blade a few inches from the scabbard. "It's a fine piece of steel, isn't it?" Silvery metal gleamed wickedly in the starlight. "And I've got this habit of losing things. I guess I'm afraid that if I ever let it out of my hands, that'll be the end of it.'' He slipped the blade back. "But you're changing the subject. Deliberately?"

"I'm not sure. Do I have to be?"

"No. I don't make the rules. Sometimes I don't even know what they are."

She bit her lower lip. "As in what the rules for you and me are."

He nodded, looking her square in the eyes. "Exactly. If I didn't know better I'd swear you're trying to get me to hate you, or at least dislike you one hell of a lot. And I'd kind of like to know why that's a stupid idea of mine." He shrugged. "I am stupid sometimes. Ignorant, too. I have it on good authority."

"Doria?"

"Not quite." He folded his fingers behind his head and stretched back. "I have bad breath or something?"

There was a lot different about Karl now, beyond the physical changes. *We could have had almost exactly this conversation a few months ago, and Karl would have been trembling inside that I'd turn him down. He isn't anymore.*

"Did anyone ever tell you you're always too goddam intense about everything?" The violence of her own words surprised her. "About whatever you happen to be majoring in at the moment, about whatever diversion you're into, about—"

"About you?" He chuckled thinly. "Is this going to be another episode of Slovotsky's Laws?"

"What?"

Karl shook his head, his eyes closed tightly. "One of Walter's ideas about life. It runs something like: 'Whatever you want too much, you can't have, so when you *really* want something, try to want it a little less.' Is that what this is all about?"

"No. It's not that. It's just that I'm not sure I'm ready for all that intensity about *me.*" She reached out to take his hand; he pulled it back. "Can you understand that? It's not that I don't like you, it's not that I'm not attracted to you—"

"Now, that is." He raised an arm and flexed his biceps. "What with the new, improved body, and all." Karl lowered his arm. "Which is one thing I'm going to be sorry to give up, once we get back."

"You're going to be sorry to get back?"

"Don't be silly," he sneered. "I like the good things in life. Bathing regularly, television, dentistry, not having a price on my head. Stuff like that. And you're changing the subject again. Which suggests that once we get back, and I'm short, skinny Karl Cullinane again—"

"Shut *up*." Sometimes he made her *so* mad. "It isn't that at all. Women aren't as shallow as men."

"Thank you, Betty Friedan."

"It's just that you're incapable of keeping things . . . casual. No, that's not the word. What I'm trying to say is—"

Fear touched the back of her neck. Ignoring her natural reflexes, she closed her eyes. Her aura wrapped her thinly; it was easy to see Aristobulus' glowing strongly, a few hundred feet away, blazing in the night like a red beacon.

But there was something else, too. Not quite distinct enough to see with her inner vision, but there. "Karl." She opened her eyes. He was shaking his head, as though to wake up, his eyelids sagging shut, despite himself.

"Andy, I—" He slumped over.

Invisible fingers wrapped themselves around her throat, cutting off her air. She tried to pry them away, but they were like steel bands.

"Don't let go of her, Ohlmin," a harsh voice whispered. "Not until she's safely gagged."

"And then," another voice answered, "we can enjoy ourselves."

She opened her mouth to scream, but a cottony softness filled it. A rough hand clutched at her breasts. She struggled uselessly.

"I want this one first. There's still a lot of fight left in her."

Karl awoke slowly. And that bothered him, even in his half-awake, just-a-few-more-minutes-*please* state. He brought his hand down to wipe at his eyes.

His hand stopped short; his wrist was tangled up with something cold and hard.

Wait a minute! I was just talking to Andy—I never woke Walter. His eyes snapped open. "What the hell—"

A small fist came out of nowhere and struck him on the cheekbone. Pain lanced through his skull. He brought his hands down in a practiced—

—his wrists jerked in their iron cuffs, fastened in heavy chains to something over his head and behind him.

"I told you that nobody ever beats me," Ohlmin rasped. "Ever."

Karl shook his head, trying to clear it. Slowly, his eyes

focused, becoming accustomed to the gloom. Hakim and Ahira sat beside him on the narrow bench of the small room, both still unconscious, both chained at wrists and ankles.

And in front of him, leaning over him close enough so that Karl could smell the reek of garlic and wine on his breath, Ohlmin stood, smirking.

"Sleep spells are handy things, no?" He slapped Karl lightly on the cheek. "Even if the wizards are resistant to them." Ohlmin smiled. "But spells of invisibility can fool their eyes, too."

"What are you—" A boot drove into his belly; Karl gasped for air.

"You speak when you are spoken to. Understood?" Ohlmin's voice was calm now, and somehow that was more frightening than his earlier rasp. "But I won't hurt you very much, Karl Cullinane. I've got to save you for Pandathaway. You're going to make me a rich man."

Karl tried to spit at him, but couldn't muster the breath to do it. Or the saliva, for that matter. His mouth was as dry as the Waste.

Stop reacting for a moment, and think. He fingered the chains. Slight ridges along the links proclaimed that they were cast iron, not forged. And that was good, possibly. If he had enough strength, if he had enough leverage, he could shatter them. Maybe. Cast iron was more brittle than forged. Just maybe . . .

His Barak-self didn't think much of that idea. *They're far too thick. But the wall behind you is wood. You may just be able to jerk them loose from the wall.*

"Feel free to continue thinking about escaping, Karl Cullinane." Ohlmin chuckled. "They always do. But"—he tapped at the wall—"the wagon is belted with iron straps, which is what the chains are bolted to."

Wagon? It wasn't a small room, then. They were in a wagon. No advantage there.

Better find some advantage, quickly. Ohlmin was close enough, just maybe. Karl lashed out with his right foot.

The cuff scraped his ankle as his foot was jerked to a halt, inches from Ohlmin's leg.

A chuckle. "We are professionals. And, just for your enlightenment, the rest of your party is well secured. Both of the wizards and the cleric are gagged. We may have to cut out the old man's tongue, eventually, but I'm sure we'll work out something else for the women. It would be a waste, wouldn't it?" He smiled, reached out, and patted Karl's head. Somehow that was more frightening than being struck. The light pat said that Karl was a harmless nothing, well secured. No danger at all.

Karl forced himself to keep his voice level. "Are you going to tell me how you found us, or are you trying to have me die of curiosity?"

Ohlmin laughed. "Ah, you did that very well. If I didn't know better, I'd think that you weren't terrified." He shrugged lightly. "But I don't see why not. The Guilds' Council finally prevailed on one of the grandmaster wizards to bring out his crystal ball, to find out who had stolen their dragon." Again, he patted Karl's head. "And you, my friend, are worth twenty-five hundred pieces of gold to me. My wizard—Blenryth; I don't think you've met him—is charging me quite a lot for those sleep and invisibility spells we caught you with, and quite a lot more for the one that kept us on your trail. But I'll still come out ahead." He spat in Karl's face. "I always come out ahead."

Karl couldn't quite reach his hand down to his face; the gob of spittle dripped slowly down his cheek.

Ohlmin sighed. "But enough of this. I had better get back to the women. The dark-haired one was quite good; I think I'll try the other. And besides, I'd better make certain that Hyrus doesn't damage them. Must keep them in shape for the block." He frowned. "No, one more thing." Ohlmin walked to the far corner of the wagon and rummaged through a pile of swords, knives, and crossbows.

Our weapons. And just about three yards farther than I can possibly reach. They might as well have been light-years away; it would take more than a sword to cut through the chains. He felt at the cuffs around his wrists. *Damn.* Even if Walter still had a lockpick on him, it wouldn't matter; the cuffs were riveted on.

Ohlmin extracted a long black scabbard from the pile. "I believe that this is your sword?" He slipped it out of the scabbard, examining the blade in the dim glow of the overhead lamp. "Very nice work. I don't think I've ever seen a sharper edge. No doubt you value it highly?"

Karl straightened his back. *I'm not going to beg for my life. It wouldn't help, anyway.*

"Oh, no." Ohlmin said, smiling. "No need to pretend to be

brave." He set one foot on top of a box, grasped the flat of the blade carefully, and brought it down on his knee.

The sword snapped.

"You don't die that easily." The two pieces clattered on the floor. "Public executions in Pandathaway take a good long time." Ohlmin opened the door. "Think about that, for a while."

The door whisked shut behind him.

"Dammit, wake up," Karl hissed. He couldn't reach Walter, and the dwarf was chained beyond the thief. Raising his voice was certain to draw attention; whispering was all he had left.

With a rattle and a shaking, the wagon started moving.

Walter opened a lazy eye. "Will you please shut up?" His voice was calm and flat. As always. "We both woke up before you did," he said, his voice barely carrying over the wagon's clatter.

"Then *why?*"

Ahira shook his head. "Because I thought that there might be some advantage in playing possum." He shrugged. "It didn't work out that way—but conceivably it might, so keep your voice low."

"But we did hear something useful, at least," the thief said. "We're not going directly back to Pandathaway. One of his men said that Ohlmin figures to make a better profit on . . ." He swallowed, he face still impassive. ". . . on the women in Metreyll than he could in Pandathaway. So we'll be skirting the edge of the Waste."

Ahira nodded. "Metreyll has a road to the Hand tabernacle, the one in the Waste. The Society might ransom Doria for a decent price."

"If she's still alive when they get there." And the same for Andy-Andy.

"Don't be silly." The dwarf scowled. "These folks are professionals, remember? They'll keep the women alive. And that's academic; apparently the Matriarch of the Healing Hand can even raise the dead. All of which doesn't do us any good here."

Karl spat. "And what else do you know that's not going to do us any good?"

Ahira shook his head. "Not a lot. There's ten to fifteen of them, including Ohlmin and his hired wizard. I also know that these chains are too damn thick, that Hakim and I are eventually headed for the block in Pandathaway. I also . . ." He trailed off, and shook his head. "I also know that either Doria's or Andrea's gag was a bit loose, for a while."

"Huh?"

"I don't know which one," Ahira said, white-lipped, "because I can't tell Doria's screams from Andrea's." He raised an eyebrow. "You want me to draw you a picture? Fine. From the sounds out there, they've been taking turns before finally deciding to—"

"*Shut up.*" Karl clenched his hands around his chains, and *pulled*.

Nothing.

He tried again, holding his breath and pulling on the chains. Sweat beaded on his forehead, lights danced in front of his eyes. The skin of his right palm split open, wetting the chains with his blood.

Karl ignored the pain, ignored the way his head was threatening to break.

He pulled.

Nothing. The chains didn't shatter, didn't stretch, didn't give. Nothing.

"Stop it." Ahira rattled his own chains. "These weren't built by amateurs."

"Amateurs?"

"Yes, amateurs—like an idiot who didn't wonder why there was a caravan following us. Like a stupid amateur who let his group take a break when he knew that there was a price on one of the member's heads." The dwarf cursed himself bitterly. "But I had to leave you on watch. Let Karl and Andrea try to straighten out their relationship, I said. And while you were doing that, they snuck up on you." He snapped a glare at Walter. "You were about to say something?"

"*I* wasn't," Karl said. "If I hadn't freed Ellegon, if I hadn't beaten Ohlmin, none of this would have happened. It's my fault."

Off in the distance, a scream trilled, fading quickly into a muffled whimper.

Walter spoke quietly, with a calm that horrified Karl more than the scream. "I think we can save the who's-at-fault session for some other time. You didn't know, Karl didn't know, and Andrea isn't as sensitive to magic as Ari is—even if they were both paying attention to keeping watch, she might not have felt that invisibility spell being used. So the two of you just *shut up and figure out what we do next*. Understood?"

Karl and Ahira drew twin breaths. They nodded.

The dwarf pointed his chin at the door. "How long do you think it's going to take them to settle in for the ride?"

"What do you mean?" Karl found his voice becoming shrill.

"I mean," the dwarf said, from between clenched teeth, "that they're all . . . enjoying themselves right now. They're all charged up. We need them to be relaxed, and a bit tired."

What you're asking is how long it will take for fifteen men to rape Andy-Andy and Doria. "A couple of hours, probably. Why all the interest?"

Visibly, Ahira forced himself to relax. "Then we wait for a couple of hours." Another muffled scream broke through the wagon's clatter. "We wait. Not a chance otherwise."

"And then?"

The dwarf nodded. "And then, I go berserk."

Ahira sat back in the flickering light of the overhead oil lamp, ignoring the fire in his shoulders. The chains' mounting had been designed for security, not the comfort of its victims; hours of keeping his arms over his head had left his shoulder joints painfully inflamed.

We wait.

It couldn't be helped. Even if they could break out of their chains earlier, retrieve the weapons, and charge outside, the odds were just too heavily against them. Ohlmin was probably their best warrior, and almost certainly the rest weren't anything near as good as Karl or Ahira, but it was still fifteen to two—Hakim wasn't very good in a fight; he'd be needed to find and try to free Aristobulus.

And if he can do that, maybe we have a chance.

But there had to be some time for the slavers to drop their guard. Just a bit. And the screams from the wagon ahead of them? Ignore them, or try to, at least. This wasn't the time for a gesture; it had to *work*.

So we wait.

But not until dawn; Hakim's skills weren't nearly as useful in daylight. In the day, bowmen could spot them easily, fill them all full of arrows before they were halfway out the door.

In the day, a dwarf's darksight was superfluous.

So we wait. But not long, now.

In the game, going berserk would have been a simple procedure. "I'm going to try to go berserk," you'd announce, rolling a four-sided die. If it came up with a zero, one, or two, the attempt would fail. You'd try again, next turn, if you wanted to.

And if it came up with a three, it would still be simple: Your Strength would double, going well past the maximum possible for a mortal, under normal circumstances. Intelligence and Wisdom would drop drastically, as would Manual Dexterity and Weapons Proficiency. Speed would be unaffected, as would Charisma—but your Endurance level would rise to the point where only a deathblow could slow you down.

There'd be a penalty to pay later, of course. For many turns after you had slipped out of your berserk state, you would be weak as a kitten.

But until you slipped out of it, you'd destroy, and break, and smash.

Or die trying.

Ahira fondled the thick chains. Possibly he couldn't break them, even berserk.

Never mind. It's h—it's our only chance.

He raised his head. "Karl. It's time."

"Right." Cullinane nodded slowly. "Try to remember to break us loose, too."

"I will. But one thing: While I'm out of it, you're in charge. Make sure you get everyone away you can. But don't worry about me; I'll—"

"No."

"Don't argue with me." This wasn't a game anymore. Amateur heroics were fine for around a mahogany table at the Student Union. But not here. "Once I set myself off, you won't be able to reason with me. I won't run. I won't be able to run."

Cullinane chuckled thinly. "I thought you said that once you're out of it. I'm in charge."

Ahira sighed. "Hakim, reason with him."

The thief shook his head. "I won't have to. Once he's got your responsibilities, he'll see it for himself. Which is why you picked him to take over, instead of me. Eh, m'friend?"

"Sure." Ahira leaned back against the rough surface of the wall. "It's time; we've waited long enough. Take care."

There was only one way to do it. Reach deep inside, find a core of hot anger, of raging fury . . .

And let it *burn*.

Special classes—that's what they called them. As though being a feeb were some sort of prize. Special classes, exceptional children—didn't that sound just dandy?

Mrs. Hennessy—that was her name. A short, pinch-faced redhead, always dressing just a little too well, oozing the slimy unction that the best special ed courses could teach. But the courses had never been able to purge from her noble head the reflexive notion that a bent body must hold a crippled mind.

She raised her head from the desk next to him, where she'd been patiently explaining to little Jacqueline Minelli, probably for the thirtieth time, that the little purple block indeed went into the little purple hole. "What *is* it, Jimmy?"

He always hated that nickname. Even his parents had started calling him James Michael when he began first grade. And that was six years ago.

But you didn't call a retard by his proper name. A nickname, preferably one that ended in a vowel—that was the protocol. And if the retard happened to be a mentally normal boy with muscular dystrophy? Didn't that call for a different protocol?

No, of course not. "I'm done with this nonsense." With the heels of his clumsy hands, he pushed at the math problem, sending the papers fluttering to the floor.

She stalked over and wearily began collecting the scattered sheets. "Jim-my, that was a bad thing to do."

"My name is James Michael. And I've been solving simple goddam algebra problems since I was ten years old."

"That isn't a nice word to—"

"And I'm goddam tired of being treated like I was half a person. Fuck you, bitch."

She slapped him.

And, of course, clapped her hand to her mouth in self-disgust, then spent the rest of the school day apologizing.

On reflection, that slap was the nicest thing a teacher had ever done for him.

Ahira tugged lightly at the chains. Then harder, and harder. No, not yet.

* * *

There was a shout out in the dorm hallway. "Hey! Anybody want to go out for a beer?"

His roommate-slash-keeper had already tucked him into bed, then headed out to the library. Granted, he could ask someone to help him out of bed again and dress him, but James Michael had invested many uncomfortable hours in the common room downstairs, putting up with corner-of-the-eye stares and hidden shudders until some of them had started to see past the crumpled body in the wheelchair.

But his roommate was gone. And if he went out for a beer with the rest, he'd have two choices when they came back. Either ask someone to carry him to the toilet three, maybe four times until the beer worked its way through his system, or . . .

Or spend the next few hours lying in his own urine.

Not yet. Try harder. Get through the wall of fire, and into the core.

Doria dropped into a chair, visibly considered the possibility that it would seem to him to be too far away, took a half-second to fight her own fear of James Michael Finnegan, and compromised by wiggling herself a scant inch closer.
Damn it, Doria, can't you treat me like a person?

Nothing. He tugged at the chains. Not even a dwarf's normal strength could break them, and he couldn't go berserk, he couldn't do it.

Here I am, just as helpless now as I've been all my life—
Just
his heart pounded, a beat like a bass drum
as helpless
a red film descended over his eyes, a fire in his head
as I've been
his skin tingled with a rush of blood, his tendons sang a hymn of power
all my life.
he went berserk.

* * *

There was an annoyance about his wrists. Ahira wanted to bring them down, to rip, to tear, to smash. But something restrained his hands.

It was an annoyance he didn't have to bear. Not bothering to clench his fists, he brought his arms *down*.

Metal squealed and shattered, and his arms were free. *Free*. He bent and ripped his ankle chains from the floor.

Two humans were chained on the bench next to him. Why didn't they free themselves? Didn't they want to smash, to break, to destroy? Maybe they were just too stupid. He reached up, grabbed the arm chains of the nearest, and pulled. Metal squealed and snapped.

Why were his hands so wet and sticky? It doesn't matter—pull, and again, and again.

Sounds came from their mouths, but they didn't make any sense.

"Walter—take some knives, and go find Ari. He's probably in the wizard's wagon, whichever one that is. I'll get the others."

"You'll need help. I'd better—"

"Move, dammit, *move*."

One of the humans picked something from the corner and bolted out the door. As though in retaliation, three others lumbered in.

"Ahira—take them. I've got to get Andy, Doria."

Words, they were just words. Didn't mean anything.

But the biggest of the three new humans was pulling a sword. That was something he could understand.

Ahira clutched the dangling end of his wrist chains and whipped the loop of chain across the face of the swordsman. The unshaven face shattered; bits of tooth and bone rattled against the wall, blood bathed Ahira in salty fountain.

He shoved the falling body out of the way. Two of the enemy to face. Just two humans, with swords thrusting for him.

He batted the swords out of the way with his loop of chain, then released the end of the chain from his hands. That was the trouble with the chain: It wasn't satisfying enough. And there were two left.

A few moments later, that wasn't true: There weren't any humans, just pieces of them, scattering the room. Ahira staggered out into the night, spitting out a warm gobbet of flesh.

There must be more to smash. There had to be.

* * *

Easy, Karl—you've got one chance at this, and you had better make it good. The hilt of Walter's scimitar felt odd in his hand; the balance of the curved sword was all wrong.

So don't try anything fancy. It was easy to tell which of the four boxlike wagons held Doria and Andy-Andy; the drunken laughter and muffled whimpers called him.

He sprinted across the broken ground. Three long strides brought him to the back door of the slowly rolling wagon. From behind him came the clatter of steel, the screams of the injured, and a constant, deep growl.

Never mind. Ahira can handle them. He jerked the door open and dived in.

And was blinded by the bright lanternlight. *So go by touch.* His questing fingers nested in a beard; he gripped it tightly and pulled it down while bringing his knee up, the man's jaw crumbling like a fleshy bagful of glass. *Don't go for the kill. A quick disable, then on to the next.* He threw the body behind him, out of the wagon.

Karl's eyes cleared, faster than he would have thought possible. Three left; two men rising slowly from the bruised naked bodies of—

Save it. There's one coming at you with a knife. Karl dodged to one side and chopped down with his sword, rewarded by the unmistakable feel of steel cleaving flesh, and a thump as the knife-wielder hit the ground outside.

Two more, drunkenly fumbling for their swords. He dropped the scimitar and grabbed the two men by their hair. Karl brought his hands together swiftly; two skulls shattered, as if they had been eggshells.

He seized Andy-Andy and flipped her onto her belly as though she was weightless.

Not now, his Barak-self said. *Take out the driver, first.*

No, not a second more. For either of them. His hands trembled too badly for him to deal with the knots. He searched the floor, found a sheathed knife, and slashed the leather straps that bound her hands behind her back. A moment later, Doria was free, too.

No time for the gags, best to let them handle that themsel—*wait!*

He slipped the knife between Andy-Andy's gag straps and her cheek, and twisted the knife's edge out. "Your sleep spell. Use it on the driver, then go invisible, and use this on him," he said, pressing the hilt into her hands.

Wild eyes looked back at him, out of a bruised face. Her left cheek was so purply inflamed that he could barely see that eye.

No answer.

"Doria." No, Doria was worse; either unconscious, or pretending to be. He turned back to Andy-Andy. "I can't wait—just do it." He shook her. *"Do it."*

She bit her lip so hard that blood began to flow. And then nodded.

He couldn't wait. There just wasn't any time. He had to find Walter and Aristobulus, and then get them all in one wagon. That was it—they'd take *this* wagon. Easier than moving Doria.

Doria's robes lay crumpled in a heap on the floor. He picked them up and wrapped them around his left arm before retrieving the scimitar.

"I'll be back." Walter and Ari first, then, if he could—

He dived out of the wagon, and hit the ground rolling.

Crushing a human's face with the outspread fingers of one hand, Ahira stumbled in front of an open wagon. The two mules reared up, hooves striking out.

He batted the hooves away with the limp form of the dead human, using the body like a flail. Ahira moved in on the driver, letting the other fall in a crumpled heap. The slim blond man raised a crossbow, pulled back the string with shaking fingers, and dropped a quarrel into the bow's groove.

Ahira laughed. And bounded to the seat of the wagon, his hands reaching for the driver's throat.

The bowstring sang.

Time, Karl thought, *time was the problem.* Surprise was on their side. It hadn't been more than a couple of minutes since Ahira had freed them. The enemy would be disorganized, startled. But that wouldn't last long. The drill was obvious: Find Walter and Ari, load them into the wagon with the two women, and vanish into the night.

But where the hell *were* they?

He ran toward the forward wagon, but stopped short. Six—no, seven men were hurriedly dismounting from the wagon's back door, swords in hand. No time to waste—Walter and the wizard weren't there.

He turned and ran, past the wagon carrying Doria and Andy-Andy, its sleeping driver lolling on the seat. The next wagon was just creaking along; no sign of any activity. He kept running.

"Greetings, Karl Cullinane," Ohlmin's voice rasped from behind him.

Karl spun around. Standing next to Ohlmin was a short, fat man in wizard's robes. The wizard raised his hands, and smiled with a wine-stained mouth.

"Leave him be, Blenryth," Ohlmin said, his eyes never leaving Karl's. "This one is mine."

Ohlmin drew his sword and lunged, in full extension. Right into Karl's left arm, the one protected by Doria's robes.

The blade *tinged,* and bounced off, as though it had hit a wall.

Before Karl could strike, Ohlmin backed away. The slim man pursed his lips. "In that case, you do it, wizard."

Blenryth raised his arms higher, a rush of harsh syllables issuing from his wine-stained mouth—

The darkness shattered as a bolt of lightning crackled past Karl from behind, streaking through the air, striking the wizard square in the center of his chest.

Blenryth exploded, spraying Karl with gobs of flesh and shards of bone, knocking him to the ground, out of breath.

Move. You don't know where Ohlmin is—

Hands grasped his shoulders; Karl reached back and up.

"Easy," Walter's voice whispered. "It's just the, umm, cavalry."

Karl bounced to his feet. Standing next to the thief, Aristobulus, looking much the worse for wear, rubbed his smoldering hands together.

And grinned.

"No time for congratulations," Karl snapped, jerking a thumb in the direction of the wagon carrying the others. "They're in that one. Get in, and get moving. I'll catch up with you." He quickly scanned the vicinity. No sign of Ohlmin. The bastard was smart enough to know when to run.

For a moment, the other two stood still. *"Now,"* Karl said. A shove sent Walter stumbling in the right direction. "I've got to find Ahira." *And Ohlmin.* He clutched the scimitar tightly. *Definitely* and Ohlmin.

*   *   *

The world was an incredibly deep, impossibly dark pit. *Or well, Ahira?*

No, I'm not well. I'm dead, aren't I?

"Pass me that last bottle." Hakim's voice was calm. As always, or almost always. "I'm going to pour a little more in the wound before it closes altogether."

"His mouth's moving," Aristobulus said. "Pour it down his throat, instead."

"But if he doesn't swallow—if it goes down the wrong tube . . ."

"Don't be silly. Those are *healing* draughts—the only way you could hurt him with that is if you hit him with the bottle."

A gentle hand behind his neck forced his head forward; a sickly-sweet, syrupy-thick liquid washed the taste of blood from his mouth. Ahira raised a distant palm, forcing the neck of the bottle away. "Save. For later." He opened his eyes. In the dim light of an overhead lamp, Aristobulus and Hakim knelt over him. "We." He swallowed, and started again. "We are not moving."

Hakim raised a palm. "No problem. We're far enough away now." He raised his head. *"Karl—he's awake."*

Far enough away? There wasn't such a thing as far enough away. "Who," he said, his voice a harsh croak, "who says so?"

Karl Cullinane leaned in through the open door, his face splotched with dried blood and streaked with soot. "I say so. They're going to be having other problems than chasing us in the dark."

"How about . . ." He gasped for breath. "How . . ."

"Shh." Karl leaned out for a moment, then returned. "They're both . . . here, anyway. Andy's not doing too badly." He shrugged. "All things considered. Doria's still kind of . . . rocky. Not physically," he said, with a wan smile. "They've both had enough of that stuff. But they've been through a hell of a lot."

"What . . . happened?"

"Later." Karl nodded reassuringly. "The main thing is that we got away. You took a bolt in the lung; if Ari hadn't found that cache of healing draughts in a box strapped under the wagon, you'd be dead. But he did, and you aren't. How's that for now?"

Ahira tried to shake his head vigorously. It just came out as a twitch. "How did I . . . get here?"

Walter patted his shoulder, then moved away, seating himself on a bench on the far side of the wagon. Idly, he picked up a crossbow, then took a quick fingercount of the quarrels in its strapped-on quiver. "Karl found you on the ground, if that's what you mean. Carried you—on a dead run, you should pardon the expression—until he caught up with the rest of us." He looked over at the big man, who was still braced in the doorway. "Eleven bolts—that's not going to be enough, not with my aim."

"Strap another quiver to your leg. And don't forget the cloth, and the lamp oil," Karl said.

"And the flint-and-steel."

"Right." He looked over at Ahira. "The other two are outside, in case you're wondering. They . . . want to be left alone for a while. And I can't say that I blame them." Karl patted Aristobulus on the shoulder. "Are you sure that you're up to keeping guard while we're gone?"

"Count on it." The wizard clenched his fists. "I've still got my Flame spell—anybody except you two who gets close, gets burned. And speaking of burned, do you think that Blenryth's spell books are still back there?"

Karl shook his head. "I doubt it. The wagon we torched was probably his. But if we get the chance, I'll check."

"Fine. And if you don't get the chance, don't worry about it."

Hakim laughed. "Ari, m'friend, I'm beginning to like you."
The wizard scowled. "Just be careful."

Ahira struggled to rise, to get his arms to push him upward. But he couldn't. *Easy.* He forced himself to relax. *It's just temporary. It's just the aftereffects.* "You two aren't going anywhere. Not back there."

Karl stepped all the way into the wagon, bending his neck to avoid bumping against the ceiling. "Out." He jerked his thumb at Hakim and Aristobulus. They stepped silently through the door; Karl sat next to Ahira. "We are going back. Just Walter and me."

"No—" Ahira tried to shout it.

"Shh. I'm going to give you the rational reasons first. One." He held up a finger. "There are two-count-them-two water barrels on the side of this wagon. That's about five too few. Two." Another finger. "We don't have our supplies here—no food, no rope, this one lamp and one oil flask—and that bottle there is the last of the healing draughts." He patted at Hakim's scimitar, which was stuck through a sash at his waist. "Three. This sword isn't worth much; I may need a decent one later on. I kind of like Ohlmin's—and once I'm done with him, he won't have any use for it.

"And lastly," Karl continued, "there's five, maybe six of them left. If they have any sense, they're not going to try to chase us, but I don't want to worry about their having any sense. Understood? We're the fox; the only good hounds are dead hounds."

"Give me the real reason. You want to play hero?"

Karl held his breath for a long moment before answering. "This isn't for show." He toyed with the iron cuffs and dangling bits of chain that were still around his wrists. "Those bastards raped two ladies I care about. Two of my *friends*, dammit. And right now, both Andy and Doria are . . . in kind of . . ." He trailed off. Cullinane closed his eyes and tightened his fists. "They're hurt, and they're scared. And if I—damn. The next time I talk to them, I'm going to be able to say that the animals that hurt them are dead." He opened his fists and rested his face in his hands. "I want to tell them that they're safe, but that'd be a lie in this goddam world. God, how I wish I were home." He took a woolen blanket from the floor and, with the scimitar, began to cut it into strips. "And if the truth be known, my little dwarf friend, Ohlmin scares the hell out of *me*. I want him *dead*."

"No. You're not going. Can't let you." Couldn't Karl see that it was just too much of a risk? The thing to do was make a run for the Gate, not try to hunt down the surviving slavers.

"You can't stop me." Karl tied the dangling chains from his left cuff to his arm, weaving the strips of cloth through the links. He shook the arm vigorously. No sound. "And don't bother calling Walter and trying to talk him out of it." He repeated the process with his right cuff's chains, then started work on his leg irons. "You left me in charge, remember?"

"That was just while—"

"Too bad." Karl shrugged. "As far as I'm concerned, you're

still out of it." He grasped Ahira's shoulder with a strong hand. "We'll be back in a while. Take care."

Two steps to the door, and Karl Cullinane was gone.

Aristobulus kept watch until dawn, sitting tailor-fashion on the flat roof of the wagon, a blanket underneath him, a waterbag at his side, his Flame spell at the surface of his mind.

At daybreak, a speck appeared on the horizon. He stood, readying himself. If it was Karl and Hakim returning, that was fine. And if not, well then that was fine, too, in another way. Out of bow range, there was no way that a small group of humans could harm him before he blasted them.

The speck grew larger, until it became their flatbed wagon, now drawn by a team of eight horses. Karl and Hakim sat on the wagon's seat, sooty but otherwise unharmed.

"Karl, Hakim," he called out, "is everything . . ." Aristobulus let his voice trail off. He couldn't think of an appropriate word.

Cullinane pulled firmly on the reins. "Easy, easy," he murmured to the animals. Taking a leather bag from the bed of the wagon, he dismounted, pausing only to pat the large mare that was his usual mount, not one of the lead horses. "No more being hitched in front of a wagon for you. It's back to the saddle, tomorrow."

He stopped on the ground in front of the wizard and craned his neck to look up at Aristobulus. "We killed all of them," he said, his voice as matter-of-fact as if he were reporting the time of day.

"You're certain?" Aristobulus asked. "Including Ohlmin?"

Cullinane reached into the leather bag. "Including Ohlmin." He pulled his hand out.

Dangling by the black hair that was gripped in a trembling hand, Ohlmin's bodiless head swayed, as though nodding in agreement.

CHAPTER THIRTEEN: *To Bremon*

> *Melancholy and despair, though often, do not always concur; there is much difference: melancholy fears without a cause, this upon great occasion; melancholy is caused by fear and grief, but this torment procures them and all extremity of bitterness.*

> —Robert Burton

Karl didn't know when it had happened, but he'd developed a habit: rubbing his wrists as though to reassure himself that the cuffs were gone. It had been almost a week since Ahira had used the tools reclaimed from the slavers to chisel them all free of the remnants of their bonds. . . .

Well, the physical remnants, anyway. Karl dropped his right hand to the saddle, shaking his head at the way his wrist was reddened and sore.

He shook himself, then gave a quick tug on the reins; the mare responded by prancing to a halt and letting the two wagons pass her by.

Karl stroked her neck, smiling fondly. "I'd give you a name, but we're going to have to turn you all loose when we reach the mountain. I can't quite see trying to take you through the Gate— and it'll be easier on me if I don't name you. Understand?"

She lifted her head and whinnied. Karl chuckled; it wasn't a response to his question. She was just irritated at being passed by the harnessed horses, twitchy at that insult to her, a member of the saddle-bearing gentry.

"Well, at least I understand you." He let her break into a slow walk, while he raised himself in the saddle, drinking in the cool, sweet air of the grassland beyond the Waste. An east wind brought him a faint, minty smell, presented him with the tang of sunbaked grass, and a distant suggestion of musk.

Walter, from his usual perch on the seat of the flatbed, cocked his head and lifted a waterbag. "Thirsty?"

More out of sociability than thirst, Karl urged his mare over to the flatbed and leaned over to accept the bag, while his mare kept to the cart's pace, her head held high, a bit of extra bounce to her step, as though to deny any association with the dusty, plodding drayhorses.

Idly, Karl wondered about the fate of the two mules. Perhaps they had run off, sometime while in the slavers' possession; possibly, the roast on the slavers' campfire had been a haunch of mule. He shrugged; the only people who knew were safely dead, and he hadn't had the time or inclination to quiz them about the matter.

But there could be others on our heels. We'll have to watch out, until we're safely away from this filthy world. Uncorking the bag, he took a shallow swig of the warm, leather-tasting water, then recorked it and handed the bag down to Walter. "When we stop to rest, I want to get in some sword practice. If you're game." Ohlmin's sword was a fine piece of steel, a rust-free length of basket-hilted saber, faintly curved. But it was barely half the length of Karl's sword; using it called for a totally different style of swordplay, with much more attention to parrying at close range. The sword was mainly a thrusting weapon rather than a slashing one on attack, although its edge was sharp enough to shave with. His Barak-self seemed comfortable with it; still, best to be sure, practice as much as possible.

I'm sure Ohlmin would want me to use it well, he thought sarcastically. It hardly seemed fair that that bastard was beyond pain, though. *Then again, life isn't fair*. "So, are you up for it?"

"Am I what?"

"Never mind."

From the high seat of the other wagon, Andy-Andy cursed in low tones at her team of horses. Six were probably more than the wagon required, but they had the harnesses to spare, and putting six on meant not having to stop twice a day to change teams.

Karl turned to Walter. "She's coming back from it. At least a bit."

Walter took a grimy rag from the seat beside him and mopped at his forehead. "Some do." His next sentence, unvoiced, was, *And some don't.* Doria was close to being an automaton, responding only to direct questions, and then only with monosyllables. She ate barely enough to keep a lizard alive, and left the wagon only under duress. Karl had tried to take her aside, to explain that everything was under control, that she didn't have to worry—

He'd only tried that once. Any touch set her screaming, a high-pitched wail that wouldn't cease until she collapsed with exhaustion.

Maybe, with the right kind of care, Doria would someday be well again. And maybe they should have taken a detour, to the tabernacle of the Healing Hand. But Ahira had overruled that; there was no way they could go directly there; they just didn't have enough water to make it to the far side of the Waste. And if there was another slaver team . . .

Ahira was right. The best thing to do was to go ahead, get home as soon as possible. Back home, psychiatric therapy might not be easily effective, but Karl would find a therapist to treat what was wrong with Doria, even if he had to break a few arms. Fine, let the shrink write off their history of the past few months as some sort of group delusion—but Doria would get the help she needed. For everything.

Walter looked up at him, his brow wrinkling. "You know, don't you?"

"About what?"

"Doria."

Karl nodded. "Yes."

Walter considered it for a moment, as he twirled the reins around his fingers. "It has to be . . . what's-its-name—that dragon—"

"Ellegon."

The thief shuddered. "With all she's gone through, do you think she'll ever be all right?"

Karl shook his head. "No."

"How sure . . . ?"

He shrugged. "Not very." There was something strange about

this whole conversation. Walter asking *him?* "I remember when you sounded a lot more sure of *your*self."

"So do I." Walter reached back for a wine bottle, uncorked it, and drank. "So do I." He offered Karl a swig, which Karl declined with a shake of the head. "Karl? What do we do about it?"

Karl shrugged, and urged his mare into a trot. "We go home. And then we do what we can." *And I'll carry a load of guilt with me to my grave. None of this would have happened if I hadn't freed Ellegon, beat Ohlmin. And if I'd known—would I have left Ellegon chained in a cesspool? Or would I have chosen to spend the rest of my life living with that?*

"And what will that be?" Walter asked, his voice drifting forward.

Karl didn't respond. It wasn't really a day for answers.

CHAPTER FOURTEEN:
The Warrens

Hence, loathed Melancholy
Of Cerberus and blackest Midnight born,
In Stygian cave forlorn,
'Mongst horrid shapes, and shrieks, and sights unholy.

—John Milton

Bremon loomed ahead, a dark, jagged mass blocking half the noon sky.

Driving the flatbed wagon, Ahira shook his head and swore softly under his breath. The damn mountain always loomed in *front* of them, even though his mental picture of Oreen's map suggested that they were finally near the known entrance. Perhaps the rough copy he had made would have differed, but that had been lost, along with much of their supplies, to the slavers.

But no, that wasn't it. Oreen's map was clear in his mind; it was just that Bremon was too large, too massive, too gently sloped to have a clear edge, a noticeably demarked base.

Next to him on the flatbed's broad seat, Hakim peered down at him. "Are we there yet?" he asked, for only the thirtieth time that morning.

Ahira jerked on the reins. The flatbed's two horses shuffled to a quick stop on the gently uphill slope.

"*You little ass!*" Andrea shrilled. Ahira turned to see her wrestle the other wagon's team to a halt, the noses of the lead horses stopping scant inches behind the back of the flatbed. "You just *stay* there." She bounded out of the high seat of her wagon, and stalked toward him through the knee-high, golden grasses.

"Excuse me," Hakim said, "I just remembered something I've got to talk over with Ari." He made a quick exit, going around the opposite side of the flatbed from Andrea's approach, and disappeared into the other wagon.

Ahira didn't blame him for manufacturing a need to talk to the wizard, or Karl for cantering his horse ahead, past the flatbed. This sort of outburst was becoming more and more common.

I can't really say that I blame her, but I don't know what I should do about it. Perhaps the best thing would be to permanently relinquish leadership of the group to Karl. No, that wouldn't do; Karl and Hakim had been lucky—but wrong.

As Andrea planted herself in front of him, he rubbed at his eyes with his thumbs, then let his hands drop. "What is it now?"

She threw up her arms. "How many times have I asked you—politely, mind—to give me a bit of goddam notice before you stop? Do you really want my team climbing into the back of this little dogcart of yours?"

Her face reddened; Ahira stifled a snapped retort and raised a palm. "Just take it easy, please." *If you're so concerned about my stopping suddenly, then why don't you just let your wagon lag behind a few yards?* That was an obvious response, but a wrong one. Clearly, she was playing me-and-my-shadow with the flatbed out of an unconscious desire to speed him up, to speed them all up. To get herself away from this world, and home. "I'm sorry," he said. "My fault—it's just that—"

He'd tried to keep his voice level, but that only enraged her. "Don't you *dare* patronize me," she said, white-lipped. "I've got a job to do, driving that stubborn, idiotic team of horses—"

"I said—"

"—fighting them, more than half the time. They've got to trust me, to know that I won't lead them into—"

"No. They. Don't." He punctuated all three words by banging his fist on the wagon's seat. Ahira vaulted heavily to the ground. "We're stopping here. Now." *Enough* of this. Granted, Andrea had been through a hard time; given, it was at least partly his fault. But enough of treating her like, like . . .

. . . like everyone used to treat me. Like some sort of feeb, giving her the job of driving the big wagon because it gives her something to do, not because she's best at it. Even if she wants that sort of treatment, it's the wrong thing to do. And it stops here. "*We* stop here; you can turn your horses loose, or butcher them for supper, for all I care." He raised his head and his voice. "Karl!"

The big man urged his horse over. "Meal break?" He jerked his thumb at the mountain behind him. "I saw some trees ahead, about a mile or so, I think. It'd be a bit more comfortable up there."

Ahira shook his head. "No. I was telling Andrea that we're stopping here. Permanently, as far as the wagons go. Hakim's in the other one, talking to Ari—you go get him, have him saddle a horse. Then you two get the joy of riding out, and seeing if you can find an entrance. *The* entrance."

"And if we can't?" Karl frowned disapprovingly.

Ahira's hands itched for his axehilt. "Then be back by sundown. You'll try again tomorrow, at first light."

Karl's horse took a prancing step back. "I've got a better idea, I think. Doria's got a Locate spell; have her find the entrance."

Andrea held up a hand. "Do you two want an opinion, or don't you give a damn what I think?" Her lips pursed; she opened her mouth as though to go on, then stopped and started again. "It would be better to leave her alone. For two reasons. First, Location spells are finicky; if she doesn't know exactly what she's looking for, the spell will fasten on something else, something that fits her . . . internal description. Besides"—her shoulders twitched beneath her robes—"I think it's best to leave her alone, in any case. Don't put any demands on her, not if you don't have to. I . . . don't know if trying to get her to do something might . . . push her over the edge."

From his perch atop his horse, Karl sighed. "I guess you're right. I . . . was just thinking that a bit of activity would be good for her, help to take her mind off . . ." He gestured absently. ". . . everything."

"What the hell do *you* know about it?" Andrea snapped.

Karl sat silent for a moment, then shook his head slowly from side to side. "Know? I wouldn't say that I know much about anything.'' He gave a thin smile, then turned his mare away and trotted back to the other wagon.

Ahira stared off into the distance, keeping his eyes on the mountain, off Andrea, not saying anything.

Finally, she broke the silence. ''What was that supposed to mean?''

Ahira moved to the flatbed and busied himself with unhitching the horses. ''Only two things that I can think of. First, that he doesn't understand you. For which I can't exactly blame him. I don't, either.''

''I was trying to explain it to him when . . .'' Her voice trailed off into choking sounds. ''When everything . . . fell apart. And now he's treating me like I'm . . . soiled.''

''*Don't.*'' Ahira spun around. ''Don't even think that. I haven't always been Karl's greatest admirer, but you're dead wrong.'' He put out a hand; she took it with trembling fingers. ''I don't think that Karl's too good at handling guilt. That's what you're seeing—not anything else. Karl knows—we *all* know the difference between a victim and . . .'' He clenched his jaw. Maybe Karl hadn't been wrong in going back to finish off Ohlmin and his slavers, despite the risk. ''Just take my word for it.''

She nodded slowly. ''You said that there were two things that he meant?''

Ahira returned her nod. ''That maybe there's a difference between knowing and caring. And Karl cares about you. As if you didn't know. He once came close to killing Hakim over you, but he stopped. Maybe it was squeamishness, maybe not.'' He squeezed her hand more tightly. ''But he didn't hold back when it came to Ohlmin, did he?''

''And for that, I'm supposed to fall into—''

''And for that,'' he interrupted, ''you're free to do whatever you want, without looking over your shoulder.'' He released her hand. ''I need a bit of help with these horses. Are you available?''

Slowly, she nodded.

Karl and Walter discovered the entrance on their second day of searching. A spiral search pattern had given them a horseback view of various naked, slightly wooded, and heavily overgrown slopes, a few dozen small animals that scurried for cover at their approach, and more than a few dozen birds, who were only too glad to interrupt their constant search for food to chitter and twerp at Karl and Walter.

The thief glared up at Karl from the back of his mount, a mild-mannered sorrel gelding. "I've got an idea—what say we take a break, let me get away from this vicious beast for a while." Walter patted at the crossbow lashed to the saddle in front of him. "Besides, maybe I could shoot us some dinner."

Karl chuckled and stroked at his mare's neck. It was dry, unsweaty; probably she could go on almost forever at this slow walk. "Why not? My horse seems a bit tired," he lied. "Although I wouldn't give odds that you could hit a bird with that bow. Your aim—"

"Was good enough when it counted, no?"

That was a good point. Karl dismounted, while from the ivy-covered rockface to their right a small bird twittered its own opinion of Walter's skill with a crossbow.

Walter jerked his horse to a stop and got off with none of his usual grace, then rubbed at his back and thighs. It was his own fault, really—if the thief had taken his turn on horseback, like the others, he would at least have the minimal horsemanship of Ahira and Andy-Andy.

The bird scolded them again.

Karl chuckled as he slipped the bridle from his horse's neck. "Seems that crow doesn't think much of your riding ability, Walter."

The thief scowled as he unstrapped the crossbow. "It's not a crow. Too small." He pulled back the string and dropped a quarrel into the slot. "Possibly it's tasty." Walter raised the bow and took aim.

Now, that was unreasonable, trying to shoot a bird out of pique. Karl shrugged. On the other hand, the thief wasn't very accurate with a crossbow. The night they had killed Ohlmin and the others, it had been Walter's ability to move silently and almost invisibly in the dark that had served them well, not his indifferent aim.

On the other hand—*hell, I've run out of hands.* "Just leave it alone—"

Twing!

The bolt went low and wide, vanishing in the ivy. With a twitter and a flutter, the bird flew away.

Karl forced himself not to smile. "Well, now we can have a

whole side of . . . mountain for supper. You like yours medium rare, or—hey! What are you doing?''

The thief let his bow drop to the ground and walked toward the rockface.

"Give me a hand up," Walter said, his eyes on the spot where the arrow had disappeared. "It should have bounced off, or stuck itself in, or something."

Karl went over and knelt on one knee, cupping his hands, then straightening and lifting as Walter settled a sandaled foot into his grip. The thief caught a handhold somewhere above and scrabbled up the ivy.

Karl looked up. Walter was gone. "Where—"

The thief's smiling face poked through the green curtain. "I believe that this is what we call *gin.*" His unseen hands clapped. "I don't have a light, but this thing looks as if it goes down and in for about a million miles. You want to go back for the others, or do I?''

"Dealer's choice," Karl said calmly, his heart beating a rapid tattoo. *We're going home. Where it's safe, comfortable.*

I'm *going home.*

Thank God.

With everyone gathered just inside the entrance, Ahira took a few minutes to check each pack, working easily in the speckled light coming through the ivy. It would have been possible to make the others check their own gear, but that would mean waiting until their eyes adjusted to the dimness. Better to get going as soon as possible.

He considered the five waterskins. Enough for four days, maybe five, if they went on a strict water ration. It would be nice to have more, but they had lost most of the waterbags to Ohlmin's group, and carrying a barrel through the tunnels would be awkward, at best.

Ahira cinched Hakim's pack a bit tighter. "No need to have things fall out," he said.

Hakim smiled. "Whatever you say, fearless leader. I've got a suggestion, though."

"Yes?"

"Ari and Doria have their Glow spells—why not save on the lantern's oil, and use one now?"

Ahira thought it over for a moment. Not necessarily a bad

idea, although the wizard's spell would be good only temporarily; the light would dim, and go out. But Doria's Glow spell was more powerful; it would keep whatever it was put on shining forever. "Karl, your sword, please."

Karl lumbered over, ducking his head under a rocky overhang. "Don't you trust me with an edged weapon?"

Ahira smiled as he hefted the blade. A decent saber, actually, but not quite the luxury-class blade that Karl's broken sword had been. "No, I'm afraid that you'll slice your foot off. Seriously, I'm going to have Doria . . ." He jerked his chin at the cleric, who was sitting slumped next to her pack. "I'm going to *try* to have her Glow it for you." Leaving Doria alone hadn't improved anything. Perhaps succeeding at something would be good for her.

"The point?" Karl's forehead furrowed. "Not to be critical, but you're not putting me in the lead, are you? Spelunking isn't exactly my specialty."

Dammit, Karl, give me a minute to finish. It'd be nice not to be interrupted. It'd be a change, anyway. "You get the spot just behind me. I won't need much light. Darksight, remember?" If the tunnels were as old as Oreen and that dragon Karl had talked to had claimed, it probably wouldn't be necessary for Ahira to go first; any sections of the ceiling that were shaky at all would have already fallen.

But no sense in taking chances. Besides, this was going to be easy for Ahira. A dwarf was built for easing through tunnels. Without adequate light, these humans would probably trip over their own feet.

The sword clutched in his hand, Ahira walked over to Doria and squatted in front of her. "doria?"

She just sat there, her robes gathered loosely around her, eyes staring blindly through him.

"Doria, I need your help."

No response.

"Please?"

Nothing.

He reached out a hand and laid it gently on her shoulder. "Doria?"

Her face came alive, creasing into a wide-eyed rictus of terror. She inhaled violently.

And screamed.

And kept screaming, until Ahira's ears rang, and Doria lay curled on the floor of the tunnel, whimpering as she gasped for breath.

Ahira looked behind him. Aristobulus, Hakim, Andrea, and Karl stood shoulder to shoulder, glowering in unison.

I had to try. We may need her later. No—make that: "I have to try," he said to Doria, pretending to ignore the way four pairs of eyes were trying to bore holes into his back. "And so do you." *I've got to do something, I have to do something.* "Doria, I'm sorry I touch—"

"Leave me alone." Her voice was low, just one step above a whisper.

"No." He said that as firmly as he could. Maybe if he acted as though she were all right, she might be. *If I close my eyes, does the world go away?* "I need you to Glow this sword. Make it give off light." As if of its own volition, his hand moved toward her; he jerked it back. "You're part of this group; you're one of us. And we need your help."

"Ahira." Karl's hand grasped his shoulder, urging him away. "Not now. We'll use the lanterns for a while. Maybe she'll be up to it later."

"No!" He shrugged the hand off. *You can't help a, a cripple by ignoring the disability. That just makes things worse. You compensate for it, but you don't ignore it.*

He shook his head to clear it. *But isn't that what I was trying to do, just a few moments ago? Maybe it isn't easy to deal with someone else's handicap, either.* "Doria, I'm not going to stop bothering you until you do it." Careful not to touch her, he grasped the sword by the blade and slid the hilt between her hands. "Take it. Make it glow."

Her lips moved fractionally, without sound.

"Do it."

At first, her voice was a whisper, a quiet, distant rustle of breath. Then the sound grew louder, nearer, stronger, a rush of airy syllables that vanished as they touched his ears.

And the sword began to glow. Faintly; the dim blue of the sky before dawn.

Then brighter; the color of a robin's egg.

And brighter, until it fell from Doria's fingers, glowing like the flame of a bunsen burner, bathing her face in blue light.

Ahira reached out a hand, halting his fingers an inch from the

216

blade. No heat, although it shone with a blue-hot fury. No heat at all—he extended a quivering finger and touched his finger to the metal.

No heat; his finger touched only cool steel.

Ahira smiled. "That's beautiful. I wish I'd gone along with Ari, to see him glow the blade for that smith, back in Pandathaway." He picked up the sword and handed it to Karl.

In the light from the blade, Aristobulus smiled. "You still would be impressed. If I'd tried to get that blade this bright, the glow would have lasted for only an hour or so."

"Doria," the dwarf said gently, "how long will this last? It's beautiful." He knew the answer, but he needed to hear her say it.

Her head nodded fractionally, her hands trembling as she knitted her fingers together. "Always."

Karl's hand fell on his shoulder. "I think it's time we got going."

"Yes," Doria whispered. "Home."

The sword held high to scatter the light as widely as possible, Karl picked his way behind Ahira, the muscles in his shoulders burning like hot wires. It was as though they were walking through the insides of some gargantuan stone worm; the tunnel twisted and turned, leading downward all the way, but never losing its tubular shape, or branching off.

His arms hurt, but he couldn't let both hang at his sides, except when they stopped to rest. The last time had been a while ago. But how long? Who could tell?

Just for something to do, he *tinged* the point of the sword against the ceiling overhead.

"Stop it," Ahira snapped from in front of him.

"Why? I just—"

"*Stop it.*" The dwarf had gotten nastier the farther down the tunnel they went.

"Ahira?"

The dwarf didn't turn around. "What is it *now?*"

"How long—"

"How long until *what?* Until we get there? I don't know."

"No," Aristobulus called from behind. "How long until we stop to rest?" His voice was ragged; the wizard wasn't holding up well.

From the rear of the group, Walter's baritone drifted forward. "I've got a better question—how long until the water gives out? And what do we do then?"

"Relax," the dwarf said, sounding anything but relaxed himself. "I've figured that out." He paused to pick his way around a pile of rocky rubble that was echoed above by a gap in the ceiling. "We go along until we either find the Gate or use up just over half our water."

Karl squeezed through between the rubble pile and the wall, barking his shin in the process. He waited on the other side, extending his hand to help Aristobulus through.

The wizard nodded his thanks.

Andy-Andy was next; she hesitated for a moment before accepting his help. "Thank you." Her voice dripped insincerity.

My, aren't we getting formal. "And you are most welcome, m'lady."

She turned away, but not before he caught a trace of a smile.

Karl shrugged, moving aside to let Doria make her own way through. Figuring out *why* Andy-Andy did *what* wasn't certain to be a waste of time and effort. But close enough.

The trouble with women is that they're too damn intelligent.

Walter moved easily through the narrow passage, balancing himself like a dancer. "Want to switch for a while?"

Gratefully, Karl handed him the sword, accepting the thief's scimitar in return. He slipped it under his belt, then folded his arm across his chest and rubbed viciously at his shoulders. Forcing someone to keep an arm overhead would make a fine torture. And probably had been used as such.

Perhaps in the Coliseum of Pandathaway? No, probably not. Too gentle; people who would chain Ellegon in the middle of a cesspool would have much worse than that in store for someone they were angry at.

But we're going home. All we have to do is tiptoe by a dragon—The Dragon.

"Karl?" Andy-Andy's form was just a silhouette in the light of the sword beyond her. "Are you going to fall asleep standing up? Or would you be so kind as to come along with the rest of us?"

He didn't bother with a sarcastic smile. She probably couldn't see it anyway. Still massaging his shoulders, he set off after the others.

Once we get to the other side, Andrea Andropolous, you and I are going to talk this out, without interruptions. And then yours truly is going to see if he can drink Walter Slovotsky under the table.

Ahira was the first to see the skeleton, of course, because of both his position at the front of the group and his darksight.

But he came close to stumbling over it; a distant, obscene reek had him distracted. It was a strange odor, far different from the cool, moist smell of the unending tunnel.

Probably just imagining it. He shook his head and sniffed twice. Nothing. He shrugged, and started to move on.

And caught himself in midstep, the blackened skull barely an inch beneath the sole of his sandal. Ahira teetered on one leg for a moment, like an aerialist on a high wire.

"Hold it." He regained his balance and motioned Hakim forward, stepping aside to bring the skull out of his shadow.

It lay on its side in the middle of the tunnel, hollow eyesockets staring blindly, open jaw leering, loose bones arrayed behind it in a charred trail.

"What the—"

"Shh," Ahira whispered. "Nobody say anything. Just stay where you are." He knelt on the rough stone beside the skull, Hakim moving the glowing sword closer without any need to be asked.

The skull had lain there a long time; dust on the upper surface was so thick that Ahira's probing finger sank into the feathery surface past his fingernail, almost to the first joint. Years, certainly. Possibly centuries.

He rubbed his finger against his chest.

Beyond the skull, a charred ribcage lay, armbones to the side, the pelvis and the long bones of the legs arrayed as though the victim had sprawled out before its flesh had vanished.

To the left of the ribcage, a round shield lay, its concavity cupping the floor of the tunnel. No design on its face, just blackness.

Blackness, and charred bones—that didn't make any sense. Unless . . . Ahira wiped his hand across the surface of the shield.

It came away black, leaving behind a dirtied outline of the design that had once decorated the shield's face: three golden circles.

Ahira wiped his other hand against the wall. It, too, came away sooty.

Hakim smiled, and leaned close. "My friend," he whispered, his lips a scant inch from Ahira's ear, "it seems to me that we're almost there."

Ahira nodded. *Take it slow, now.* "Pass the word down. Everyone is to take his pack off, and leave it. Sandals, too—we go barefoot from here on in."

And quietly, quietly. But as he turned to look into the others' fear-whitened faces, he knew that there was no need to say that.

Ahira's heart pounded. *I can send them home. And if I don't make it out of here in half the time it took to get in, I deserve to die of thirst.*

Hakim turned back from his whispering to Andrea. "I think we can quit the pretense, James. This is the end of the line for you, no? You aren't coming with us."

Ahira smiled. "I'll see you to the Gate—I'll see you *through* the Gate. But . . ." He trailed off, shrugging.

Hakim nodded. "I understand. Do you explain it to the others, or . . . ?"

"I'll leave the explanations to you. For the other side." *It's almost done, over. And how can I say goodbye to all of them?* His eyes started to mist over. He caught himself. This wasn't a time to get sentimental. "Oh," he whispered, as gruffly as he could, "we won't want that sword anymore. Drop it right here."

Hakim smiled, shrugged, and dropped the glowing blade, snatching it out of the air scant inches before it would have clanged on the stone. His smile, and his wide-armed shrug, said, *Sorry, I couldn't resist it.*

Ahira's glare answered, *Try real hard, next time.*

CHAPTER FIFTEEN: *The Dragon at the Gate*

> From generation to generation it shall lie waste,
> none shall pass through it for ever and ever. But the
> cormorant and the bittern shall possess it; the owl
> and the raven shall also dwell in it; and he shall
> stretch out upon it the line of confusion, and the
> stones of emptiness . . .
> . . . and it shall be an habitation for dragons.
>
> —Isaiah Ben-Amoz

As the distant glow of the abandoned sword faded behind, a rainbow phosphorescence fingered the walls of the tunnel ahead.

Karl furrowed his brow. Just a lucky coincidence, or had Ahira spotted it back at the skeleton?

He clenched the hilt of the scimitar. It probably didn't matter. If it hadn't gotten brighter ahead, Ahira would have sent him back for the sword. Stumbling around in the dark was almost certainly more dangerous than a bit of light. The other choice, of course, would have been for all of them to link hands, but—

—no, that wouldn't have been another choice. Not unless they left Doria behind.

The tunnel curled like the coils of a snake, winding downward, ever steeper. He was glad that Ahira had forced them all to rid themselves of their sandals; any grip less sure than that of bare feet, and Aristobulus, at least, would have fallen.

Just in front of him, Andy-Andy stumbled; he whipped his free arm around her waist, catching and lifting her before she could fall. As he set her on her feet, she gave his hand a quick squeeze and favored him with a slight nod.

Now isn't the time to work that *out,* he thought. *There'll be plenty of time when we're back, on the other side. Home.*

Ahead, Ahira motioned for a stop, then beckoned to Walter. A few whispered words passed between the two, and then the thief crept on hands and knees downward, around the next bend in the tunnel.

Seconds passed. Karl was sure it was only seconds; he counted eighty-nine of his own heartbeats before Walter returned, and Ahira urged them all back away from the bend, and into a kneeling circle.

Chance put Karl between Andy-Andy and Doria; he pressed away from the cleric, noting that Walter, on the other side of her, was similarly squeezing up against the smaller form of Aristobulus.

"I saw it," Walter whispered, so quietly that Karl had to strain his ears to hear the thief, over the beating of his own heart. "It's about a hundred yards away from where the tunnel dumps out. At about ten o'clock, if your back's to the tunnel—understand?" Karl nodded in unison with the others.

"And The Dragon is sleeping," Walter continued. "But we've got to pass in front of It, to get to the Gate. And I don't know if we'll need Ari to operate it for us." He raised a quizzical eyebrow.

The wizard shook his head. "Either we're in a very bad way, or it's as I think: It's automatic. Does it look like water? Good. Then we're safe."

"One more problem," the thief whispered. "There's only enough room for us to go single-file—or just one at a time."

Ahira rubbed at his temples with blunt fingers. "One at a time—Hakim first."

"No," Karl shook his head, pointing to Andy-Andy. "She goes first, it's—"

"We do it my way!" the dwarf hissed.

Well, it made sense, in a way: The thief was best at moving silently. Karl nodded slowly. "But she's next." *I got her into this; I've got to see that she gets out of it.*

The dwarf hesitated for a moment. "Agreed. Then Doria."

You're not thinking, Ahira. Doria could easily turn out to be a problem. "No, then Ari." *You and I can take Doria out, if need be. And, each in our own way, you and I are responsible for her.* But he couldn't say that, and didn't need to. A few seconds of thought would let the dwarf reach the same conclusion.

Ahira sighed. "Perhaps you're right. Hakim, get going."

"See you." Walter briefly clasped hands with Karl, then Aristobulus, then chucked Andy-Andy under the chin. She jerked her head away and grabbed his hand.

"Just be careful," she whispered. "I'll be along."

Walter took a slow, long look at Doria, then threw his arms around Ahira. Karl couldn't make out Walter's whispered words, except for the last two: "Be well."

The thief crawled away, then rose silently to the balls of his feet and disappeared around the bend.

Silence.

Ahira tapped Andy-Andy's shoulder. "Go."

Karl smiled. "See you in a little while."

Her chin trembled; a stray lock of hair fell across her nose. Karl brushed it away. "Go."

She nodded, and left.

Ahira beckoned at Aristobulus. "Get ready."

Aristobulus started to rise, then stopped. "No. All at once."

"No," the dwarf said, shaking his head. "You next—Karl and I will take care of Doria."

Aristobulus shrugged and seated himself carefully on the floor, a study in simulated nonchalance. "I'll wait."

We've all grown, Karl thought. *I think he's wrong to pull this, but it's not coming from that damn self-centeredness that I used to hate in him.* "No time to argue." He reached for the wizard—

—and found his wrists caught in Ahira's huge hands. The dwarf's mouth quirked; he dropped Karl's wrists and spread his arms, shrugging, as though to say, *What can we do?*

"Fine," the dwarf said, unlimbering his axe from his chest. "Single-file—first Karl, then you, then Doria, then me."

The wizard nodded, and stood.

Karl rose silently to his feet, as did Aristobulus. Ahira urged Doria to stand. Sullenly, clumsily, she did.

Karl took the lead, and tiptoed around the bend—

* * *

—and into a brightness that stung his eyes, and a silent, moldy reek that ached in his nostrils. It smelled of age, and cruelty, and hatred . . . and Dragon.

The Dragon lay sleeping in the huge chamber, a cavern lit by glowing rainbowed crystals that lined the walls arching hundreds of yards above the rough floor. Its huge head, wickedly saurian, rested on crossed forelegs the size of centuries-old oak trunks.

Ellegon had been right. He *was* just a baby, a miniature, smoother version of *This*. The smallest of The Dragon's mottled scales was easily Karl's height; Its mouth could have swallowed an elephant.

And the teeth sent chills running down Karl's back. They stood tall and sharp, threatening yellowed edges through which The Dragon's fetid breath whistled, like a wind through a horrid forest.

He wrestled his eyes from The Dragon and looked around the cavern. Beyond the creature's left shoulder, a mirror gleamed, a surface rippled.

The Gate. Karl tiptoed slowly forward, his feet numb on the cold stone floor.

The Gate hung unsupported in the air, just above a narrow ledge. Its surface rippled, shimmering in the cavern's light, as the Gate stood, silently waiting, like a pool of water tipped on its side.

A stone ramp led up to the Gate, tapering from a wide base to where it became a stone ledge. There was no way that more than one person could stand on that ledge; it couldn't have been more than two feet square. They would have to go through one by one.

He turned and waved for Ahira and Aristobulus to bring Doria forward.

Both of them beckoned to her.

Come on, Doria. Just a little farther.

No response. She stood still, staring wide-eyed at The Dragon, her jaw clenched and quivering. A trickle of blood ran out of the corner of her mouth and dripped, one drop at a time, onto her white robes.

Ahira shook his head as he turned to face Karl. *No good,* he mouthed. *We need a diversion. Diversion.* He pointed to Karl, then Aristobulus, and then the Gate. *You two wait at the ramp. I'll bring her.*

Karl nodded, then walked slowly by The Dragon's head, Aristobulus at his side. The hundred-yard walk to the ramp took him past The Dragon's bulging midsection. If only he had a decent sword he could—

—*what? A mosquito could do more harm to me than I could do to That.* He gripped the hilt of Walter's scimitar. *Not unless I stuck It in the eye. And I couldn't reach that with a stepladder.* And perhaps he wouldn't even be able to stick this sword through Its lids. Then again—

Doria screamed, shattering the thick silence.

HUMANS. A roar shook the cavern, sending light-bearing crystals tinkling to the floor, knocking Karl off his feet.

Slowly, ponderously, the head lifted and turned, the man-high eyelids retracting.

"Over *here*," Aristobulus shouted, his voice breaking. "The eyes, Karl, the eyes—"

Karl bounced to his feet, the scimitar held in his right hand. "I know. I'll . . ." His voice caught in his throat as the head turned, two immense liquid eyes staring directly at him.

Behind Karl, Aristobulus' voice murmured harsh syllables, spoken and then gone, while over at the entrance, Ahira threw Doria's struggling body over his shoulder and broke into a sprint.

The Dragon's mouth opened. *BURN.* Its eyes gleamed—

"And done!" Aristobulus clapped his hands together.

—and shone, brighter and brighter until they flared with the light of a thousand suns.

Ari's light spell—The Dragon was blinded!

Karl ducked to one side as a gout of flame scoured the stone where he had stood. Aristobulus hiked up his robes and wordlessly sprinted up the ramp, not slowing as he reached the top, dived through the Gate, and was gone.

A heavy, limp mass knocked Karl off his feet. Doria!

"Over here! Burn *me*, you son of a pig," Ahira shouted, his battleaxe drawn. He raced away from the Gate. The Dragon's head following him. "Get through—take her. *Move*."

Karl snatched up Doria as though she were a piece of fluff and ran with her up the ramp, to the Gate. A quick one-handed throw, and she was gone.

He turned. Ahira ducked a flamebreath, and dashed for the tunnel's opening. Like a felled tree, The Dragon's tail slammed down in front of the hole, the impact on the floor of the cavern knocking Ahira over.

"*Over here, now,*" Karl shouted. "We'll take turns with your attention, Dragon."

The light in The Dragon's eyes was already beginning to dim; Aristobulus' light spell was wearing off. A few seconds more, and Karl and Ahira would be trapped in the cavern, The Dragon's sight restored.

YOU WILL BURN.

Ahira ran toward Karl, The Dragon's head following him.

Karl hesitated in front of the Gate. Ahira couldn't run fast enough; it didn't seem to take The Dragon long between flamebreaths, and the gaping mouth was coming to bear on the dwarf.

"*Not him!*" Karl shouted. "Try and burn *me*, Dragon."

At the base of the ramp, the dwarf stumbled, and started scrabbling up it on all fours. "Karl, *go.*"

A rush of flame caught Ahira. The force of the gout of fire slid the dwarf up the ramp as he crackled and screamed in the flame, his arms waving aimlessly.

Karl turned and dived for the Gate, his legs burning behind him. A searing mass struck him in the back . . .

. . . and the world dissolved into a white-hot nightmare that faded only slowly into utter black.

PART FIVE:

And Beyond

CHAPTER SIXTEEN:
The Way Back

It is easy to go down into Hell;
night and day, the gates of dark Death stand wide;
   but to climb back up again, to retrace one's steps
to the upper air—there's the rub, the task.

   —Publius Vergilius Maro (Virgil)

Walter Slovotsky's huge hand shook him, while the damp night grass pressed against his shirt and bare feet.

"Karl, we're back." The big man wept almost silently. "We're back."

Bare feet? That made sense; they had left their sandals behind. But why did his back hurt so? As if he'd been sunburned. Worse.

"Easy, now." Her hand at the back of his neck, Andy-Andy propped him up to a sitting position.

Karl opened his eyes, moonlight off the water in front of him hitting him like a slap. Moonlight? "We did it."

Lou Riccetti knelt in front of him, barefoot in now-tattered workshirt and jeans. "Not quite." His voice was somber, his round cheeks were wet. "We don't even have Jason's body with us, and . . ."

"And what, *dammit?*" Karl peeled back the right leg of his jeans. No wonder it ached so; it was covered with blisters.

"Look over there." Riccetti pointed. Doria lay curled on the grass, her eyes wide and unblinking, her chest barely moving. "She's gone, Karl. Catatonic."

Karl shook himself And it was himself; smaller, skinnier. *Barak?*

Help me?

Nothing. No answer, not even the feeling of the presence of his other persona. *Then I'll do without.* "Where's Ahi—James?"

"Later," Andy-Andy breathed. "Just take a moment. You need—"

"Show him." Riccetti's voice was firm.

She caught a breath, and held it for longer than Karl would have thought possible. "Look to your right."

Walter Slovotsky knelt weeping over the dead body of James Michael Finnegan. The third-degree burns that had killed James Michael still smoldered, sending up light traces of mist and smoke.

Ohgod. "He didn't change enough."

Walter wept unashamedly, his huge hands reaching out as though to shake little James Michael Finnegan awake, then drawing back.

Just think for a minute. Mirror Lake spread out in front of him in the moonlight, the Commons all around. "We're on campus." A chill wind blew across the lake, sending a rush of leaves tumbling around him. "How long?"

Riccetti shook his head. "Deighton didn't lie about the different time rates. I snuck into a dorm; we've been gone just about eight hours—it's four in the morning. Jase is . . . gone, James Michael is dead, Doria is—"

Karl backhanded him across the face. "Shut *up*." Shaking off Andy-Andy's helping hands, he got to his feet, ignoring the shooting pains from the blisters on his soles. "We've got to get moving."

"And do *what?*" Andy-Andy shrilled.

"*Shut up*, I said." He hobbled over to where Walter knelt weeping over the burned body that had been James Michael Finnegan. "And you, stand up and clear your head. Now. We don't have time for this shit."

Walter bared his teeth and growled, "You leave me alone. You—"

"No time for that. Where do you keep your car?"

"Car?"

"Yes, car. Automobile—where do you keep it parked?"

The big man's forehead crinkled. "Over in B-Lot. What are you—"

"Not close enough. *Lou?*"

Riccetti trotted over, a faint smile peeking through the grimness of his wet face. "Yes? Are you thinking what I think—"

"You've got it. S-Lot's closest—get there, find a big car, and steal it. Spare key under the front fender, cross some wires, do whatever you have to, but get a *big* car, and get it here. *Fast.*"

"Got it." Riccetti nodded and ran off.

"Karl?" Walter looked up at him. "What's going on?"

"Lou worked it out. You should have listened more closely to Ahira. The Matriarch of the Healing Hand may be able to raise the dead. Now, we don't have Jason's body, but we do have James Michael's. And we have Doria." He took a deep breath. "So we're going back. You know where that bastard Deighton lives?"

"Faculty Row—third house from the—"

"Fine. Run up there—act like you're out for a jog, or something—and cut the phone lines. Don't go in, but if he notices you and tries to get out, *stop him.*"

Slovotsky stood. "Are you sure we should handle it this way?"

Karl grabbed him by the front of the shirt. "Ahira's out of it, and I'm in charge. Understood?"

Slovotsky smiled and nodded. "You really think we'll be able to get away with all this?"

"No. But we're going to try. Get moving." Karl released his grip.

Slovotsky turned and jogged away, not looking back.

"Karl?" His feet aching hideously, he turned to face Andy-Andy. "What have you got for me?"

"Diversion." He jerked his thumb toward the road. "If anybody comes this way, you distract them. Particularly if it's Security. If we get stuck on this side, James'll get buried, Doria gets committed to some nice funny farm, and that's it. So make it good."

She nodded. "But if it's Security, and I get busted?"

"Then you stay here. So make sure you don't. If we lose you, meet us up at Faculty Row. Third house from the west end." He forced a grin. "It'll be the one with the big stolen car in front of it. Now get up to the road, and keep watch."

She nodded and started to walk away, then turned back to face him. "But what if Deighton won't send us back? Or can't?"

Karl crossed his arms over his chest. "He will. Believe me, he will."

They huddled in the bushes next to Deighton's back porch. A light shone through the drawn curtains, casting their faces into yellow shadow.

"Last chance," Karl said quietly. "We've all got family and friends on this side. Our lives are here. I promise I'll do my best to bring anybody back who wants to come back. . . ." He shrugged.

Walter smiled. Not amiably. "But there's no guarantee we can slip by The Dragon again." The big man shrugged, not noticing how that split the shoulders of his shirt. "I'll take the chance. For James."

Riccetti rubbed at his face. "I've got no problem. I've always wanted out, wanted to make some miracles." He spread his hands. "And what am I here? A ninth-semester engineering major with maybe enough money for another semester. Haven't spoken to my parents in—" He shook himself. "I just want to know how we're going to do it."

"In a minute. Andy?"

She laid a hand on his arm. "We'll talk about it later. Right now, I'm more worried about Doria and Ahira. You said that they can help them on the other side?"

I don't have time for explanations. No, that wasn't true. It wasn't a matter of time, but of nerve. *If we don't do this quickly, I don't know if I can do it at all.* "Somewhere in the Waste is the home tabernacle of the Healing Hand Society. Doria's sect."

She nodded. "And she's one of their own, so they're likely to help her. Probably." She paused for a moment, fingering the bend in her nose. "But only probably—what if their . . . records don't show her? I mean, on this side there's institutions—maybe Doria would be best here?"

"No." Karl forced a smile. "I'm an ex-psych major, remember? The prognosis for catatonia is bad. Insulin therapy, shock treatments—none of it has decent odds. That's one.

"Two. If she could be brought out of it here, what do you

think her chances are of ever getting out of the rubber-room set? Even a good shrink will diagnose her as having heavy delusions— and the rest of us won't be around to back her up, not if we're going to try to get James brought back. I can't see a chance that she could persuade anyone that what happened, well, happened. As far as I can see it, we're her only chance." He turned to Riccetti. "You crack a window in the car?"

"As per instructions. The . . . bag is still in the trunk, Doria's safely under a blanket in the back seat, and after I dropped you two off, I parked it well away from a streetlight."

"Fine," Karl said. "Go back to it, start it up, and pull it into the driveway when you see the light on the front porch blink three times. If that doesn't happen within, say, fifteen minutes, get going. Take care of them, and make another try when you think it's right. Got it?"

"Got it." Riccetti walked away, stooping low as he passed under Deighton's kitchen window.

Walter straightened himself. "What have you got for me?"

"Free safety. If the bastard gets past Andy and me, stop him. Don't kill him, don't give him a concussion—but stop him. On the three blinks, you come in, too. And if we blow it, you get back to your dorm and play Football Hero until you hear from Riccetti—Andy and I will keep our mouths shut. You weren't at the Student Union tonight, you didn't know anybody was missing or dead—understood?"

"Understood. We could just *ask* Deighton, you know." Walter held up a hand. "I know—but if he tells us to go to hell and starts screaming for the cops, we're in trouble."

Karl turned back to Andy-Andy. "You still haven't said whether you're in or out."

She gripped his shoulder. "In. Idiot."

He took a deep breath. It wasn't all that bad, not here. If something had gone wrong on the other side, he would have ended up as the main feature at a Coliseum torture session; here, the worst possibility was being arrested for kidnapping, assault, and first-degree murder.

No, make that second-degree. No way any prosecutor is ever going to prove my motive, show that I premeditated it.

Karl exhaled, forcing himself to relax. "Anybody got anything else to bring up? Then let's do it, people." He stood. "Now."

*   *   *

Ten minutes later, Arthur Simpson Deighton sat bound to a kitchen chair, glaring at Karl with his left eye. He couldn't quite glare with the right one; it was swollen shut.

Karl finished the last knot on the ropes that bound the old man's left ankle to the chair, then stepped back to admire his handiwork. Deighton was secure: His wrists were tied tightly with two of his own neckties, and the gag was letting little else besides muffled groans through.

He walked over to the sink where Andy-Andy stood, her right hand under the cold running water. "Nice shot," he said.

"Thanks." She winced. "I wish you could have taken him down a bit faster; I think I broke my thumb."

"You shouldn't make a fist with the thumb inside. Besides, that looks like a sprain to me. You want to go down to the infirmary, have it X-rayed?"

"And miss all the fun? No thanks. And no thanks for the sympathy, either."

He shrugged, then turned as the kitchen door swung open. No problem; just Walter.

"Everything okay in here?"

Karl nodded. "Just fine. You two go out and sit in the living room with the rest. Doc and I have a couple of things to talk over."

He checked three of the kitchen drawers before he found the one with the knives. Selecting a long, thin skinning knife, he looked around for a whetstone. No luck.

And that was too bad. Sharpening the knife in front of Deighton would have been good theater.

Still, Deighton's unbruised eye widened as Karl, knife in hand, pulled up a chair, spun it around, and seated himself ass-backward, his arms resting on the chair's back, the knife held lightly between thumb and forefinger.

"Deighton," Karl said, in his best Charles Bronson monotone, "I'm going to make this short." *And as frightening as possible; I don't want you thinking about anything except that you're terrified of me.* "You used us as a bunch of guinea pigs; everything that happened on the other side was your fault. Agreed?" *And what does he know about what happened on the other side? He said in his letter that his visions were erratic, that*

234

*the time differential makes it hard for him to follow what happens—
does he know that Jason is dead?*

Deighton shook his head violently.

Karl smiled. "Relax. You may just have a way out of it. As I
was saying, when you shoot craps with people's lives, you're
responsible for the result. It's a sound legal principle—take my
word for it. Say, if you torch a building for the insurance, and
someone dies in the fire, you don't just spend a year or two in jail
for the arson. It's murder one." Karl raised a palm. "I'll give you
this: You tried to see that we were well enough equipped. You
didn't know that Ari—that Riccetti was going to blast the treasure chest." He set the point of the knife under Deighton's chin,
sliding the blade through the gray goatee until it touched flesh.
"But that doesn't make any difference, professor. Agreed? *I
said, agreed?*" He drew the knife back, just enough for Deighton
to move his head.

Slowly, Deighton nodded.

"And how many times a murderer does that make you, Art?
Blink once for each."

Deighton's left eye closed, then opened. He looked toward the
door from the kitchen to the living room, then back at Karl.

*Good. He's not sure if I want him to count Doria, but he
doesn't know about Jason.* Karl forced himself not to breathe
a sigh of relief. *He doesn't know that Jason is dead.*

"Now," Karl went on, "it's your fault that James Michael is
dead, and Doria's . . . in bad shape. If killing you would bring
them back, I'd do it here and now." He touched the blade to
Deighton's neck, just over the jugular. "A little push, and it
would be all over." He dropped the point of the blade. "But that
wouldn't bring them back, would it? It's too bad that the only
way I can see to fix things requires that you stay alive."

Hope brightened Deighton's lined face. Karl went on: "So,
you're sending us back. Can you do that? I mean, because it
worked once with us, can you be sure that it'll work again?"

Deighton nodded.

"Good. Next question—and in case you haven't guessed, the
answer had better be yes—can you transfer us from here to that
green spot in the Waste of Elrood, the home tabernacle of the
Society of the Healing Hand? Better nod, Art. Otherwise"—Karl
touched the knifepoint to the center of Deighton's forehead—"we
go to Plan B."

Deighton drew his head back.

"You don't want to know what Plan B is, do you?"

Deighton shook his head as though he were trying to shake his ears loose.

Good. Because I don't know what Plan B is, either. That was the trouble with threatening Deighton; what if he called Karl's bluff? There was no way to get back to the other side that didn't require Deighton's cooperation, and Karl wasn't sure that he had either the stomach or the knowledge to cause Deighton enough pain to make him cooperate—without killing the bastard.

So we keep him too scared to think of calling my bluff. "One more thing: Only six of us are going back; Parker is staying behind. I've got him safely away from campus, holed up in a motel. If we don't get back in a reasonable time . . ." He let his voice trail off; Deighton's imagination would work better than an explicit threat.

Karl shrugged. "Are we agreed? Good—I'm going to free your mouth now." He slipped the knife between Deighton's cheek and the cloth strips that held a balled-up dishtowel in Deighton's mouth. "Go ahead and yell. Once." Karl sliced the strips.

Deighton spat out the dishtowel. "You . . . misunderstood me." His voice quavered only a little. "I didn't mean for any of this—"

"Shut up. What equipment do you need?"

"I haven't said that I'd do it."

Karl shrugged. "Got a pair of pliers around here? I bet you'll do it after I've pulled a few teeth." He started to rise.

"Wait. There's a wood box in the living room. Oak, approximately two feet by one, six inches deep. I'll need that, and I'll have to have my hands free."

Karl reached out and patted the old man's cheek. "No problem. But if you try to free your legs before we're gone, I'll break them. At the kneecaps." He couldn't resist adding, "Shweetheart."

"You are lying in the short grasses of the well-kept lawn surrounding the tabernacle of the Society of the Healing Hand, a group of six adventurers, seeking the revivification of one of your number, the healing of the soul of another, and fleeing the shame of a distant wizard, who regrets with all his heart that you were hurt. That *any* of you were hurt.

"The tabernacle towers above you, several hundred yards to the west, blocking the setting sun. In the harsh glare, it is difficult to make out the details, but you see that it is of the same general shape as the Aztec pyramids, although easily twice their height.

"The wind is hot and dry; blowing across the Waste of Elrood, it has lost almost all of its moisture. . . .

CHAPTER SEVENTEEN: *Payment*

> *I have always thought that all men should be free;
> but if any should be slaves, it should be first those
> who desire it for themselves, and secondly those
> who desire it for others. Whenever I hear anyone
> arguing for slavery, I feel a strong impulse to see it
> tried on him personally.*

> —Abraham Lincoln

A white-robed acolyte led them inside, with Karl in the lead, carrying the sewn-leather bag containing Ahira's remains. A distant uneasiness kept his right hand on the hilt of his new sword, a longish saber with a strange leather grip that sucked all the sweat away from his palm. Having the steel quickly available comforted him—just as well he'd kept that skinning knife in hand while Deighton transferred them; it had translated well.

Behind him walked Andy-Andy and Aristobulus, both clutching their leather-bound spell books as tightly as Karl held his swordhilt.

One thing you can say for Deighton, he doesn't equip us poorly. The packs they had left outside lacked only magical implements—Deighton had claimed that he hadn't any left, other than the spell books, and Karl hadn't wanted to argue the point. But they did bear food, and additional weapons, and several puptents, along with other necessities.

Last in their ragged line was Walter Slovotsky, Doria's limp form held chest-high in his arms. Karl turned to see Walter nodding reassuringly to Doria, as though she could see him.

Dark corridors led to a vast, high-ceilinged hall, where the sounds of their footsteps echoed off marble walls and the smooth gray floor. Lit dimly by three ornate candelabra that hung from the ceiling, it was empty, deserted save for a high-backed throne on a white stone pedestal, three-quarters of the way across the room. Beyond the throne, a narrow slit of a window gave them a view of the greenery on the east side of the tabernacle. In the morning, no doubt, it brought more light into the room, but not now, at sunset.

Karl lowered the bag to the floor.

The acolyte nodded. "The Matriarch will see you here," she said, extending her arms for Doria. "And I will see to my sister."

Walter looked over to Karl. *Well?* his half-shrug said.

We're on their turf, but . . .

"Really," the acolyte said, a half-sneer passing across her smooth face, "do you trust us so little? If so, then why are you here, Karl Cullinane?"

We haven't exchanged a single word, but she knows my name. I'm not going to ask her how; undoubtedly, that's what she's expecting.

"We will heal her, and take care of her. Doria is one of us, now—not one of you," the acolyte said. "I must warn you that you are now prejudicing your case."

That sounded ominous; he quelled the warrior's natural response to a challenge. "Go ahead, Walter," he said. "If they're as powerful as we hope they are, we couldn't put up much of a fight anyway."

The acolyte accepted Doria's slack body, not straining with the effort. Clearly, she was stronger than she looked.

"The Matriarch will be with you shortly," she said, walking easily toward the hall's entrance. And then she was gone.

Andy-Andy put a hand on his shoulder. "Take it easy, Karl—they won't hurt her. Besides," she sighed, "what could they *do* to hurt her, the way she is?"

Walter chuckled grimly. "And if the little bitch was lying, we can still try and take her apart later. Or frighten the hell out of her, like you did out of Deighton. Nice bit of acting, that—or *would* you have carved little pieces out of him until he gave in?"

Karl smiled. "I'll never tell." *And I'll never know. I know that I could have killed him without any regret; torture is something else.* "Apology time, Ari—if I'd leaned on him a bit harder, we might have been able to get better out of him than a couple of spell books."

Clutching the leather-bound volume tightly, Aristobulus' lined face broke into a smile. "You haven't heard me complaining. For someone with no talent for leadership, you haven't done a bad job. Besides, *I'm* not the one who's wanted in Pandathaway—now I can go back, and qualify for the guild, and—"

"Not necessarily," a low, reedy voice said from behind Karl's back.

Karl turned, his weight on the balls of his feet, forcing himself to move slowly. The throne wasn't empty anymore.

An almost impossibly thin woman sat there, faintly glowing white robes gathered about her. The collar of her garment was different from Doria's or the acolyte's; it covered her head as a sort of cowl, casting her face into shadow, her features, if any, hidden as well as if she were masked. *"Greetings. You may approach me."* There was an eerie quality to her voice; it had the airiness of an old woman's, but no hint of fragility or weakness. And it was loud; if this was her normal speaking voice, her shout could well shatter stone walls.

Karl bent to pick up the bag containing Ahira's body, then straightened. They all walked across the floor, Karl carrying the bag in cupped arms. "We're here to—"

"I know why you are here."

They stopped in unison, ten yards from her throne. Karl's forehead wrinkled; she hadn't given a command, she hadn't said anything or made the slightest gesture, yet all four of them had stopped suddenly, as though responding to a compelling order.

"The issue at hand," the Matriarch said, *"is whether or not we shall honor your wishes. Clearly, the Society is in debt to you to some extent; you have done us a service by protecting one of our own, and bringing her here."*

"Then—" Karl started.

"But that is not sufficient payment for what you ask. Reviving the dead is immensely difficult, immensely draining. We require further payment."

241

Aristobulus took a half-step forward, then stepped back. "What sort of payment? I've still got some spells in my—"

"That is insufficient. Your spells are trivial by my standards, wizard. Did you look about our preserve? Once, the entire Waste was that lush, that fine. I protected this tabernacle against the magic of greater than you."

Walter raised his hands. "Look, Lady—instead of telling us what isn't enough, why don't you just tell us what you want? You want gold? I'll go steal you a few tons. You want diamonds? I'll—"

"Be silent." The Matriarch raised her hands to her face, the first motion they had seen her make. *"The one who spoke of you, Karl Cullinane, was correct. You are not terribly bright. But this one, this Walter Slovotsky, is worse."* She lowered her hands. *"Then again, that is hardly your fault. You are, after all, merely a human."*

And what are you, old lady? Karl thought. *God? Or is it just that you think you—*

"No. And yes. It's simply that . . ." Her voice trailed off into gibberish. She sighed. *"But you do not understand the High Tongue, and that is the only language in which I can clearly explain myself. My requirements are so necessary and so obvious—but this Erendra and this English of yours . . . the words do not cover the territory. So I shall speak as simply as I can, so that you each can understand what I require of you, if not why I require it—*

"Aristobulus."

The wizard shook himself. The voice was somehow different now, less . . . diffuse?

"True. I speak only to you, wizard. Only one of the others can hear me, and will know if you decline to offer your portion of the payment."

Aristobulus nodded. *Very well,* he thought. *You don't want what my spells can do for you—what do you want?*

"Your magic. All of it. Your . . . Aristobulus-ness. Your portion of the payment is to be but Louis Riccetti evermore. An ordinary human, unable to even read a word—to even see a word—in that book you clutch so tightly. Agree to that, and Ahira may live again. Decline, and he will surely stay dead."

How could she be sure of that? Certainly, the Healing Hand

wasn't the only sect in the world; possibly there was some other cleric, somewhere, who could raise the dead.

"No. There is not. And soon, there may be none at all who can."

His aura wrapped him tightly, seething. For James Michael, could he give that up?

"Your reasons don't matter to me. It's . . . the distance between us that makes our communication so difficult, just as you could never teach your cat to fetch. You may give up your magic for whatever reason you wish. Or not. She sighed. *"But I see that you will not. You do not see enough worth in your other self, in that engineering nonsense you used to almost worship—"*

"Nonsense? Listen to me, you: There's more magic in a suspension bridge than in all these books, and—"

"Then you agree?"

To hell with her. "Engineering nonsense" indeed. "Yes," he snarled. "I'll give it up." *And I'll build bridges, here. I will. And horsecollars, and steam engines—*

"As you wish." She gestured lightly with one hand, murmuring words that could only be heard and then forgotten.

He *changed*. Aristobulus' slim form bulged out, the old, dry skin of his body becoming once more firm with youth. It dizzied him; he stumbled . . .

. . . and Lou Riccetti, clad in workshirt and blue jeans, picked himself up off the floor to glare at the Matriarch. He crossed his arms defiantly over his chest. And, to his own surprise, found that he was grinning from ear to ear.

"Andrea."

"Yes?" Why was *she* first? That didn't seem fair. After all—

"One of the others has the same reaction. Curious."

Andrea tried to turn her head, to see which one of the others the Matriarch was talking about, but she couldn't move.

I'm not even breathing. She tried to force her lungs to draw in air, and couldn't. Panic burned her throat.

"Be still. Do you need to breathe?"

Well, no—and that was strange. Why didn't she need to?

"You stall. Which is typical of you. You lack commitment, Andrea Andropolous. You wait, and you see, and you never decide until you absolutely have to. Your payment is this: You must agree to decide about something important. Yes or no; in or out; together or apart."

243

Fine. But what "something important"? I have to say yes without knowing?

"No. You neither have to say yes, nor commit yourself without knowing. But an important promise will be made here, perhaps. Your payment is to agree to participate, or to reject participation in that promise. Without hesitation; without time for contemplation; without stalling. Will you make payment? Or will Ahira remain dead?"

She shrugged mentally, irritated at the way her shoulders refused to move. *I can't see that that's such a big sacrifice—and I can't see what you're getting out of it.*

"True. Will you make payment?"

Yes, but— The thought cut off as she heard the Matriarch and Walter.

"Walter Slovotsky."

I'm first. I knew I'd be first.

The Matriarch chuckled. "You are always first, are you not? The center of your pitiful little universe. Your portion of the payment will be that egotism, that idiotic notion that everything centers on you, that as long as all is right with you, all is right with the world—and that always, all is right with you."

He wanted to reach up and scratch his head while he puzzled that out, but his arms hung limp by his sides. No, not limp—unmoving, that was all.

"Time works somewhat differently around me, when I so command it. Your mind is free, but the nerve impulses won't reach your arms until we have finished our conversation."

Well, then, we can finish it quickly. I gave up on seeing myself as some sort of superman back in Lundeyll. I'll tell you—a knife in the shoulder can do wonders for your perspective. Is that what you wanted to hear?

"No. That is what I wanted to know."

Karl's ears buzzed with the sounds of the Matriarch carrying on three conversations at once; with Riccetti renouncing his wizardry, Andy her indecisiveness, and Walter his self-centeredness. But it was as though Karl had three separate sets of ears, three separate minds: The words didn't jumble together; each word, each thought, stood out from the others, with crystal clarity.

"Karl Cullinane," the Matriarch said. *"It is your turn to offer payment. Or not."*

Payment? How was all this payment? What possible benefit could she get from this? *I just don't see what she's gaining from—*

"True. You do not see. And, quite probably, you never will. Are you prepared to make payment, or will Ahira remain dead?"

Of course he was prepared to do something for her—but what did she want? Some of his possessions?

"No."

The sacrifice of some of his abilities, like the way she had made Aris—

"No."

A portion of his psyche, as with Walter?

"No."

That left some sort of commitment, like the way she had made Andy agree to decide about something or other. *Does that have something to do with this?*

"Correct. And what will you commit yourself to?"

What do you want, Lady? Why don't you just come out and ask?

"Because I have limitations that you can never understand. I am far wiser, far more intelligent, than you can ever hope to be, but the perspective . . . limits me."

Wonderful. Power doesn't just corrupt, it limits, too. Eh?

"You stall, dilettante. You delay. Answer my question."

There was something strange about this whole payment business, as though the other three had gained, instead of lost—

"True."

Lou Riccetti had always been sort of an oddity, a misfit. No real self-respect, back in the days when he used to trail around behind Jason Parker, like some sort of obedient spaniel. But that had changed when he was transferred over to this side, when he became a wizard.

No. It hadn't. Aristobulus was just the other side of the same coin, seeing himself as worthwhile through his magic. *Only* through his magic.

And that was it. Lou Riccetti hadn't seen *himself* as worthwhile until the moment that the Matriarch had required he give up his wizardry, turned him back into a normal human being.

"Again correct. Go on."

Now, Walter was a different case. Slovotsky had always seen himself as worthwhile, perhaps too much so. Until Lundeyll, Walter hadn't understood his own mortality, his own limitations.

And the Matriarch wanted Walter to know that mortality, to see those limitations.

But what did that imply? So what if Walter knew he could hurt?

"Perhaps he can now truly understand that others can hurt, as well."

Karl nodded mentally.

And then there was Andy-Andy, who forestalled committing herself. *Which sounds a lot like me, actually. Psych major, soc major, bridge player, gamer, et cetera and ad nauseam. If she's got a mild case of indecision, then I'm close to terminal.*

"Precisely."

Then what do you want me to decide to do? I can see that you want me to agree to do something, but what?

"That which you have enjoyed most. That one thing which has made you feel most alive. To agree to do that, for the rest of your life, is your payment."

Karl let his string of former majors and hobbies run through his head. No, none of those. The Matriarch had hardly gone through all of this to get him to agree to finish his acting degree.

But she said that I have to take up—what was it?—"that one thing which has made you feel most alive."

And then, it all clicked into place. Normality. Commitment. Lack of self-centeredness. The commitment to understanding that there were others out there, that they had feelings, and that those feelings *counted*.

Jefferson's words swam in his brain: "We hold these truths to be self-evident, that all men are created equal—"

And in this world, they *didn't* hold that self-evident. Ellegon was a person, if not a human, and he had been left chained to a rock in Pandathaway just for the convenience of the rulers of that city. And in the slave markets, whips cracked and flesh parted. Ohlmin and his slavers had chained and abused them, because people were property here.

And the last piece: *The two things in my life that I enjoyed most were the time that I freed Ellegon and when I got us away from Ohlmin and killed those bastards.*

Matriarch, that's to be my payment. Free all the slaves. But how? Slice up all the slavers? Break all the chains? How?

"*That is your problem. Do you commit yourslf?*"

"Of course." Karl tried to spread his hands, and found to his surprise that he could. "But that isn't a sacrifice."

"*But it is payment, in the only coin I will accept.*"

The others stirred around him. Andy-Andy glared up at the Matriarch. "And you can count me in on it, too. Is that a quick enough decision for you?"

"*Yes.*" The Matriarch's voice held a hint of amusement.

Lou Riccetti, arms crossed over his chest, smiled. "I'm in."

Walter Slovotsky raised his hands and shrugged. "You'll probably get us all killed trying, but . . ."

Karl threw an arm around the other's shoulder. "But he's in, too. Now, about Ahira . . . ?"

"*We have accepted payment. It will take slightly more than a year to effect his revivification.*"

Walter shook his head. "We can't hang around here; there's a price on Karl's head, at least, and the Pandathaway Guilds' Council has already managed to nail him with a Location spell once—"

"*That could not happen here. This preserve is . . . defended. But,*" the Matriarch sighed, "*I could hardly have the four of you within the tabernacle for that length of time, making noise and—ahh. Of course. Length of time, indeed.*" She gestured, and spoke, the words vanishing as they left her mouth.

Through the window beyond the throne, night fell, the darkness only momentary as the sun rose like a glowing balloon across the sky.

And darkness, again. And light, and darkness. And light and darkness. Andlightanddarkandlightandark as the days strobed past.

And then it slowed, until a brilliant sun hung motionless, casting bright light into the hall, with its empty throne.

Karl brushed a year's accumulation of dust from his shoulders. "Is everyone all—"

"I'm fine, in case anyone's interested," Ahira's voice rasped behind him.

Ahira?

Karl turned. The dwarf glared up at him, hands on hips,

head cocked to one side. "Well," Ahira said, "don't I get a hello?"

"James!"

It was physically impossible for all four full-sized humans to hug the same dwarf at the same time, but they tried.

"And I have arranged some company for you."

Karl turned to look at the empty throne. He had heard her voice, but the Matriarch was nowhere to be seen. *"Nor will you see me again."*

"Now wait—" he started. "What if we need some help? Won't you—"

"No," the voice answered, coming at him from every direction. *"Never will the Hand aid you again. I'm . . . sorry, Karl Cullinane, but we . . . can't."*

"I don't understand."

True. I told her you were a decent person—for a human, that is—but I never claimed you were intelligent.

"As I said, I've arranged some company for you."

A huge, triangular head peeked in through the door.

"Ellegon!"

Yes, I'm Ellegon. And you are Karl Cullinane. A paw slapped against stone. *And this is a floor . . .*

"Enough. I take it you're the company."

Very clever. I am also transportation. We will camp on the edge of the forest tonight. Just in case you're interested, I've spent a good part of the past year ferrying some of your possessions here, things you left at the base of Bremon. Including one red mare that emptied her bowels all the way across the Waste. I don't think she likes me. But she does look tasty.

We are not eating my horse. And are you certain you can carry all of us?

No. Actually, I just want to see how high I can get before we crash. Any other stupid questions?

"Well, I wanted to ask the Matriarch about—"

She wouldn't answer. You are on your own.

"Isn't that *we?*"

No. Not until you introduce me to the other three. I already know Walter Slovotsky.

"And then?"

Karl, it took me three centuries of being chained in a cesspool to learn what you found in months. You just may be able to do it.

"You call that an answer?"

The dragon's head cocked to one side. *As a matter of fact, I do.*

CHAPTER EIGHTEEN: *Profession*

Give me where to stand, and I shall move the world.

—Archimedes

Karl walked a few hundred yards from the fire before spreading his blankets on the damp grass.

Slipping out of his leggings and tunic, he slid between the blankets and lay back, pillowing his head on his hands. High above, a coal-black sky winked its million eyes.

How the hell are we going to do it? Where do we start? With Pandathaway's Slavers' Guild, I suppose, but . . .

He shrugged. Slavery had been alive on this world for millennia. He wasn't going to figure out how to end it tonight.

But tomorrow was another day.

And besides, I've been told that thinking isn't my strong suit.
He chuckled, and then sighed deeply.

Well, you're correct for once.

Thanks.

He sighed. Doria was gone, now. He probably wouldn't see her again. Would she be happy with the Society?

They take care of their own, Karl.

"Probably. Do me a favor; get out of my mind for a while. It's been kind of a tough day—"

Year.

"—year, then. I could use some rest."

I was just going to ask if you minded if I hunted up some food.

"Not my department; take it up with Ahira. Where are you, anyway?"

Down by the stream. I thought I might snatch up a few fish while I'm on watch. I can see Walter and Ahira and Riccetti from here, sitting around the fire, arguing. And Andrea's worrying—

"Arguing and worrying? About what?"

Riccetti's talking about going back to the other side for a book of tables, of all things. Why he's so interested in furniture, I don't know.

"Engineering tables, Ellegon. Different sort of thing." Although Karl had had quite enough of Riccetti's arguing about books. First the spell books, and now this. "What's Andy worried about?"

Parents, relatives, friends. How they'll miss her, not know what happened to her. And—

"Hmm—remind her about the time differential on this side. It's a problem for all of us, but we've got a few years to figure out what to do about it. It'll be at least a day or so, on the other side, before we're seriously missed. And that'll stack up to . . ." He trailed off, too lazy and too tired to worry over the calculation. *Save it for morning. Save it all for morning.*

But I was wondering about the food. I'll keep alert, I promise. Young dragons don't sleep much at all, you know.

"Young dragons also don't stop bugging the hell out of me."

True.

Ellegon went silent. Karl let his eyelids sag shut, his muscles unkink. Loosen the neck, slow the heart, rest the mind . . .

Silently, she slid into his arms. He sat up with a jerk, bowling her over. "What the *hell*—"

Andy-Andy propped her chin on one hand. "If you're going to bounce me around the meadow, I'll go elsewhere." A loose strand of hair fell across her nose. She blew it off and moved closer to him, brushing the blankets aside.

No, there weren't any bikini marks. Amazing.

After a while, she pushed him away. But gently, and only a few inches. "Looks like you finally found yourself a profession—"

"This?"

"—hero."

"Don't talk dirty."

Whether he reached for her, or she for him, he was never quite sure.

But he couldn't have cared less.

ABOUT THE AUTHOR

Joel Rosenberg was born in Winnipeg, Manitoba, Canada, in 1954, and raised in eastern North Dakota and northern Connecticut. He attended the University of Connecticut, where he met and married Felicia Herman.

Joel's occupations, before settling down to writing full-time, have run the usual gamut, including driving a truck, caring for the institutionalized retarded, bookkeeping, gambling, motel desk-clerking, and a two-week stint of passing himself off as a head chef. His majors, while at UConn, surpassed Karl Cullinane's in number and scope.

Joel's first sale, an op-ed piece favoring nuclear power, was published in *The New York Times*. His stories have appeared in *Isaac Asimov's Science Fiction Magazine*, *Perpetual Light*, *Amazing Science Fiction Stories*, and TSR's *The Dragon*. He is now a Contributing Editor at *Gameplay* magazine, writing a monthly backgammon column.

Joel's hobbies include backgammon, poker, bridge, and several other sorts of gaming, as well as cooking; his broiled butterfly leg of lamb has to be tasted to be believed.

He now lives in New Haven, Connecticut, with his wife and the traditional two cats.

The Sleeping Dragon is his first novel.

Ø

SIGNET Science Fiction You'll Enjoy

SIGNET Science Fiction You'll Enjoy